REA

P9-BIO-318

THE PALE
GREEN HORSE

Also by Michael I. Leahey

Broken Machines

THE PALE
GREEN HORSE

...

Michael I. Leahey

THOMAS DUNNE BOOKS
ST. MARTIN'S MINOTAUR
NEW YORK

THOMAS DUNNE BOOKS.
An imprint of St. Martin's Press.

THE PALE GREEN HORSE. Copyright © 2002 by Michael I. Leahey. All rights reserved. Printed in the United States of America. No part of this book may be used or reproduced in any manner whatsoever without written permission except in the case of brief quotations embodied in critical articles or reviews. For information, address St. Martin's Press, 175 Fifth Avenue, New York, N.Y. 10010.

www.minotaurbooks.com

Library of Congress Cataloging-in-Publication Data

Leahey, Michael I.
The pale green horse / Michael I. Leahey—1st ed.
p. cm.
ISBN 0–312–27813–6
1. Sick—Crimes against—Fiction. 2. Insurance crimes—Fiction. 3. New York (N.Y.)—Fiction. 4. Consultants—Fiction. I. Title.

PS3562.E215 P35 2002
813'.6–dc21

2001054454

First Edition: April 2002

10 9 8 7 6 5 4 3 2 1

For My Parents, Ed and Mary

When I behold the sacred liao wo my thoughts return to those who made me, raised me and now are tired. I would repay the bounty they have given me, but it is as the sky: it can never be approached.

—Anonymous

When he broke open the fourth seal, I heard the voice of the fourth living creature cry out, *come forward*. I looked and there was a pale green horse. Its rider was named Death, and Hades accompanied him. They were given authority over a quarter of the earth, to kill with sword, famine, and plague, and by means of the beasts of the earth.

Revelation 6:8

PROLOGUE

∎ ∎ ∎

Michael Adams lay on his bed staring out the window. It was spring, his favorite season. From the seventh floor of his New York City apartment, Michael had a clear view over the trees and down into Gramercy Park. He thought about the walks he'd taken there and remembered lovers' quarrels acted out on the little wooden bench still visible below him, just inside the gate. There was an old man sitting on his bench now, spreading bread crumbs for the pigeons. Michael smiled and closed his eyes.

Twenty years earlier, when he'd first looked down into the park, Michael had felt excited and inspired. But now, with the illness slowly draining his energy, the park was merely a pleasant distraction. He opened his eyes again and watched enviously as a dark-skinned nanny carefully parked her stroller, facing it into the warm sun. How he longed to trade places with the sleeping child she protected.

Michael's mind was still wandering lazily through the park when the sound of his front door opening and closing brought him back. It's only Sheila, the night nurse, he thought, and tried to sit upright in the bed. The sudden movement disturbed the infection in his chest and he started coughing. Spasms wracked his frail body, burning his lungs. Michael's face turned bright crimson and the sweat ran off of him, soaking into his bed-clothes. His eyes filled with tears and he was on the verge of panic, when strong arms gently lifted him and rolled him onto

1

his side. The head of the electric bed rose, and experienced hands began rubbing his neck and beating softly, steadily, against his back.

"There, there, not to worry. You can relax now, my lamb, Johnny will take care of you."

It was a man's deep voice; unfamiliar, but pleasant. At first, Michael tried to focus through the tears, then gave up, exhausted. When the coughing subsided, the new man expertly suctioned his throat, clearing the airway, then cleaned and massaged Michael's weary frame before helping him change into dry pajamas. Later, as his breathing became more regular, Michael was able to watch the male nurse as he moved about the room.

Johnny was a large, powerfully built man of medium height. He was middle-aged, perhaps even older, yet he seemed strong and vigorous. His dark, healthy tan contrasted sharply with the sickly pallor and purplish skin lesions Michael saw reflected back at him in the mirror. Johnny wore the traditional white uniform of a male nurse: buck shoes, trousers, and a short-sleeved shirt that buttoned up the side. A mane of blue-white hair crowned his head. To Michael Adams's weary eyes, the nurse seemed to shimmer in the fading afternoon light.

Johnny moved quickly and efficiently as he went about his routine tasks. After tending to his patient, he rearranged the bedding and straightened up the room. Next, he turned his attention to Michael's chart, which hung from the frame at the foot of the bed. The chart listed the doctor's instructions and detailed time and dosage for all his medications. As Johnny worked, he talked. He said nothing really, but he was friendly and the sound of his voice was comforting.

"Poor Sheila, the old girl's come down with a terrible cold. Let's hope she's tucked in bed with a box of tissues and the blankets pulled up under her chin," he said at one point.

Michael didn't mind the change in nurses; thanks to Johnny, he was feeling warm and safe again. He could hear the sound of his medicine bottles bumping into each other as Johnny measured solutions into dosing cups and counted out pills and vitamins. Closing his eyes, Michael tried to picture himself basking in the sun like that child in the park.

Before long, the nurse was supporting his neck and the medicines were going down. Last came the cough syrup, heavily scented and exotic. He drank it gratefully, not minding the mild, burning sensation as the narcotic coursed through his body and set him drifting toward sleep. Michael Adams looked up into the coal-black eyes of the white-haired stranger.

"Thank you," he whispered.

"Good-bye, my lamb," Johnny whispered back.

Half an hour later, the room was cool, but it still wasn't cold. Johnny preferred it cold. He turned up the air conditioner, then lingered at the window, looking down into the park where an old man was feeding the pigeons. The dusk was cloaking the old boy in shadows. Johnny smiled knowingly.

He stared for another minute, then closed the blinds and walked over to the green-leather club chair in the corner, across from the bed. He eased himself into the big chair, then shut his eyes and tried to direct his mind, willing himself to relax. He could hear Michael Adams's uneven breathing, growing worse now that the head of his bed had been lowered again. The rasping noise was distracting, but Johnny forced himself to be patient—it was the least he could do. When he felt reasonably composed, Johnny opened his eyes and took in the setting.

The lighting wasn't right, that was obvious. He switched off the standing lamps and the overhead, leaving only the dim glow from a small night-light near the bed. As his eyes adjusted to the semidarkness, Johnny felt more comfortable with the ambience, but there was still something missing. He slowly rubbed his left temple as his mind wandered.

When the image he sought refused to come into focus, Johnny decided to search for inspiration. Moving carefully from room

3

to room, he took his time, studying the mementos his patient had collected in a lifetime. It was a stylish one-bedroom apartment, tastefully furnished and spacious. Johnny lingered in the classically appointed dining room, running his fingers over the burled-mahogany furniture, examining the Irish crystal in the cabinets. The walls were papered with a colorful floral print, and there was a large arrangement of fresh white lilies in the center of the table. Johnny smiled.

He carried the vase of lilies back to the bedroom and carefully balanced it on the nightstand. Michael Adams's breathing was extremely labored and his color had begun changing again as his body demanded oxygen.

"Cyanotic," Johnny said softly, shaking his head. "Prognosis, very grim."

It was time. The room was as cold as a meat locker, the lighting darkly theatrical. And now there was a bouquet of white lilies to commemorate the passing. Johnny stood motionless, gazing down at Michael Adams's shrunken form for several minutes, his lips moving to the words of a silent prayer. When he could no longer contain himself, Johnny picked up a pillow and placed it over Michael's face.

" 'Worthy is the Lamb that was slain to receive power, and riches, wisdom, and strength, and honour and glory, and blessing,' " he recited.

Then he pressed down firmly with both hands.

ONE

. . .

The sun was inching its way into the sky, dusting the blue-green waves with sparkles. It was dawn in the Caribbean and a light breeze had set the mahogany trees dancing. In that quiet time, alone and listening as the day awoke, the thought of death never entered my mind.

I remember the cool, salty aroma of the sea and the steady rhythm of the waves. I was leaning back against the trunk of an old palm tree, digging my toes into the sand and sipping hot tea, feeling warm and safe, like a kid nestled on his mother's lap. When I think about it now, I tell myself that it was just a dream, that it was never meant to last, which is almost true. Within a few short hours, the warm, fuzzy picture warped into something stark and distorted, and my world turned inside out.

Dr. Boris Koulomzin, my partner, says I've developed an unhealthy preoccupation with death, and maybe he's right. On the other hand, that's coming from a man so afraid of skin cancer that he wears long-sleeved shirts and gloves in the summer. Believe me, I know you can't put things back the way they were. But late at night, alone in the dark, I can still see Johnny's eyes. Coal-black eyes that didn't reflect light.

Just before sunrise, I'd fallen out of bed and stumbled down to the beach. There had been a wee party in our shack the night

5

before and I needed fresh air and cool water. Before leaving the bedroom, I brewed some hot tea and watched my beautiful Kathleen, the sensible one. She slept peacefully, the hint of a smile on her lips as she nuzzled a goose-down pillow. I really wanted to pat myself on the back for that little wrinkle, but far too many brain cells had been sacrificed in the name of fun to be sure I could take the credit.

Walking down the path to the beach, I was flanked on either side by brilliant red and white bougainvillea spilling off the rock walls in a tangle of color. The ground was still damp from an early morning rain, and the path was cool against the soles of my bare feet. Pretty soon, the fog inside my head began to lift. In fact, after a few sips of tea, I felt so much better, I decided I really was responsible for the contented expression on Kate's face.

I sat on the beach and happily sipped my tea as the sun rose, banishing the shadows. Before long, there was nothing but a clear blue sky and warm sunlight all the way to the horizon. As the wind picked up, blowing the hair out of my eyes, I noticed white sails and brightly colored spinnakers weaving and bobbing out beyond the barrier reef.

Another day had dawned in paradise and I decided to celebrate the event by taking a nap. I dragged a couple of lounge chairs farther down the beach, into the shade, then lay down and quickly fell asleep.

"Mr. Donovan?" she whispered.

James Joseph Donovan to you, kid, I thought without opening my eyes. The woman had a deep, silky voice. Instead of opening my eyes, I lay there like a dope, listening to my heart pick up speed as I pictured someone tall and tan, in a string bikini.

Then I heard the ice cubes rattling. It wasn't much of a warning; like hearing the hammer cock on a pistol just before you get shot. There was perhaps a moment's pause before I felt the ice water and bolted upright, my eyes wide open at last. The first thing I saw was the smirk on Kate's face; then I noticed the empty glass in her right hand.

"Mr. Donovan?"

That voice again. I turned to my left and found a very small, very wrinkled old woman in a faded hotel uniform. She smiled pleasantly.

"Yes, for God's sake, yes, I'm Donovan. Now, could you *please* wait a minute?"

I didn't wait for an answer; a tumbler of ice cubes was melting in my swim shorts. I ran down to the water and flushed them out. When I came stomping back to the lounge chairs, Kate was reclining with the newspaper as if nothing had happened. The little old lady with the lounge singer's voice had disappeared.

"Good morning, darling," Kate said sweetly.

"What's with the ice cubes?" I demanded. I felt like a kid who'd been caught looking at dirty pictures.

"Don't bother, Jamie. I know you too well."

I tried to look shocked, but she ignored me, returning to the paper.

Kathleen Mary Byrne is a beautiful, obviously ruthless woman. Her large hazel eyes were hidden behind dark sunglasses, and even though her light-brown hair was pulled back into a tight braid, the natural blond highlights still sparkled. Seeing her in the morning light, her skin glistening with tanning oil, I forgot all about the ice cubes.

"Actually," she said, lowering her voice, "I'm surprised you had the energy to even contemplate such a fantasy. After last night, I thought you'd be needing a physical therapist."

"Really? Well, maybe you don't know me as well as you think."

I smiled and tried to squeeze next to her on the chair, but she knocked me off the edge with a swift kick.

"Don't go getting yourself all puffed up again," she teased. "Which reminds me, how's your head this morning? You drank an awful lot of punch last night."

7

I got up, dusted the sand off my shorts and moved to the other lounge chair. The question about the rum punch sounded an awful lot like "I told you so." I ignored her, and shading my eyes with the palms of my hands, made a thorough survey up and down the beach.

"What happened to that old lady?" I asked finally.

"That sweet old lady has a name," Kate said, peering at me over the rim of her sunglasses. "It's 'Magda,' and she came all the way down from the main house just to tell you about a telephone call."

Kate picked up the newspaper again. I waited a minute or two, but she didn't say anything else.

"And?"

Kate lowered the paper just enough to look at me.

"And I told her to forget about it."

"Did you bother to ask who the caller was?"

"No, I didn't."

"I see. And why was that?"

"Because we have a deal. Remember? No outside intrusions, no phone calls, no business. We're on vacation."

"Except in the case of an emergency?"

"Right."

"Well, how do you know this wasn't an emergency call?"

"I don't," she said patiently, as if I was really stupid. "If it *is* an emergency, they'll call again."

That was more than my tired brain could handle, so I settled back on the lounge chair with a section of the paper. While I was leafing through the pages, Kate decided to inspect the polish on her toenails. She'd already read the paper—the crossword puzzle was done.

When I got to the obituaries, I stopped. Reading the death notices is like sitting in the seat that faced backward in those old Country Squire station wagons—you get a chance to take a longer look at the things that have already passed you by. I

8

usually start by calculating the average age of the deceased. In this case, the average turned out to be more than eighty, which was encouraging.

"Did you read the obits?"

"Oh, no, I didn't," Kate said, hopefully.

We connect in some very strange ways.

"Okay, let's see," I began, scanning the notices. "Hey, wait a minute, these notices are a month old!"

"I know, the plane from the mainland was late again this morning. I found that paper in the closet. But go ahead, read them anyway. I mean, it's not like these are developing stories."

She had a point. I started scanning again.

"Looks like we have a pretty boring group."

"Well, at least read me the headlines and captions. There might be a hidden jewel."

" 'Dr. Alfred P. Johnson, Eighty-five; Trained Physicians in Surgery.' Any interest?"

"Keep going."

" 'Martin A. Devine; History Professor and College Dean, was Fifty-five.' "

I stopped to check the cause of death, which was leukemia, then looked over at Kate. She shook her head.

" 'James Shulty,' " I continued. " 'Philanthropist and Manufacturing Chief, Hundred and two.' "

Mr. Shulty's company made rolling overhead doors. That earned a yawn.

I looked up from the page.

"They all have pictures."

"Aren't there any smaller announcements?" Kate asked, hopefully. "You know, for someone who'll probably get overlooked if we don't take the time."

"Just one," I reported, double-checking. "A guy named Michael Adams. It's very small."

"Okay, read me that one."

9

Kate dug a bottle of polish out of her purse and began to touch up her toenails.

" 'Michael Adams Memorial: A memorial service for Michael Adams, an interior designer who also painted cityscapes, was held last evening at the Fashion Institute of Technology, Seventh Avenue at Twenty-seventh Street. Mr. Adams died on March nine, from an AIDS-related illness. In lieu of flowers, friends are asked to send donations to the Gay Men's Health Crisis.' "

"How old do you suppose he was?" Kate wondered.

I didn't say anything. Reading about ninety-year-old generals and famous statesmen was interesting. Bearing witness as AIDS erased the lives of talented young people was not. For Kate, it was personal. She published a big fashion magazine and had lost quite a few close friends and business associates to the epidemic. She just sat there, an open bottle of nail polish in her hand, and stared out across the water.

"I think I'll move on to the Sports Section," I sighed, turning the page on Michael Adams and the others.

By two o'clock that afternoon, the sun had risen high enough to melt a hole in the sky. There was still a stiff breeze coming across the bay, but the beach had gradually heated up and we were both covered with tiny droplets of perspiration. The day had started badly and gotten worse: we'd let the newspaper invade our sanctuary, and it had pulled us dangerously close to the world we were trying to avoid. I got up and dragged Kate down to the water. I hadn't dunked her in at least twenty-four hours and we both needed it.

She pretended to resist, but once we reached the surf, she dove right in and started swimming around cheerfully. I did not. I never do. I like to take my time entering the water. As usual,

Kate couldn't resist the temptation to splash me, and that made a dunking inevitable. I swam out beyond the reef, then leisurely paddled back in, sizing up my prey. When I was pretty close, I slipped below the surface and made my final advance underwater.

It is usually a very effective tactic. This time, however, the victim gave in too easily. I hesitated for a second, wondering if something was wrong. As soon as my grip relaxed, Kate rolled over, grabbed my swimsuit and pulled it down around my ankles. She was back on shore before I knew what had happened. I quickly pulled my trunks up, then chased her down the beach and would have caught her, too, if I hadn't run into that old lounge lizard Magda.

She was waiting for us by the beach chairs, holding a piece of paper in her hand. Kate had been right—if it was an emergency, they'd call back.

"Mr. Donovan?"

The same old question.

"Yes, I'm Mr. Donovan," I said sweetly. "Is there a message for me?"

She just grinned and carefully handed me the envelope.

I ripped open the telegram. It was from Manny Santos, the superintendent in my apartment building on Amsterdam Avenue near 101st Street in New York City. Santos is a tiny old man, with a big gut and plenty of brass. There's an unconfirmed rumor that he actually does some work around the building, but I doubt it. Manny generally holds court in the lobby and keeps himself busy by running the local numbers game and by placing members of his extended family in odd jobs around town. He also works part-time for my consulting business, which operates out of two apartments on the seventeenth floor. The message was simple and direct, just like Manny:

DONOVAN, WHERE YOU BEEN? DOC IN BAD ACCIDENT.
QUIT FOOLING AROUND. CALL BACK. NOW. MANNY.

11

I stood there dripping-wet, up to my ankles in the sand, and stared at the telegram. Kate took the wire from me and read it. "Let's go," she said, throwing me a towel.

As I followed Magda and Kate up to the main house, I tried to imagine what could have happened. The "Doc" Manny referred to is my business partner, Dr. Boris Mikail Koulomzin. Boris and I operate a private consulting business out of our apartments, which are connected by a hidden passageway and occupy the entire seventeenth floor of the building Santos pretends to manage. The jobs we take on vary a lot in plot and setting. They can lead us into the presence of the exalted or, just as easily and quickly, drag us down into the mire. The one central thread running through our body of work is that the cases usually involve a problem nobody else wants to fix.

Dr. Koulomzin is a brilliant, somewhat eccentric scientist. He dresses almost exclusively in black, chain-smokes dark, gold-tipped Turkish cigarettes, and avoids exposure to sunlight, even when he's fully clothed. Boris reads voraciously, plays the cello like a professional, and is a merciless competitor when engaged in a game of chess. Except for the smoking, however, these are not high-risk activities. The man just doesn't lead the kind of life one associates with accidents. Unless he'd fallen off the balcony, or his computer had blown up, it was difficult to picture him having an accident.

I was trying to imagine what might have gone wrong as I stood at the front desk, listening to the buzz and crackle while my call raced along the circuits to New York City. Manny Santos answered on the second ring.

"Manny? It's Donovan."

"Donovan, where the fuck you been, man? I been callin' all day. You get ma telegram?"

"Yeah, I got it."

"Yo, them people won't take no swear words in a telegram, otha-wise, I got some shit to say to you, gringo. Where you been? The doc's hurt bad, man."

Manny was scared and angry.

"Listen, Santos, this isn't the time to be ragging on me. Just tell me what happened."

He took a deep breath.

"You shoulda called soona."

"Fine. Point taken."

"Okay. Lemme see." He paused and took another deep breath. "We went to openin' day ova at the stadium like usual. Took the leem-o, man. Rode in style."

Just before I left on my vacation, Manny had talked my partner into a new business venture, which Manny dubbed "Fly Rides." They purchased an old stretch limousine, a relic, and started a car service. The big car was quite a prize. At night, you could barely see the dents and scratches, even if it was parked near a streetlight. Boris supplied the start-up funds and Manny agreed to run the business. It seemed like a pretty good deal for both of them. Manny put a few more relatives to work, and Boris, who's a menace behind the wheel of an automobile, was guaranteed a ride whenever he left the building.

"Anyways," Manny said, warming, "afta the game, I when to call ma cousin Moses on his cell phone, ya know, so he could come an' pick us up. An' the doc was waitin' out on the street. He had his umbrella, so's everythin' was cool wit the sun, ya know?"

I could picture Boris, dressed in a khaki-colored safari outfit, with a pith helmet and sun umbrella, standing on the street outside Yankee Stadium, like a Victorian explorer among the natives.

"When I came back, I seen a big crowd ova where the doc was standin'," Manny said, growing more excited. "I pushed them people outta ma way and there he was, down on the ground bleedin' bad, and a cop was callin' for an amba-lance. I started askin' what happened, an' this kid tole me, man, he saw the whole fuckin' thing."

There was another pause.

"Motherfucka hit him wit a car, Donovan. Drove right up on the sidewalk an' hit the doc. Used the driver's door to lay him out."

Manny's voice was cracking. The tough little man was blaming himself for not being there to protect Boris, even though my partner could lift Manny Santos over his head with one hand. I covered the phone and turned to Kate.

"What's wrong, Jamie?" She looked scared.

"As far as I can tell, Boris was hit by a car on the street in front of Yankee Stadium. Call the airport and see how soon we can get out of here."

Kate went to find another telephone. Our vacation was over.

"Manny, we're coming home. Okay? You still there?"

"Yeah, I'm wit you."

The poor guy sounded like he'd gone a long time without sleep.

"Where's Boris now, what hospital?"

"They moved him to Columbia-Presbyterian real early this mornin'."

It was a good hospital, but it probably meant that he needed specialized care.

"Manny, tell me straight, how is he?"

There was a long interval.

"Manny?"

"I dunno. You ask me, I say bad, man, real bad."

14

TWO

. . .

We managed to get off the island within two hours of my call to Manny Santos, but it wasn't easy. We stuffed our belongings into suitcases, checked out of the resort, and raced to the airport just in time to catch the last flight. Unfortunately for us, the little plane we boarded wasn't heading in the right direction.

Many hours later, we finally landed at Kennedy Airport, in New York City. Santos and his cousin, Moses, picked us up in the Fly Rides leem-o and drove us to the Milstein Hospital. Milstein Hospital is just one piece of Columbia University's Health Sciences campus, which includes Schools of Medicine, Dentistry, Nursing, and Public Health, as well as the New York State Psychiatric Institute. The whole center is built on the site of American League Park, which was the original home of the Yankees, back when they were known as the "Highlanders." The historical significance was ironic, considering where Boris was run over. The neighborhood around the Medical Center is called Washington Heights, and it surrounds the George Washington Bridge on the Manhattan side, which is a long haul from Kennedy Airport; with traffic, the ride took almost two hours. It seemed even longer.

When we finally pulled up in front of the hospital, Manny took charge. He arranged for visitors' passes, led the way to the elevators, and made sure we got off on the right floor. We were just rounding the corner into a hall of private rooms when I heard a familiar voice.

"I do not, I repeat, DO NOT wish to have my blinds opened. Now, if you've finished meddling, I insist that you LEAVE ME ALONE!"

"I thought you said he was hurt real bad," I muttered, looking down at Manny suspiciously.

"I said he was fucked up, but that don' mean the man can be shut up."

Kate ignored us. She was walking ahead, checking the room numbers. We'd been traveling for nineteen hours and it showed; our days of rest and romance were a fading memory.

"You can carry on all you want, but it won't change a thing, Doctor," a woman's voice shot back. "And by the way, don't think I can't tell that you've been smoking. When I find out who's been supplying your cigarettes, I'll put an end to that nonsense, too."

Manny's ears flushed.

"WOMAN, BE-GONE!" the patient bellowed in a voice much too strong for a dying man. A tall, broad-shouldered nurse, who looked about forty, came sprinting out of the room and almost ran us down.

"Excuse me, please," she begged, looking flustered and angry.

"Why don't you go in first, dear," I suggested, looking at Kate. She made a face, then pushed the door open.

"I thought I told you—" Boris growled, then stopped abruptly. "Oh my, Kathleen, is that really you?"

There was a moment of silence.

"It was . . . so kind . . . of you . . . to come," he finally stammered weakly.

"You can stop the acting right now, Buster," Kate announced.

But as she marched toward the bed, I heard a little gasp.

"My God, Boris! You poor thing."

"Yes, I guess it looks bad," he sighed pitifully. "But it's nothing, really. Nothing that won't heal, with time."

16

It was an impressive performance, even for Boris. I knocked on the door, then pushed Manny into the room in front of me, just in case. Boris is an intimidating figure. He stands six feet five inches tall and weighs as much as my refrigerator, but his pale complexion and thick, wire-rimmed glasses usually render him a benign, if not friendly, giant. The figure in that small hospital bed wasn't what I'd expected.

The only light in the room came from a fluorescent fixture hanging high on the wall behind him. The illumination cast heavy shadows across his face, but the shadows didn't hide the damage. From the doorway, I could see that his right leg and left wrist were in plaster casts, propped up on pillows. As I began moving toward the bed, I noticed a long, dark line of blood-encrusted sutures on his face. It began midway down his right cheek and continued diagonally across both lips, then ran down the line of his jaw to the left earlobe. The surrounding tissue was bright red and swollen, and he was badly bruised, like a prizefighter after a losing bout. Set against his pale skin, the wound had a chilling effect.

"James. Manuel. I'm happy to see you both," he said, nodding as if he were welcoming dinner guests.

"Yeah, I'm glad to see you, too," I said. "We've been up all night worrying."

"Thanks to a steady diet of Percodan—" he blinked his eyes and smiled weakly "—I have not."

I felt like an idiot.

"Why don't you all sit down?" Boris suggested. "You're making me nervous looming over me. I'm starting to feel like the corpse at an Irish wake."

Kate sat on the edge of the bed, picked up his good right hand and held it. I don't know if Boris liked that or not, but he didn't try to pull his hand away. Santos drifted over toward the windows, peeked outside, then squatted down and leaned against the wall looking miserable. There was a chair in the corner. I pulled it up to the bed and sat down.

17

"That's better," I began, taking a deep breath. "Now, tell me how you feel, because you look terrible. To be honest, I didn't know what to say at first."

"What? Kathleen, Manuel, did you hear that? I believe a precedent has just been set. On this date in history, Mr. James Joseph Donovan was rendered speechless. Let the record show that the silence lasted for nearly two whole minutes."

He twisted his sutured face into a grotesque smirk.

"Under the circumstances, I suggest you watch the sarcasm, pal," I warned. "You never know, I might decide to bring the Polhemus sisters up here for a visit."

"You wouldn't dare," he said, looking worried.

"Or I could tell the nurse where you get your cigarettes," I continued thoughtfully.

He shot an accusing glance at Manny, who shrugged his shoulders.

"You leave Boris alone," Kate snapped. "J. J. Donovan, if you were in that bed, the melodrama would be so thick we'd need violins and a harp for background music. I think the poor man is being very brave."

Dr. Koulomzin batted his eyelashes modestly.

"How was the vacation?" he asked, changing the subject. "If you weren't so dangerously tanned, I'd apologize for interrupting the trip. But, my God, look at yourselves! I may just have saved your lives. Did I or did I not warn you about the ultraviolet rays in that latitude?"

Sidestepping the ultraviolet debate, I told him about our crazy trip home.

"You should not have gone to all that trouble," Boris said gravely. "I mean, really, there's nothing either of you could have done."

There was something in his eyes I wasn't expecting. It was fear.

"Is that so?" I asked, watching his face. "Well, suppose we talk about that later, after you've told us what happened."

18

He began to fidget.

"What's the matter, is there a problem?" I asked.

"No, there's no problem," he sighed. "It's just that I doubt I will ever erase the memory of being deposited, like a cheap cut of beef, in the emergency ward at Lincoln Hospital. And the ride in the ambulance, that was as bad as anything I can remember from the war."

Boris lost his parents during the Second World War and was shuttled between relief camps and orphanages until his Uncle Ivan finally rescued him and brought him to America.

"I was dazed and somewhat disoriented when the ambulance arrived, but I distinctly recall hearing people yelling, and I remember the lights flashing. It was very surreal."

"The yellin' was me tellin' them people to be careful wit you," Manny said softly.

"I don't know what I would have done without Manuel," Boris added quickly. "He's the only reason I survived. He rescued me."

Manny's scowl melted into a proud grin.

"As I said, I was left unattended in the emergency ward, in that terrible hospital. I tell you, Abraham Lincoln would be ashamed to find his name associated with such a facility. The place was badly overcrowded and dirty. All around me, people were screaming and yelling, and my stretcher was repeatedly bumped and pushed as the staff rushed back and forth in the midst of all this confusion. Had it not been for Manuel's persistence, I might have bled to death right there in the hallway!"

Boris paused for a breath.

"I grabbed that son-of-a-bitch doctor an' I told him he bedda fix the doc or he was gonna be sorry," Manny beamed.

"They wheeled me into a treatment room, stopped the bleeding, and finally gave me a thorough examination," Boris continued. "That led to X rays and splints. In the meantime, Manuel located Richard Steinman, and Richard spoke with the doctors at Lincoln Hospital via the telephone. I was moved into a small, private cubicle and given a shot of something potent enough to carry me into a deep sleep. When I awoke, I was in this bed."

He looked around the room, probably expecting applause. Kate continued to pat his hand and Santos smiled. I wasn't as easily satisfied. Boris still hadn't told us about the accident.

"I'm afraid that won't be easy," he said slowly when I asked again. "You see, in addition to my other physical injuries, I seem to be suffering from a slight case of retrograde amnesia."

"Consider the audience, dear," Kate said politely. "Perhaps you could explain?"

Boris thought for a moment.

"Retrograde amnesia is the loss of memory associated with a specific incident. For instance, a person hurt in a car accident might not remember driving in the automobile or, for that matter, anything else leading up to the accident. Actually, these symptoms can also occur with the use of certain anesthetics, but it's less common."

"That's just fascinating, Boris," I said, eyeing him closely. "How much memory did you lose?"

"The memory loss," he continued, without looking directly at me, "varies widely from case to case. It may cover a very few minutes or a much longer period. In my case, the loss of memory seems to be spotty . . . there are gaps."

He turned his head slightly and finally looked me in the eye. It was a request. He didn't want me to push the issue, not in front of the others.

"In that case, why don't you just tell us what you do remember?" I suggested.

"Well, I suppose I could do that," he said slowly.

We all waited while Boris collected his thoughts.

"It was opening day at the stadium. You know how much I love opening day." He looked at Kate. "The old park was dressed in its finest bunting, and the pennants lining the facade were snapping in the breeze. For the first time in years, even the weather was cooperating. It was a perfect day for baseball, unseasonably warm under a cloudless blue sky."

The Bob Costas imitation was part of the stall, but I humored him.

"Down on the field, the players looked sharp in their starched white pinstriped uniforms. They were soft-tossing baseballs and running sprints. Ignoring the reporters and players, the grounds crew kept on working—drawing chalk lines on the base paths, tracing out the batters boxes, and hosing down the infield clay. Seen from the stands, the freshly painted white bases made the points of the infield diamond just sparkle."

He closed his eyes, obviously enjoying the memory.

"Joe DiMaggio, the Yankee Clipper, was announced, and when he walked onto the field to throw out the first pitch, fifty thousand people rose to their feet and began to whistle, stomp, and applaud. It was really quite exciting."

Boris stopped speaking again and smiled. His mottled face was all black-and-blue, and he had more crusty stitches than the Frankenstein monster, yet he was smiling. I wondered if his lips hurt.

"Hello," I said, snapping my fingers. "Are you still with us?"

He blinked like someone waking from a nap.

"We were sitting in our usual box, in the loge section," Boris said softly. "First tier, first-base side, right behind the dugout."

Kate smiled, remembering. We had chosen that particular section because it's covered by the upper deck and, therefore, shielded from direct sunlight.

"Just as the ovation for Mr. DiMaggio began, a stranger approached Manuel and began to harass him. I was preoccupied with events on the field, so I can't tell you exactly what transpired between them, but the exchange became rather heated. I finally turned to the stranger and suggested that he leave us alone."

"You did more than suggest, Señor," Manny volunteered from the corner.

"What was that all about?" I turned to Santos.

"He was a *pendejo,* man, a fuckin' chump."

"Manuel, there's a lady present," Boris reminded him.

"Awright, Doctor B, but he was a chump."

"Which means what?" I asked. "Who was the guy? What did he want? You know, Manny, give me some details."

"Fact is, the guy was a 'Rican chump who tried to get cute wit me."

Santos twisted his face into a sour expression, reminding us all that he's from the Dominican Republic, not Puerto Rico.

"Listen to me. This *maricon* comes up and shoves a packet in ma face, an' he says he wants a tip. So I said, 'You wanna tip? Get that fuckin' papa outta ma face.' Like that. Sorry Miz Kate, but the man asked for details."

"So keep going," I coached. "What happened next?"

For a guy who loves to talk, Manny wasn't doing so good.

"He said I gotta take the envelope, even if I am a cheap bastid, 'cause he already been paid. So I took the papers and threw 'em on the chair wit the doctor's otha papers and told the chump to get lost before I smacked him. So he did."

Manny is tiny and he's getting pretty old. Having a full-grown albino bear like Boris standing behind him probably helped make the point.

"Did you look in the envelope?" I asked.

"No way, man. We was watchin' Yankee baseball."

"All right, let me see if I've got this straight. A guy came up to your seats and insisted that you accept an envelope, the contents of which were unknown. You thought he was a pest, but you took the envelope anyway, because it was the easiest way to get rid of him."

"Yeah, that's it, man."

"That can't be *it,* Manuel," I said. "I still don't know how Boris got hurt. Unless, of course, this guy with the envelope came back in his car and managed to run Doctor Koulomzin

22

over while he was seated in the loge section munching on a hot dog."

"That's stupid," Manny snapped, sounding hurt.

Boris cleared his throat.

"We watched the game. Obviously, the accident came later, outside the stadium."

"Thank you. Who won?"

"The Yankees won. Naturally."

"Naturally."

I took a deep breath.

"Listen, guys, I'm losing my patience. Will one of you please just tell me about the accident?"

They looked at each other.

"I really don't remember much, not until they put me in the ambulance," Boris lied.

"Is that so? What about you, Manny? Don't tell me you've got amnesia, too."

"No way, man. Like I told you before, the doctor was waitin' for me on the corna."

"What corner?"

"One-fifty-seven."

"One-fifty-seventh and what?"

"And River Avenue."

"After the game, Boris was standing at the corner of One Hundred Fifty-seventh Street and River Avenue and you were making a telephone call."

"That's what I said."

"Fine. Where'd you make the call?"

"I went to a pay phone inna bodega. When I come back, the doc was down and the whole place gone crazy."

"I don't suppose you have anything to add?" I asked, turning back to Boris.

He shook his head without looking at me.

"Manny, you said there was a witness. Did he see the man driving the car?"

23

"Oh yeah, Donovan, he seen him, and so did a buncha otha people. Got the license plate and everythin'. The police caught up wit that *maricon* pretty quick."

"That's great. Where are they holding him?"

Boris and Manny looked at each other again.

"Where are they holding him?" I repeated, looking first at Manny, then at Boris.

"The man driving the car that hit me is in the Bellevue Hospital morgue, James," Boris said slowly. "I've seen a photograph of the body, and so has Manuel. It's the same man who was bothering us before the game. There is no question in my mind about the identity. His car was found in Manhattan on the day after my accident. It was left in Riverside Park, off the Westside Highway. The driver's body was in the trunk."

This story had too many wrinkles. I was getting a headache.

"And now you know almost as much as we do," Boris said quietly. "So if you don't mind, I'm very tired and would like to rest. Perhaps you could come back later?"

Kate was tired, too. She gave Boris a good-night kiss, then turned to me.

"Let's go back to your place and get some dinner," she suggested.

"I've got a better idea," I said quickly. "Let Manny take you home in the leem-o. I'll get something to eat in the cafeteria, then come back up here and sit with Boris."

"Okay, fine," she said, forcing a big smile. Something was wrong, but she knew enough to stay out of it.

"I'll be back in about an hour," I told Boris as Kate stepped into the hall. "Get plenty of rest, my friend, because we've got a lot to talk about."

Boris ignored me. He was busy watching Santos crawl under the radiator. When Manny reappeared, he was smiling happily. I watched Boris take a couple of Balkan Sobraine cigarettes and a pack of matches from him and slip them into the top of his leg cast.

I made a point of shutting the door on my way out.

24

THREE

■ ■ ■

Kate and I stood in the quiet, carpeted hallway, a short distance from the nurses' station, and waited for the elevator in silence. Manny, who joined us when his smuggling assignment was complete, kept busy by pressing the Down button until the car arrived. We were all too tired for conversation.

Boris has a faculty appointment in Columbia University's Department of Mathematics at the main campus, which is located on Morningside Heights at 116th Street, fourteen blocks north of our apartment building. This professorial distinction had earned him a private room on the ninth floor of the Milstein Hospital, which was quite an honor. The ninth floor is the top floor, and it is usually reserved for people like the mayor of New York City or Mohammed Ali—which explained the carpeted hallways and the neat, well-appointed private rooms with river views, new television sets, and fresh-cut flowers.

On the ride down, the elevator made local stops and we saw hallways with worn linoleum flooring and dirty walls. The lower floors were crowded with patients and staff. There were attending physicians in long white lab coats, nurses in blue or green surgical scrubs, baby-faced medical students in short white jackets, transporters in dark-blue-and-gray uniforms, and maintenance people in tan. All of them, regardless of their color-coded outfits, wore identifying security badges. The elevator filled quickly and we found ourselves squeezed up against the right-hand side of the cab, listening to a couple of medical types earnestly discussing the treatment of a terminal patient.

When the doors opened on the fourth floor, the crowd thinned a bit as the conferring doctors departed. A tall, gaunt young man wearing a surgical mask and faded red pajamas shuffled aboard. He was connected by intravenous lines to several plastic bags hanging from a rolling metal pole that he dragged behind himself like an unwilling friend. Nasty black-and-blue marks streaked his arms and the backs of his hands, and his eyes were watery and vacant. When more people entered the car at the next stop, I was pushed up so close to the man that our noses could have touched.

I have never liked being in hospitals, though I can handle a visit now and then if I'm not the center of attention. But finding myself in such close proximity with an obviously sick person made me really uncomfortable. This guy looked like a breeding ground for all sorts of deadly microbes. Believe me, if the elevator trip had been more than a few floors, I probably would have developed symptoms. I held my breath and tried to look natural.

When the doors opened on the main floor, I made a dash for the great outdoors, where I gratefully filled my lungs with New York City air. Disinfectants don't hold a candle to the good old-fashioned diesel fumes produced by city buses. Manny's cousin, Moses, had the big car parked and running near the front door, so I leaned against it, catching my breath, and waited for the others.

Kate took her time walking across the lobby, pretending that she didn't know me. But when she stepped outside, I could see the smile forming. I grabbed her before she could say anything smart and held her in my arms.

"I'm sorry about the trip, Kate," I whispered in her ear as we hugged. "There are still so many things I didn't get to tell you. I wasn't ready to come home."

She held me tightly and began to tremble.

"Don't you think for one moment that I've forgotten anything, you big dope," she said softly. When she let go of me, she was still smiling, but there were tears in her eyes.

Manny was holding the car door open, looking embarrassed. Kate turned away quickly and climbed into the battered old limousine. J. J. Donovan knows how to send a lady home in style. As the Fly Rides Leem-o pulled away from the curb, I noticed the electric license-plate holder, flashing and blinking like the neon sign outside a strip joint. The doorman at Kate's condo, over on Sutton Place, was going to be really impressed.

I stood at the curb and watched until the leem-o turned the corner and disappeared from sight. Right on cue, my stomach began to growl. It led me back to the lobby, where a security guard directed me to the public cafeteria. It was clean and bright, and there were comfortable little tables set out on a balcony overlooking the entrance foyer. I got in line with a tray and managed to fill it before I even reached the dessert section. The hospital food looked good and smelled better, which was a really pleasant surprise.

I had a napkin tucked in my shirt collar and was poised with fork and knife, when I noticed a pair of legs the size of tree trunks coming my way. The tree trunks wore green surgical scrubs and I could see the white skirt of a lab coat. I started to eat with a vengeance, like a condemned man who's just seen the warden and the priest coming down the hall.

"Hello, Donovan, how's the shoulder?" Hiram Parker asked, sitting down uninvited and grinning at me.

Dr. Parker is a very tall, ebony-skinned man who comports himself with an air of supreme confidence. His speciality is orthopedic surgery and he considers himself the best in the business. A lot of people agree with him. They've even named a screw after the good doctor—"The Parker Screw." It's made of titanium and they use it to fix broken pelvic bones. I've fed

Hiram straight lines about his device a few times, but he's never amused.

The best thing I can say about Parker's bedside manner is that it's unforgettable. He took care of my shoulder when a bad guy broke it with a baseball bat. The shoulder managed to heal, despite getting rebroken in a little gas explosion, and I showed my gratitude by contributing to the renovation of his outpatient clinic. So, technically speaking, we're even. Doesn't matter, I still get the willies around the guy. My shoulder began to throb as soon as I saw him.

"I presume you've come to look after your friend, Doctor Koulomzin," he remarked.

I wasn't about to let Hiram Parker or anybody else interfere with my dinner, so I just nodded and kept right on chewing. Two days of airline food can do that to a man.

"Son, I think you'd best take some air with that protein. The food won't do you much good if you're not breathing," he advised.

I lifted my head, stopped chewing, and took a deep breath through my nose. I exhaled slowly and satisfactorily. Then I started chewing again.

"You know something, Donovan? For a man your age, there's still an awful lot of the little boy comin' out." He shook his head back and forth ruefully.

That wasn't much of a revelation, but I let him believe it was profound while I swallowed the food in my mouth and washed it down with a long, cool drink of Diet Pepsi.

"Hiram," I began, then belched into my napkin as politely as possible, "less than twenty-four hours ago, I was in paradise with a beautiful woman. I woke up with a hangover, got doused with ice water, and then learned that my best friend and partner had been struck down by some sort of maniac in the Bronx. For all I knew, my friend was clinging to life by the thinnest of threads."

I started to carefully butter a cube of fresh corn bread, making sure I got butter on all four sides of the little square before continuing.

"So I raced home, forsaking food, sleep, and more important, the aforementioned beautiful woman. And what did I find upon my arrival? Well, my dear friend is very much alive and, if possible, more cantankerous than ever. Having confused and frustrated me, I suspect that he's tormenting the nursing staff even as we speak. All things considered, I thought it would be wise to eat some food and relax a little, lest I started doing my imitation of a disgruntled postal worker. Now, does that sound like the reasoning of a child?"

"You know something, Donovan? Every time I run into you, I gotta hear a long, sad story, like you're the only poor thing in town." He was still shaking his head.

"What can I tell you, Hiram? Stuff happens to me."

"That it does, J. J. That it does."

"Have an apple," I suggested, rolling one across the table to him. "It'll help you relax, you're starting to repeat yourself. Look at me, I've been eating an apple a day ever since you worked on my shoulder."

"Very funny," he said, even though he doesn't really have a sense of humor. "Look, I came over here to talk to you about your partner. He happens to be my patient."

I already knew that. I'd called Richard Steinman from the plane. Rich is my close friend and neighbor. He's also the internist unlucky enough to have all of us for patients—me, Boris, the Santos family, and just about everyone else in our building. Richard hadn't appreciated the four-o'clock wake-up call, but I learned that Parker was in charge and managed to get a brief overview of the case before he hung up on me.

"I thought you worked down at St. Luke's–Roosevelt," I said, just to bust Hiram's chops. "What happened, they trade you for future draft picks?"

"I have attending privileges at both hospitals," he growled. "Now, about my patient."

29

"You referring to the strange-looking creature who's been threatening all the nurses up on the ninth floor?" I asked cheerfully.

"One and the same," Parker confirmed, putting on his serious face. "He's a lot more banged up than you think, Donovan. Don't let him fool you. Frankly, for a man in his fifties, Doctor Koulomzin has shown a remarkable amount of physical strength and resilience. I'm surprised he's come around so fast."

This didn't sound like my friend Boris. Not the guy who thinks splinters should be removed under general anesthetic.

"Why don't you tell me what's wrong with him?" I asked, stirring my coffee. "He's claims to be suffering from something called 'retrograde amnesia.' I think the amnesia's a ploy."

"I don't know the good doctor very well, but I agree that the memory loss is suspicious," Parker acknowledged, scratching his chin like a college professor. "We've had him checked and rechecked by the neurologists, and there is no obvious mental deficit. Doctor Koulomzin pulled this memory-loss stuff on the nurses a couple of times, but I didn't make a big deal of it. You got any idea what he's up to?"

"Not yet, but I will soon," I said confidently. "By the way, if your patient does anything else you don't understand, just remember, he can be rather eccentric."

I smiled weakly.

"Why don't I finish telling you what ails him?" Hiram suggested, looking unhappy.

"Okay," I said. "Fire away."

"Well, in addition to that ugly facial laceration and the obvious abrasions and bruising, he sustained three broken ribs on the right side of his chest, a compound fracture of his right femur, and a broken left wrist. The femur and ribs were probably broken upon impact with the vehicle, and I'd bet that he hurt the wrist trying to break his fall. But the laceration across his face is a different animal, I can't figure out what could have caused such a clean wound."

I was starting to feel guilty for not showing Boris more sympathy.

"Doctor Koulomzin was originally taken by ambulance to Lincoln Hospital," Parker continued, as if he were lecturing an intern. "I don't know if you're familiar with Lincoln Hospital— it's over on a Hundred Forty-ninth Street, near the Grand Concourse, in the South Bronx."

I'd been in the neighborhood a few times, with my windows up and the car doors locked. To be badly hurt and alone in an emergency room in the South Bronx would have left an indelible scar on my psyche.

"Fortunately, they didn't keep him very long," Dr. Parker said. "Somebody named Santos managed to track down Richard Steinman, and Rich found me. We had Boris transferred to Columbia as soon as possible. To Lincoln's credit, they followed instructions. By the time he arrived at our shop, the patient was stabilized, the facial wound had been dressed, and there were X rays. Given the volume of business they get, the boys and girls at Lincoln did a pretty good job."

This was generous praise from the great surgeon.

"When I first saw Doctor Koulomzin, he still had a Philadelphia collar strapped around his neck, so they hadn't moved him very much. I looked at the pictures and examined him, but it was obvious that we had to get him into the O.R."

"The operating room? I didn't know he needed surgery," I said, feeling guiltier by the minute.

"I told you, he's more seriously injured than it appears."

Hiram didn't like repeating himself.

During the next fifteen minutes, I learned all the grisly details. Boris had spent more than two hours on the operating table having his bones repaired. The right femur, the piece connecting the knee to the hip, had been snapped in half. To fix it, something called an "interlocking intramedullary rod" had been inserted into hollowed-out portions of the bone on either side of the break. The rod was held in place at either end by a screw. It

31

wasn't the Parker screw, but he assured me it was still a very good screw. The fractured left wrist had been easier to fix. Parker realigned it, then put on a plaster cast to hold the placement while the bones healed.

These weren't the only problems. In addition to the big laceration across his face, Boris had lost a lot of blood. Dr. Parker didn't understand the facial wound. It was too clean, as if it had been made with a very sharp knife or a razor. But that didn't make any sense because there had been no reports of a slashing. While the orthopedic team worked on the broken bones, a plastic surgeon had been busy closing the ugly laceration. She'd used more than two hundred stitches, and everyone was hoping the scarring would be minimal.

Finally, as if Boris didn't have enough broken parts, there were also those three cracked ribs to mend. They'd been taped, but that wouldn't make them any less painful. Hiram said that Boris should expect to spend at least four more days in the hospital, and he predicted six weeks at home, followed by physical therapy. When he started going back over the finer points of the operation, I tuned him out. A precise description of Dr. Parker's surgical technique wasn't on my short list of postprandial topics, though I do remember thinking that Boris should stay inside the building during electrical storms.

While Parker lectured me on the best packing material to use when anchoring a stainless-steel rod in a broken shank, we slowly made our way back up to the ninth floor. I'd been gone for more than an hour, and it should have been safe to return. As we approached the door to Boris's room, we heard a woman's voice. It sounded strained.

"Now you listen to me, Doctor Koulomzin. I've taken enough crap from you for one day. You better knock it off or I'll page Doctor Parker."

"Did someone mention my name?" Parker asked, pushing the door open and striding into the room.

We met a wall of silence. The nurse I'd seen earlier had frozen in position while shaking an angry finger at the big lump in the bed. Boris was pouting, but he didn't say anything.

"I'm sure I heard my name spoken, Ms. Nangle. Is there some sort of problem?" Parker asked.

She looked down at Boris and I could see how badly she wanted to rat on him. But she couldn't bring herself to do it. Boris was her patient; she'd settle this score some other way.

"No, Doctor, there isn't anything wrong. Doctor Koulomzin and I were just having a discussion and your name came up. It was nothing, really."

She forced a crooked smile, then scowled at Boris. He owed her big-time.

"I see," Parker said, rubbing his chin again. "I don't suppose that's cigarette smoke I'm smelling? Cigarette smoking is strictly forbidden in this hospital, and I will not have patients of mine abusing either the fire code or my personal instructions."

Six and one half feet of menacing surgeon stared down at the patient, who flushed a bit but kept mum. Ms. Nangle tried very hard to keep a straight face as she picked up a paper cup half filled with water, ashes, and cigarette butts and hid it under the towel she was carrying.

"If there's nothing else, Doctor, I'll be getting back to my other patients," she said, slipping past him out the door.

"Fine, fine," Hiram mumbled, turning his attention to the patient's chart. "So, how are we feeling tonight, Doctor Koulomzin?" he asked without looking up. "Are we experiencing any pain?"

"I don't have a clue how *we're* feeling, Doctor Parker," Boris grumbled. "However, I am feeling miserable. The pain has been constant and I cannot seem to find a position comfortable enough to allow for sleep. The sleep depravation has, in turn, made me somewhat disagreeable. And if this weren't bad enough, they—" Boris gestured toward the nurses' station "—*they* have refused me decent food and are constantly invading my privacy. Does that answer your question? I am one miserable human being."

I had to bite my tongue.

"Good, that's very good. If you've got enough energy to be angry, you're doing just fine." Parker smiled reassuringly, like he'd just cured cancer. "Now, about your complaints, I think I can be of some help. Your diet was restricted on my orders, but those orders can be changed. The average person finds solid foods difficult to keep down so soon after surgery. I'm sure you'll agree that it makes no sense to put food into the stomach if it's going to come right back out. However, if you're feeling up to it, I think we could arrange for some soup and crackers."

"Soup and crackers be damned!" Boris shouted. "Get me some solid food right now or I'm leaving!"

Parker raised his eyebrows and turned to me.

"I think you should ignore the Park Ranger's signs and feed the old bear," I said.

"Very well, Doctor Koulomzin, have it your way," Parker conceded. "I'll instruct the nurse to bring in a menu. But don't cry to me if you vomit the whole thing back up."

"Thank you," Boris said, his eyes shining with pleasure.

"You're welcome," Parker said without enthusiasm. "Now, about the pain. They gave you morphine over at Lincoln, then we switched you to Percodan after the surgery. I had hoped to switch again as soon as possible, to something milder, perhaps just extra-strength Tylenol."

"I tell you honestly, Doctor, I am in pain and I need some assistance. At this point, I'd considered chewing my leg off at the hip if it would bring relief."

"That won't be necessary," Parker said, making notes in the chart. "I get the point."

He finished writing, returned the chart to its place at the foot of the bed and stepped out of the room, presumably to make the necessary arrangements. Boris made an ill-advised stab at the pitcher of ice water on the stand next to his bed and knocked a large pile of books and papers onto the floor. While I was cleaning up the mess, Parker reappeared with the nurse. She was carrying a small tray of medical supplies.

"Ms. Nangle has the instructions, Doctor Koulomzin," he said, arranging the utensils on the tray. "Now, I'm going to give you a shot of Demerol. This should ease your pain considerably. When it wears off, we'll try Tylenol with codeine. I think you'll be much more comfortable after that."

Hiram stood up straight, checked the syringe in his hand, flicked it a few times to remove air bubbles, then turned and advanced on his target. Boris was too banged up to move, or even to defend himself. He looked over at me, made a face, then winced as the point was driven home.

"Okay, boys, that's it for me, I have other patients," Parker announced, straightening back up to his full height and looming over Boris. "I'm going to leave you in Ms. Nangle's care, Doctor. I advise you to cooperate."

Parker left the room, but his words seemed to linger. Nangle moved to the foot of the bed and folded her arms across her chest.

"I'm told you can eat solid food, Doctor Koulomzin. Did you have something in mind, or would you prefer to see the menu?"

The question was wrapped in sarcasm, but it wasn't a joke. Turned out, ninth floor VIPs could order à la carte from a special dining room. The news didn't immediately register with Boris, so the shot must have been working. His rigid, combative mask slowly dissolved into a benign expression.

"Ms. Nangle . . ." he slurred, the way he does after a third martini ". . . please accept my apology for being such a difficult patient. I merely wish to have some real food, solid food, if you will, so that I can begin the process of restoring my diminished blood supply. I would be happy to accept anything you think appropriate, though I should mention that I cannot tolerate brussels sprouts."

With that said, Boris promptly fell sound asleep. The nurse

removed his glasses and straightened the blankets. Under the circumstances, food was out of the question. She took her menu and left me to contemplate the sound of Boris snoring.

There weren't many options. If I wanted to know what was going on, I had to stick around until he woke up. I got a blanket and a pillow from the closet and curled up as best I could in my little chair. When sleep eluded me, I tried to will myself back to the island by thinking of Kate lying next to me on the beach in that little bikini of hers. But it just wasn't meant to be. Every time the action started to pick up, wrinkled old Magda popped into my mind, interrupting things as usual.

FOUR

■ ■ ■

A man who stands six feet two inches tall and weighs nearly two hundred pounds isn't meant to rest comfortably in a tiny, straight-backed chair, especially if he's twisted up like a pretzel. To make matters worse, the snorting and rasping sounds coming out of my partner were so unnatural they made the hair on my forearms stand on end.

After a while, I got up and quietly opened the blinds. The sun had long since melted from the sky, so I didn't have to worry about deadly ultraviolet rays startling Boris into consciousness. The view from the windows was spectacular. To my right, the George Washington Bridge stretched out across the Hudson River, its steel-gray girders and cables firmly grasping the banks on either shore. Turning left, I was able to look straight down the West Side of Manhattan, following the highway as it snaked along the riverbank. And directly across from me, over in New Jersey, bright lights were beginning to sparkle in the luxury condos dotting the cliffs.

As I lingered at the window, I began to organize the books and papers I'd rescued earlier, when Boris had knocked them off his nightstand. Wherever he goes, Boris creates these tiny paper stalagmites by stacking books, journals, magazines, computer printouts, newspapers, or just about any other readable material that catches his fancy. Sorting through the pile, I was reminded of how much stuff his brain needs to absorb in order to satisfy its craving for information. I once snooped through a pile of his papers that included a dog-eared issue of *Statistical Method in Medical Research*, a copy of a journal called *Biometrics*, two months of the *New York Times* Sunday Magazine sections, a research paper comparing the mating rituals of Asian and African bull elephants, volume three of Winston Churchill's *A History of the English Speaking Peoples*, the libretto for the opera *Siegfried*, and finally, beneath the Wagnerian strata, an April 1978 issue of *Soap Opera Digest*.

The stack of goodies I was sorting on the windowsill included all the reading material he'd lugged to the baseball game up in the Bronx. There was a six-hundred-page paperback copy of the *Baseball Encyclopedia*, the opening-day game program, the Yankee team's yearbook, two copies of the *Journal of Biostatistics*, a small notebook of formulas written in Boris's compressed scribble, a hardcover copy of William Manchester's *A World Lit Only By Fire*, a spiral-bound book of game scorecards, several pages of the Yankees' preseason statistics printed on our office letterhead, and finally, an unlabeled manilla envelope.

I took the envelope back to my chair, where the lighting was better. It was nine-by-twelve inches, slightly larger than a standard pad of writing paper. I turned the package over several times, examining it closely for identifying marks or labels. It was spattered with blood and dirt, but the flap had been glued and then taped shut, so it was still sealed. I balanced the envelope on the palm of my right hand and guessed the weight to be about three ounces. It was pretty flat, and there didn't seem to be any hard or strangely shaped objects inside.

I quietly wheeled the dinner tray over to my chair, lowered the tabletop and cleared it off. Using the sharp ceramic blade on my pocketknife, I carefully lifted the tape, then slit the flap. When it was open, I blew some air into the envelope and peeked inside. I wiped the surface of the table with my handkerchief, then gently shook the contents out of the envelope. The complete inventory consisted of three black-and-white photographs. Each photograph had a six-by-eight-inch index card stapled to its back. Each card had neatly typed medical jargon on it. But that was all—no cover letter or note to introduce or explain the pictures. The person receiving this package was expected to understand the contents.

I spread the photographs out on the table in front of me and examined them carefully, looking for identifying marks or labels that might have helped me trace them back to a photo lab, but the prints were on common stock and it was clean. The first picture showed three men in T-shirts, their arms draped around each other, standing in front of a bar or restaurant. Behind them, etched in the storefront glass, was a derby hat. The man on the left was a burly fellow with a full, thick beard, who looked to be about fifty years old. His counterpart, on the right side in the photo, was a tall, sinewy man, probably in his early forties, with graying blond hair and a neatly trimmed mustache. Both men were looking at a much younger fellow who stood between them. All were smiling happily.

I gazed at the young man in the middle of the picture for a minute. He was probably in his early thirties, with the trim build of an athlete and a confident, handsome face. He was clearly the center of attention in this print; but you could tell that the picture had been cropped or enlarged to capture this particular section of a larger group photo. Turning the picture over, I read: *Micro-bacterium Avium Complex Infection (MAC). New York University Medical Center (Lieb). 9–16 months.* The r's were irregular and some of the ink had smeared; the card had been typed on an old machine with a ribbon.

I picked up the second picture. This time, the subject was a woman and she was alone, standing in front of an abstract sculpture. It was an inviting face, the kind to which you'd confide your secrets. The lady could have been thirty or forty or fifty, it was hard to pinpoint. There was something about her comportment that suggested the kind of wisdom one develops over time, but her complexion and carriage was that of a younger woman.

Perhaps it was the sculpture; a finely polished, white-marble nude, reclining. When I turned the picture over, I got more of the medical mumbojumbo: *Acute Myelogenous Leukemia. No bone marrow TP; failed standard chemotherapy. Yale–New Haven Hospital (Newman). 8–11 months.*

The third card could have been part of a corporate press kit. It showed a serious-looking character in his middle fifties, with a studied touch of gray at the temples. He wore an expensive-looking pinstriped suit and a starched white shirt with a silver tie. He was staring at the camera, his expression daring it to disagree with him. I had an urge to tweak the end of his pointy nose. Flipping the picture over, I read: *Kaposi's Sarcoma, Pneumocystis carinii pneumonia. Mount Sinai Medical Center (Conners). 10–12 months.* The same irregular r's, the same smudged ink.

I sat back heavily and started chewing my thumbnail.

"Well, what was he looking for?" Boris asked, startling me.

I turned to him, but he was staring out the window, looking depressed.

"Was it worth it?"

"I'm not sure what you mean," I answered. "The package was delivered to the wrong party. Obviously, he wanted to get it back."

"Was it worth dying for?"

"How should I know? Look, Boris, the man wasn't very bright. Think about it. He runs you down with his car and then what? Was he planning to pull over and casually search your pockets while you lay in the street?"

"What are you talking about?" he snapped.

"I'm talking about the Puerto Rican deliveryman," I said calmly. "You know, the driver of the car that almost killed you. The man whose body is chilling in the morgue. This should be familiar ground."

Boris looked really disgusted.

"I know *who* you're talking about," he said, "but you're not making sense. I wasn't referring to the driver, I was talking about the other one, the one who tried to slit my throat. And for the record, I was wondering about the value of my own life. I could have died, you know."

I sat up straighter in my chair.

"What other man?" I stammered.

Boris lowered his voice dramatically.

"The devil's helper," he whispered slowly, making it sound creepy. "The man with the black eyes."

I blinked a few times.

"Nobody has said anything to me about another person, let alone a spirit from the netherworld," I said. "How could I have known about someone you've never mentioned?"

"Well, he was there, and he was a demon."

I assumed the painkillers were playing games with him.

"Listen, Boris, maybe I should come back tomorrow."

"No, please!" he insisted. "I don't want you to leave, not just yet. Please, James, we need to talk."

"Okay, okay, relax. I won't go anywhere if you don't want me to, but man, you've got to admit, you're not acting like yourself."

He sat up a little in the bed.

"There is absolutely no need for you to pander to me," he said, drilling into me with those bloodshot, black-and-blue eyes. "I understand exactly what's happening and I have complete control of my mental faculties."

Before he could continue, Ms. Nangle reappeared.

"I see Sleeping Beauty has awakened," she boomed, trying to be pleasant. "Are *we* ready for dinner?"

Boris made a rude noise and turned his head away.

"This might be a good time to place the dinner order, Ms. Nangle," I suggested when it became obvious that Boris wasn't going to answer her. "You go ahead and pick something tasty. But remember, no brussels sprouts."

"I see," she nodded, looking at Boris like he was a specimen on a slide. "Well, I've brought his medication. Would you plant these pills in him while I arrange for the meal?"

I took the little paper cup from her hand, but she wasn't paying attention. Nurse Nangle was slowly backing out of the room, trying to diagnose the change in Boris's mood. When she was gone, I gave him the medication and filled a glass with water.

"What was that all about?" I asked, sticking a straw in the water glass.

"What do you mean?"

Boris stirred enough to swallowed his medicine.

"What do you think I mean? Why'd you snub Nangle? She's only trying to help."

"Oh, that," he nodded. "Yes, well, I am very sorry if I was rude, but the woman is loud and cloddish, and she arrived at a bad time, James. I simply cannot abide these constant interruptions."

I got up and stood over him like a frustrated parent.

"Okay, now listen up," I said. "You are out of control and it's got to stop. You have been rude and abusive to that nurse ever since I got here. At your worst, Boris, you are weird and annoying, but you are never abusive. Everyone's allowed some leeway, especially under these circumstances, but you crossed that line a while back. Do I make myself clear?"

He turned his head away, but I wasn't through.

"In addition to abusing the nursing staff, you've just informed me that a second man, not the one who hit you with his car and later died, but a second man, came along and tried to slit your throat. According to you, this second man was a disciple of Satan's. Be honest, wouldn't this new story raise questions in your mind?"

A tense interval followed, during which Boris pouted and stared out the window. It seemed unnatural; I don't usually get the last word.

"Tell me what you found in the envelope," he asked at last, speaking softly.

"There are three photographs," I began, relieved to get things moving again. "Two are pictures of men, the third photo is of a woman."

I went back to the rolling bed table and collected the pictures.

"Attached to each of the photographs is an index card with some medical information typed on it. The typing was probably done with an old machine—some of the letters are irregular and the ink is smeared around the edges. Aside from the pictures and cards, there was nothing in the envelope. There are no identifying marks on the inside or outside of the package."

I held the photographs up, one at a time, and read him the information typed on each card.

"Maybe the creep was delivering material to a blackmailer and he got his box seats mixed up," I suggested.

Boris shook his head back and forth very slowly.

"I think not," he muttered. "There's been a mix-up, but it wasn't with a blackmailer."

"Boris, you're starting to give me the creeps," I said honestly. "Why not go back to the beginning and tell me the whole story? You're not suffering from amnesia any more than I am, and I can't help if I don't know what happened."

"You're right, of course. I will need your help," he said, the fear creeping back into his eyes. He fought with it for a second, before deciding to continue.

"The explanation you heard earlier was essentially true, though, as you guessed, incomplete," he began. "For reasons that should become apparent, I edited the story when I told it to the police and the doctors."

"Do the cops know about this envelope?"

I held it up.

"That depends on what you mean by 'know about' it."

"Don't start the evasiveness again, Boris. You've already told me that you and Manny each identified the driver from pictures the police provided. Since Manny wasn't there when the car hit you, the only time he would have seen the driver was during the

43

little argument at the beginning of the game. If the cops asked him to look at pictures, then they must know about the botched delivery."

"That's very good reasoning," he conceded.

"Just answer the question. Do the cops know you have the envelope?"

"Yes and no."

"Boris, I'm getting annoyed."

He sighed dramatically.

"Very well. They know that an envelope was mistakenly delivered to us during the game by the driver of the car that later struck me. But they think the envelope is missing."

"And you haven't done anything to change their minds about that?"

He shook his head no.

"What is wrong with you?" I asked seriously. "This is a problem for the police."

"I wasn't in a position to give or tell them anything for almost twenty-four hours. When the time came, I just decided to wait."

"Wait? For what?"

He didn't respond.

"And the other guy, the one who cut you, do they know about him?"

"No."

"Why not, for God's sake?"

"I have my reasons."

He hesitated again, and made a face.

"It's too late to stop now, Boris. Just tell me what happened."

He looked up uncertainly, but I didn't waver.

"Very well," he sighed. "I was standing across the street from Yankee Stadium, on the corner of One Hundred Fifty-seventh Street and River Avenue, as Manuel described. It was late afternoon, and the game had just ended. I was watching the crowds of people leaving the area, as one does while waiting for time to pass. I'd forgotten about the trouble over the envelope at the beginning of the game, so the assault caught me completely off guard.

"The details are still fuzzy, but I remember looking up and noticing the brilliant colors in the sunset, which got me to thinking about the effects of carbon monoxide on this otherwise beautiful natural phenomena. I was in the midst of this contemplation when I heard a woman cry out. Naturally, I turned toward the source. When I did, I saw a large American-built automobile heading directly for me. The tires on the driver's side of the car were up on the sidewalk and people were diving out of the vehicle's path as it accelerated. There was very little time to act, but I managed to take a step backward. That single step saved my life, James. The driver was forced to slow down and had to swing his door open in order to strike me. And strike me he did, though it seemed better to be bludgeoned with the door than to absorb the full force of the moving automobile.

"Anyway, I took the blow and fell to the ground. Fortunately, I didn't land on or injure my head, so I was able to remain conscious. I lay on the sidewalk in a state of shock, badly injured, unable to move, surrounded by hundreds of strangers. As you might imagine, it was terribly confusing and frightening. Then a powerfully built, white-haired gentleman pushed his way through the crowd and knelt down beside me like a Good Samaritan. My bag and papers were by my side and he dragged them closer, as if to protect them from theft.

"At first I felt relieved that someone was trying to help me. But then the stranger began to chuckle under his breath, and the sound made my skin crawl as I realized that my new friend was planning to help himself. He spread a coat over me and pretended to tend to my wounds while he skillfully searched through my belongings.

"It didn't take him long to find a manilla envelope in my bag. I watched as he deftly slipped it into his jacket, all the while fawning over me and calling for assistance. Then he leaned down, smiling, and whispered in my ear. His breath was cold,

45

James, cold and foul. He said: 'I came to sacrifice a lamb and I've been given a fatted cow.' Then he cackled."

Boris stopped and looked at me. His eyes were rimmed with red, and tears welled up.

"He leaned over me again, as if to check the back of my head, but he only wanted to shield his actions from the crowd. You see, there was a razor blade hidden in his left hand. He calmly raked the deadly instrument across my face. He meant to open my throat, but his position was awkward and I wasn't very co-operative. As it was, he inflicted a wound from which I might have bled to death. When I felt my own blood, warm against my chest, I finally regained my voice and let go a terrific scream. The white-haired man jumped to his feet, taking his coat with him, and innocently renewed his call for assistance. I watched him as he melted back into the crowd and disappeared. It was easy for him to flee—the crowd was pressing forward, hungry for the sight of blood."

Boris stopped for a moment, breathing hard, fighting back anger and fear.

"When he bent down to speak to me, I looked into the man's eyes, James. They were black, like his soul. I know this man, I saw his kind when I was a child in the war. He is the devil's instrument, and I believe he has only just begun to haunt us."

"There isn't going to be any haunting, Boris. This man, who-ever he is, won't bother you again. It's over."

"It's not over, James. Look in front of you—that is the pack-age he sought. The manilla envelope he snatched from my bag contained the draft manuscript of an article about balance points in chaotic systems. I doubt that my assailant considers it a fair trade. The article will, however, provide him with my name and address. Do not forget the fate of his unfortunate accomplice, the Puerto Rican deliveryman and driver. He failed twice. For this, he was murdered and stuffed into the trunk of a car. I predict that this white-haired ghoul is very, very angry. We have his things and he won't rest until he retrieves them."

Boris shuddered.

"What do you make of these medical terms?" I asked, turning the photographs over and looking at the index cards.

"Read them to me again," he sighed.

I picked up the first photograph, the picture of three happy men.

" 'Microbacterium Avium Complex Infection (MAC). New York University Medical Center (Lieb). Nine to sixteen months,' " I read, struggling a bit with the words.

Boris took slow, deep breaths while he thought.

"One of those men has the AIDS virus," he said finally. "MAC is a serious, fatal complication, symptomatic of advanced immunological deficiency. I don't know what 'Lieb' means; it could be the name of the patient's physician or his nearest relative. Nine to sixteen months probably refers to his life expectancy."

He sounded very tired, as if the explanation was sapping all of his energy. I quickly read him the next card, which was stapled to the picture of a woman with a sculpture.

" 'Acute Myelogenous Leukemia. No Bone Marrow TP; failed standard chemotherapy. Yale–New Haven Hospital (Newman). Eight to eleven months.' "

This time, Boris didn't make me wait.

"This woman has a very active form of leukemia. It has not responded to standard treatment and is apparently too advanced for consideration of a bone-marrow transplant. The disease is fatal. Eleven months strikes me as an optimistic projection of her life expectancy."

The last card was attached to the picture of the executive.

" 'Kaposi's Sarcoma, Pneumocystis carinii pneumonia. Mount Sinai Medical Center (Conners). Ten to twelve months.' "

Boris winced slightly.

"Like the first case, this man probably has the AIDS virus. Kaposi's skin cancer is a common expression of the active disease, though it doesn't necessarily indicate imminent death. The

47

Pneumocystis pneumonia, however, is a very dangerous indication that the disease has advanced."

"How do you know all this stuff?" I asked, amazed.

"I fulfill my responsibility to stay informed," he said simply, like it was as easy as reading box scores in the local newspaper.

I turned back to the photographs and looked at each of the innocent faces.

"They're all dying?"

"Yes."

"What could your white-haired friend possibly want with sick people?" I asked. "There's no profit in blackmailing the dying—they've got nothing to lose. Do you think he's planning to go after their families?"

Boris stared straight up at the ceiling, as if he were imploring heaven to send him help.

"No, James, my cold-blooded friend isn't contemplating blackmail."

"Then what's he up to?"

The silence returned, and the room seemed to grow cooler. I watched Boris as he concentrated on the ceiling, and saw the tears welling up in his eyes again.

"Boris?" I asked, after a long interval.

"Yes."

"What's going on?"

He blinked his eyes several times, fighting back the tears.

"Boris?"

It was my turn to get scared.

"The white-haired man intends to kill them, James," he said.

FIVE

■ ■ ■

It was well past midnight and the lobby of my apartment building was completely deserted. Most nights, Manny Santos and his boys sit up late, drinking cerbeza and playing dominoes. As far as I could remember, they hadn't interrupted play since the night Carlos Diaz shot Manny's cousin Hector. And even then, they picked up the game as soon as the cops left.

My loafers echoed in the empty foyer as I walked slowly toward the elevators. I pushed the call button and the tired old lift started to moan and groan as it came to life and headed down to the lobby. When the doors finally opened, the cab was at least a foot higher than the ground level, forcing me to step up and into the little box. I made a mental note to call Harry Noble, the landlord. It was time for the old cheapskate to dig under his lumpy mattress and part with some of his buried treasure.

The apartment building stands between 101st and 102nd Streets on Amsterdam Avenue, not far from Central Park. The neighborhood's not great, so I tell people it's in transition, like that's a good thing. Unfortunately, the area's been in transition for years, it just hasn't gotten any better. Neither has the building. Our beloved Amsterdam Avenue Hilton is a dilapidated, forties-vintage high-rise. If it were a person, you'd think it needed a shower and a shave. The final insult came a few years back when Harry decided to rent the southern face of the building to a billboard company. Now there's a fancy full-color advertisement painted on the wall, stretching from the fifth floor to the tenth: SMOOTH TEXTURE, ORANGE FLAVOR—METAMUCIL! #1 DOCTOR-RECOMMENDED FIBER LAXATIVE. You can see the ad from a mile away.

Inside, there are still some remnants of the building's former glory. There's a very grand penthouse apartment on eighteen, and there are quite a few large, spacious apartments on the floors below. Boris and I live in renovated quarters on seventeen, just below the penthouse. Seventeen isn't as swank as the penthouse, but there are only two apartments on our floor and we happen to own them both. Just how we became *very limited* partners in Mr. Noble's building makes for a long story, but it boils down to the fact that we once did him a very big favor. In a moment of weakness, Harry decided to show his gratitude by rewarding Boris and me with these tiny pieces of his tangled real estate empire, and we were lucky enough to get it in writing and no-tarized before he sobered up.

The elevator made a last, desperate groan, then lurched to a stop. This time, the cab was more than three feet above the floor level. I hopped down quickly, just in case it decided to free-fall into the basement, then hurried over to my front door. It took a minute to dig the key out of my pocket, but I finally heard the familiar sound of the dead bolt slipping back and stepped into my front hall. The week-old air was hot and stale, but I didn't care, it felt good to be home. I was still sniffing critically and groping for the light-switch, when I heard the sound of canine toenails clicking on the hardwood floors.

In the dim glow cast by the overhead fixture, I could just make out the dark outline of a very large, uncoordinated animal as it started loping down the hall to greet me. It was Boris's dog, Angus. Manny had told me to expect him, but nothing prepares you for the real thing. As Angus gained momentum, I quickly realized that one hundred and thirty-five pounds of hyperactive, slobbering puppy was more than I could handle. While he was still several feet away, I stepped quickly to my left and threw open the front door. The big guy really showed me something as he tried to stop and change direction on the polished floor, but it was too late. He'd gotten himself so twisted up, he was actually moving backward when he shot past me into the hall.

The hall carpet stopped his forward motion and Angus sat for a moment, trying to sort out what had just happened. When the light of understanding failed to ignite, he jumped to his feet and ambled over to me, his tail swinging like a metronome. The poor guy was lonely and very confused. I gave him a big reassuring hug and scratched behind his ears. When my fingers got tired, we headed for my kitchen, where a couple of pounds of dry dog food, two Budweisers, and a gallon-sized chaser of fresh cold water helped to restore his equilibrium.

While Angus was busy eating and drinking, I brewed myself a pot of decaffeinated coffee and made a quick inspection tour of the apartment, turning on lights and opening windows along the way. When I got back to the kitchen, I finally paid some attention to the little green light on my answering machine, which was blinking impatiently. There were lots of calls on the tape, but most of them were personal messages from friends who'd heard about the accident. In between the messages, there were plenty of hang-ups. At one point, I had to wait through a string of clicks and beeps so long it sounded like Morse code. It was annoying, but I kept listening. The last message was from Kate, calling from her home over on Sutton Place. When I heard the sound of her voice, I put my coffee mug down and closed my eyes.

"Jamie, it's seven-thirty and Manny just dropped me off. Boy, did the leem-o cause a stir over here. Billy said to tell you that he knows a good body shop," she giggled. "Oh, and he says you owe him twenty bucks."

Bill Jackson's the night man in her building. He takes care of my car when I visit, and I was *maybe* a little behind in showing my appreciation.

"Anyway, home safe and sound," she said cheerfully. "I hope you got things squared away with Boris. I can usually tell when you two lunkheads shift into the world of shadows. But remember, the poor man's been through a really bad experience. Try to be patient."

Kate paused, cleared her throat, then paused again.

"Jamie, when we said good-bye tonight, there were things I wanted to say, too. And now . . . well, now I feel a little empty inside and I thought you should know why."

I could hear pages turning.

"Don't faint, but I was planning to read you a poem, only it doesn't sound right talking to this dumb machine. The poem's called '*Mezzo Cammin*' and it was written by Henry Wadsworth Longfellow in eighteen forty-two. These aren't my words, J. J., but they are my thoughts. Look, I just want you to know what I'm thinking. Read the poem for me if you get a chance, and don't overreact. Okay? It's a good thing."

She paused again, and I heard the book close.

"I miss you, Jamie, and I really do love you."

There was a sharp electronic beep as the message ended.

Angus was stretched out on the kitchen floor, dozing. He let out a deep, contented sigh and seemed to smile as he rolled onto his back. I refilled his water bowl, poured myself some more coffee, then went into my living room, where a nice soft couch was waiting. Angus got up slowly and took a few gulps of water, then stood in the doorway and waited. He wanted to make sure I wasn't going to move again before he got comfortable. Once I was settled, he ambled over in front of the couch, flopped down, and immediately began to snore.

I propped a quilted pillow under my head and started sorting through the pile of mail Manny Santos had stacked on my kitchen counter. I didn't get very far. First came a yawn and then I decided to shut my eyes for a minute. The next thing I knew, the telephone was jolting me out of a deep sleep. I started to grope for the receiver, but instead of the phone, I latched on to a hard, furry object that turned out to be Angus's right ear. He lifted his head slightly and opened one eye. I smiled weakly, then let go.

The telephone kept trilling at me, which was annoying because it was wireless and I couldn't immediately locate the handset. When I finally put the receiver to my ear, Boris's voice came thundering out at me like a front of bad weather.

"What in the name of all that is sacred do you think you are doing?" he demanded.

I had to stop and ponder for a minute.

"What do you mean, what am I doing?" I yawned. "What time is it, anyway? And don't yell at me."

"It is nearly eight-thirty in the morning. People may be dying and you are lazing about in bed!"

I looked at my wristwatch. It was eight o'clock.

"First of all, it's eight o'clock, not eight-thirty," I said with feeling. "Second, I'm not lazing in bed, I'm on the couch, where I spent the entire night. And third, you've got a lot of nerve calling me with this attitude. I warned you last night, you're out of control."

There was an icy silence.

"Okay, okay, I'm getting up," I muttered.

"What are you going to do first?" he demanded.

"We discussed my itinerary last night, Boris," I said patiently. "Wait, don't tell me, your retrograde amnesia is coming back?"

"Very amusing," he growled. "Now, answer the question."

It was easier to repeat the plans than to argue with him. First thing on my list was getting the photographs copied. I wanted the originals back on the windowsill in Boris's room as fast as possible. That way, when the cops finally learned about their

53

missing evidence, we could innocently point to the pile of personal effects and shrug. "Gee, Officer, where'd that stuff come from?" It was weak, but better than getting caught with a hand in the cookie jar.

Next, I wanted to drive over to Yankee Stadium for a look-see, after which I planned to visit the 33rd Precinct.

"When I've finished with the boys in blue, I'll start tracking down our friends in the photographs," I explained. "Is that all right with you?"

"I don't think you should waste any time in the Bronx," he said impatiently. "Start looking for these people immediately, while we still have a jump on him. After all, we have the pictures, he doesn't."

Boris wouldn't explain why be believed that a crazy white-haired man with black eyes and bad breath was planning to kill three critically ill, probably unsuspecting people, but it didn't matter. He believed they were each in mortal danger. I wasn't sure what I believed, but it seemed reasonable to try to locate them. After all, these folks had a right to know that someone was trying to exchange privileged information about them. If people listened and didn't slam the door in my face, there was a chance I'd actually get some credit for being a good citizen.

"Okay, calm down," I said, remembering Kate's plea for understanding. "I'll make a few calls before I leave."

Cradling the phone on my left shoulder, I walked over to the kitchen counter and picked up the photographs. The images weren't much to go on, but the index cards were full of data. The information might just as well have been written in Chinese for all the good it did me, but it was a place to start.

"Tell you what, Boris," I said, spreading the pictures out on the counter. "I'll start digging into the medical angle over the phone. Okay? In the meantime, I can still go ahead with the original plan."

He snorted.

"In that case, if you're going to be at the Thirty-third Precinct, perhaps you could swing by the Medical Center?" he asked politely. "You'll be in the neighborhood."

The car that hit my partner was found in Riverside Park, off the West Side Highway, near 155th Street in Manhattan. Because the police also found a dead guy folded up in the trunk, the Bronx hit-and-run case had turned into a Manhattan homicide investigation. When a murder has been committed, the police usually tow large pieces of evidence, like a car, to the nearest police precinct for a detailed forensic examination. It just so happened that the nearest precinct to Riverside Park was right down the street from the hospital.

"What do you need?" I asked cautiously.

"Well, it would be extremely helpful if I had my laptop computer," he began.

In addition to the computer, he *really needed* a couple of reference books, the Bible, his portable CD player, the boxed collection of Beethoven's symphonies, and a mixed assortment of chocolate-covered nuts.

"Is there anything else?" I asked sarcastically.

There was another uncomfortable silence.

"Boris, I'm sitting here in the same clothes I was wearing when I left the island two days ago . . . just tell me what you want."

He cleared his throat.

"I see. Well, actually, I was hoping you would do me a special favor."

"Okay, what is it?"

There was another pause.

"I need a pistol," he said.

"Not possible."

"What do you mean, *not possible*? Are you suggesting that I, of all people, cannot be trusted with a handgun?"

"You asked a question and I gave you an answer," I told him. "For starters, you aren't licensed to carry a weapon in New York City. Next, you're in a hospital. People don't bring guns into

55

hospitals, they go to hospitals after they get shot. On top of that, you're left-handed and your left wrist is broken. Switching hands isn't easy. If I brought you a handgun and you tried to use it, chances are good that you'd miss the target and kill someone innocent, like Nurse Nangle."

"She's hardly innocent," he muttered.

"Let's just back up a minute here," I said. "Why do you need a gun?"

"I have legitimate concerns about my safety," he said evenly.

"Fine, then we should call the cops right now. You can tell them the whole story this time and we'll demand protection. Let the police drive all over the tristate area looking for three sick people and a white-haired maniac with a razor blade."

I wasn't kidding.

"Look, I have told you that is not an option right now," he growled. "I'm serious, James. Do as I ask or I will make other arrangements."

Threatening me was not a good idea. Besides, I'm not in the habit of loaning handguns to unlicensed citizens, especially when they're being fed a steady diet of mood-altering painkillers. Boris was wrong and he knew it, but that didn't mean he wouldn't bribe Manny Santos and get a gun off the street.

"You do whatever you want, Boris," I snapped, then hung up on him.

It was not a good start to the morning. I splashed cold water on my face, then brewed some high-test java and started looking for food. After ten days of neglect, the inside of my refrigerator was pretty scary. Fortunately, I had an emergency supply of bagels in the freezer. Angus wandered in looking like he could use a cup of espresso. I gave him a few super-sized dog cookies and a bowl of fresh water instead. For myself, there were toasted bagels, with butter and blueberry jam, and a large mug of coffee. Ten minutes later, I was in the study, sitting in front of the computer. Thanks to the caffeine, my right foot was tapping impatiently as the machine went through its start-up applications.

It is probably worth mentioning that I do not have a great affinity for computers. And my relationship to the infamous Internet is even more tenuous. As a rule, I prefer to read things I can hold in my hand and I like to do my shopping in stores where I can actually sample the goods. The Net reminds me of a multilane road through a badly zoned industrial area, where the signs and billboards are so dense it's impossible to find anything. I realize this is a bit like my grandmother standing on a street corner in the Bronx and shouting "Get a horse!" when the first motor cars drove past her, but ignorance is one of my rights. Boris, on the other hand, is a technological wizard. Unfortunately, he wasn't available to do my grunt work.

After logging onto the computer, I dialed our Internet provider. When the search engine appeared, I picked up the first index card, the one clipped to the picture of the three men outside a bar. It described something called Microbacterium Avium Complex Infection and referenced NYU Medical Center and somebody named Lieb. Boris said this MAC was an AIDS-related disease. Without too much trouble, I navigated my way to the New York University AIDS Clinical Trials Unit. The Web site listed active clinical trials at the center and gave a nice description of the clinical research unit, but that didn't help very much. Fortunately, there was also a phone number, which was a piece of data I knew how to use.

I dialed the number and spoke to a nice woman named Susan. There were only four doctors in her research unit and none of them was named Lieb. In fact, although two of the physicians saw patients part-time in the virology clinic at Bellevue Hospital, none of them had private practices. I told Susan that Dr. Lieb had been recommended by a former patient, but that I didn't have any contact information other than the doctor's name and NYU Medical Center. She suggested I call the NYU Doctor Referral Service. Turns out most of the 350,000 metropolitan-area residents infected with AIDS are either seen by private practitioners or not at all. She was trying to be helpful, but in the end, all she could do was to give me the 800 number for the referral service.

A few minutes later, I was listening to an automated phone service. One of the few things I like even less than the Internet is a computerized telephone system. I listened to the recorded instructions and eventually learned that the referral system was designed to randomly select ("on a rotational basis") a physician specializing in my area of need. If my area of need was a specific doctor, whose name I already knew, there was a different number to call. I hung up again and called the new number. On the second ring, a very pleasant human being answered and was able to locate a Dr. Harold Lieb, the only Dr. Lieb in her directory. Unhappily, he specialized in dermatology, not infectious diseases. I took his number anyway and thanked the nice human.

It was ten-thirty. The morning was half over and I had nothing to show for it. I gulped down the rest of the coffee and headed for the bathroom; two days in the same clothes is one day too many. Since I had to wait for the hot water to slowly work its way up to my shower on the seventeenth floor, I called Santos and asked him to get my car. After a good night's sleep, Manny was back to his old tricks. In exchange for the car, a service he was already paid to perform, he extorted the loan of forty dollars for a trip to the beer wholesaler up on University Avenue, in the Bronx. I was so glad to hear him sounding like himself again that I gave in without a fight, setting a really dangerous precedent.

When I was clean again and dressed, I walked down to the kitchen and opened the old broom closet in the pantry. The cupboard was empty, but there was another door at the back. I stepped into the passageway, turned the knob directly in front of me, and walked into Boris's front hall through a space that had been his coat closet.

Once inside Boris's apartment, I had to stop and get my bearings. The Koulomzin domicile takes some getting used to. It is cold, dark, and very cluttered. To protect the precious computer equipment, the central air-conditioning system is always set at sixty-four degrees, and Boris has blue-gelatin sun shields on all the windows, which add a cool tint to the rooms during the day. Because of the semidarkness and the mess of books, papers, and machines, it can be difficult to maneuver in the cramped space. Less than a year earlier, our young friend Clifford Brice had spent a few weeks with us while we looked for his mother's killer. During that short time, Clifford, a very gifted ten-year-old boy, organized the workroom so well that you could actually figure out the pattern in the Oriental carpet. I had to shake my head. It hadn't taken very long for the chaos to return. Fortunately, I knew where to look for the light-switches.

I found the portable laptop computer, the compact-disc player, and most of the Beethoven symphonies right away. Finding all the reference books wasn't so easy. While I was searching through the bookcases, I noticed a thick collection of nineteenth-century American poetry and snatched it off the shelf. Longfellow's picture was on the cover, so I added the book to my pile. I was going to read that poem for Kate, no matter what.

In the meantime, I still had one more book to find and it took longer than I'd planned. After a frustrating search, I eventually located the *Physician's Desk Reference* under a pot of moldy old tea Boris had left on his desk. I flipped the book open and discovered that it describes all the prescription drugs available in the U.S. Apparently, Boris was going to review the medications he was being given. He had also asked for a copy of the Holy Bible. If he was planning to second-guess Hiram Parker's medical judgment, he was going to need it.

I loaded all the books and electronic toys into a big canvas tote bag and turned to leave the apartment. When I got back to the foyer, I found Angus waiting patiently by the front door. He had a dark-blue leash in his mouth, and his tail was keeping time again. I'd forgotten all about his morning walk. It didn't seem fair to quickly march him up and down the street and then lock him up in the apartment all day. Besides, a passenger his size and general description would be helpful in the neighborhoods I was planning to visit.

"Hey, Angus, want to go for a ride?" I asked.

He bounced straight up and started dancing around. In his joy, the big guy knocked over several large stacks of books and magazines, sending little clouds of dust into the air. The dirt was more than I could stand. I opened a few windows, letting in the sunlight and airing the place out. While I was busy destroying the dark, gloomy atmosphere Boris had worked so hard to create, the telephone rang. I hesitated for a moment, then answered it.

"Doctor Koulomzin?"

The voice was strong and deep, but unfamiliar.

"No, this isn't Doctor Koulomzin," I said. "Would you like to leave a message?"

"With whom am I speaking?" the man asked politely.

"That depends," I answered. "Who are *you*?"

"Ah, now I see."

The caller chuckled, and the hair on the back of my neck stood up.

"You must be Donovan."

When he spoke my name, his tone implied something unpleasant.

"Well, Mr. J. J. Donovan, this is Mr. St. John, Johnny St. John. Doctor Koulomzin and I met the other day, in the Bronx. You know, I do hope he's feeling better than he did the last time I saw him."

I reached out and pushed the Record button on the desk console. We have sophisticated electronic equipment for situations just like this one. Mr. Johnny St. John must have been a mind reader.

"Tut-tut, James," he scolded. "Don't tell me you're making a recording. Well, that's nice, but it really isn't necessary. I have a very simple message for your partner. He has something that

60

belongs to me. I want it back. I'll call again to tell you where to send it. Do you hear?"

"What I didn't hear was you saying *please*," I told him.

He laughed long and hard, then stopped again, like he'd turned a switch.

"Do you have any idea with whom you're speaking?"

"Yeah, sure. A piece of garbage who likes to cut up defenseless people," I said, warming to the subject.

For a few seconds, there was only the sound of St. John breathing heavily into the receiver. Then he began to recite:

> " 'In the midst of the lamp stands one like the son of man. . . . The hair of his head was as white as white wool or snow, and his eyes were like a fiery flame. His feet were like polished brass refined in a furnace, and his voice was like the sound of rushing water. In his right hand he held seven stars. A sharp two-edged sword came out of his mouth, and his face shone like the sun at its brightest!' "

His voice rose and fell dramatically, growing louder and stronger with each syllable, until he was shouting. St. John finished, panting into the receiver, then started to cackle like a madman. Before I could say another word, he slammed the phone down.

The recorder automatically turned off when the line went dead. I waited for a minute or two, just in case he called back, then replayed the tape. If possible, it sounded even spookier the second time around. When the recording finished, I pushed the Rewind button and left it on the machine, so Boris could listen via the telephone in his hospital room.

His story about a crazy white-haired man didn't seem so unreasonable anymore. The guy was clearly unstable, but he was also well-spoken and educated. This Johnny was clever, too. Finding our phone number was one thing, but he'd also done enough checking to know about me. I started wondering just how carefully the hospital guarded the identity of those important patients up on the ninth floor. Because one thing was for sure—Boris didn't need another visit from Johnny St. John.

I carried the tote bag into my apartment, then went back and closed both doors in the passageway. I left the bag in the front foyer, then headed down the long, narrow hallway to my office, where the computer was still humming. The office is a good-sized room, with two walls of bookcases, some filing cabinets, and several nice big windows. Not an executive suite, but more than enough space for my needs.

Angus followed me, as usual, then squeezed under my desk and got comfortable. I climbed up on a stool and took down the dusty, leather-bound copy of *New York State Tort Law* that I keep stored on the top shelf. Years ago, I had hollowed out the core of the big book and put it to practical use hiding my small collection of revolvers.

If I need to carry a gun, I like to wear a light .38-caliber Beretta hidden in a clip holster that fits inside the rear waistband of my trousers. But I also own an old .32-caliber Browning model 1910, and a .45-caliber Colt Anaconda. The Anaconda is a heavy, long-barreled, five-shot revolver, with the kind of firepower you'd expect from a .44 Magnum. It's a big piece of metal and it looks scary.

I opened the Colt and spun the empty chamber out of habit. Boris was right, he had legitimate concerns about his personal safety. I balanced the big gun in my left hand and weighed my options. I certainly wouldn't have wanted to lie helplessly in some hospital bed waiting for a madman to pay me a visit. On the other hand, I couldn't trust Boris with a loaded gun, not while he was taking all that medication.

Ten minutes later, I was still sitting there, rocking back and forth in my leather desk chair, when an idea came to me. I got up and strolled over to the big oak filing cabinet in the corner and rooted around in the drawers until I found a box of blanks. Boris couldn't injure anybody using dummies, but he could make a lot of noise. I loaded the gun with blanks and flipped the cylinder back into place. If all went well, no one would ever know that I'd given Boris the weapon. But if he did have trouble, just looking down the barrel of a Colt Anaconda would make most people think twice.

I took a deep breath and spun the cylinder. It was a crapshoot. And if things didn't go right, I was going to have an awful lot of explaining to do.

SIX

■ ■ ■

The Donovan family motto is: "Never give up, never give in!" With those words echoing in my head, I turned back to the computer, which was still on, and took another stab at the Internet. This time, I decided to follow up on the picture of the business executive whose index card also listed AIDS-related diseases. In addition to Kaposi's Sarcoma and Pneumocystis carinii pneumonia, the card had the *Mount Sinai Medical Center* and the name *Conners* typed on it. I went to a search engine and typed Mount Sinai Hospital. The search found ten sites. Number seven read: *Mount Sinia IPA Drs., Physicians—Doctors in New York Affiliated with Mount Sinai Hospital, all Specialities and Managed Care.* Confirming my prejudice that computer geniuses, other than Boris, are illiterate, the word Sinai was misspelled.

Without knowing for sure what IPA meant, I clicked on the *Mount Sinia IPA* and found myself transported to a Web site that promised to find me a doctor; all I had to do was type in a name. I tried *Conners*, but there were no matches. Next, I tried *Connors*, thinking the name could be misspelled. Again, no luck. Giving up on *Conners* for the moment, I typed in *Lieb* and got two matches; there was a cardiologist named Mary Lieb and a pathologist named Simon Lieb. I took down the doctors' phone numbers just in case, but it didn't get me any closer to finding an infectious-diseases specialist named Lieb.

I picked up the third picture, the one with the sculpture and the lady with the nice face. Her card referenced *Yale–New Haven Hospital*, after which the name *Newman* was typed in parenthesis. I went back to my trusty search engine and found the Yale–New Haven Medical Center Web site without any trouble. It had two different options when searching for physicians. You could ask about doctors on the faculty of the Yale School of Medicine or about doctors on the medical staff of the hospital. Even I knew there would be many cases where the same doctors would be on both lists. I clicked on the faculty page first and was given the choice of submitting a computer form or making a phone call. I wrote down the phone number. Next, I went to the medical-staff page. It worked just like the Mount Sinai Web site; you typed in a name and it searched for matches. I typed in *Newman* and hit the jackpot—more than fourteen names appeared. Unfortunately, there were no phone numbers and most of the doctors' titles and specialties were missing. As usual, the information you got out of a computer was only as good as the information they put in. I hit the Print button.

While my desktop printer made a beautiful full-color print of the referral list of *Newmans*, I put my notes and the original photographs in a file folder. When the print job was done, I put the list in the file and turned the computer off. It was time to get moving or the day would be lost. Angus climbed out from underneath my desk and we both headed to the front hall, where the canvas tote bag was waiting. Before leaving, I ducked into the kitchen and grabbed my cell phone from the cradle; for once, the thing was fully charged.

The light-panel above the elevator doors slowly counted down the floor numbers as we inched toward the lobby. To pass the time, I looked for new graffiti on the scarred walls of the cab. When we finally reached street level, the doors refused to open. Angus rolled his eyes and sighed, then sat down patiently. I jumped up and down, pushed the Emergency button and started banging on the doors. About the time my hands began to get sore, the doors finally opened. When I stepped into the lobby,

Manny Santos was sitting off to one side playing dominoes. He acted as if nothing had happened.

"Didn't you hear the Emergency bell?" I asked.

He shrugged. It was out of his control, like all the great mysteries of life. Manny was wearing a busy, floral-patterned silk shirt, pressed slacks, and all the gold jewelry he owned. A trip to the beer distributor followed a set protocol.

"Your car, she is waitin' out front, Señor Boss."

He smiled, and his gold front tooth sparkled.

"An' now, if you don' mind—" he held out his hand "—sixty dollas, please."

"We agreed on forty," I reminded him, reaching for my wallet.

"Yo, Donovan, that was before I checked the stock," he said seriously.

I started to put the wallet back in my pocket.

"Okay, okay, forty dollas," he sighed.

I handed over a couple of twenties, then had to listen to a lot of moaning and complaining when I asked him to load the car. Manny's never satisfied.

Angus and I left the little extortionist muttering to himself and strolled up Amsterdam Avenue to Westside Photo. The owner, Geoff Weir, is a friend of mine. For a couple of those crispy twenties I was handing out, he agreed to make me copies of the three black-and-white prints, but he needed about thirty-five minutes. It was a bright, clear spring day, and the cool breeze coming out of Central Park felt refreshing. I took Angus up to the park and let the pooch burn off some adrenaline. While he pranced around, I sat on the grass and let the springtime air clear my head. We stayed longer than I'd expected, but it did us both good. When we got back to Westside Photo, Geoff Weir was waiting for us with the copies.

"Hey, Donovan," he said, giving me a queer look, "somebody just come in here and told me about Boris. What's up wit that?"

"You don't want to know," I said seriously.

"Yeah, right, just business as usual." He was shaking his head.

67

"What's that supposed to mean?" I asked, grabbing the copies.

"Nothin'," he added quickly. "But, man, you gotta admit you guys are really snake-bit. I mean, you must be carryin' a lot of insurance."

I just smiled. Back when we were helping that kid, Clifford Brice, I managed to get blown up in a little gas explosion and they put my picture in the paper. Ever since then, people had been making wisecracks.

When we got back to the car, Manny was long gone. Angus hopped in and took his place in the copilot's seat. I fired up the old blue Nova, jammed a disc into the CD player, and pointed her toward the Bronx. We crossed the park at 97th Street, took the FDR Drive to the Willis Avenue Bridge, and from there, navigated our way up side streets to Yankee Stadium.

It had been four days since Boris lay stunned and bleeding on the sidewalk, which was old news by New York City standards, but I still wanted to take a look at the scene myself. Parking the Nova in front of a hydrant on 157th Street, I clipped the leash to Angus's collar and let him pull me around the block. It was not a friendly neighborhood, especially on a day when the ballpark was closed. There were small mountains of black garbage bags piled along the curb, and there was lots of graffiti on the walls of the buildings. As we walked along Gerard Avenue, we passed teams of young Hispanic men, beepers clipped to the pockets of their baggy jeans, leaning in doorways or making deals through the open windows of cars. I remember thinking that those skinny little boys wouldn't have been very tough in my old neighborhood. Then again, today you don't have to be tough to be dangerous.

We turned left at 158th Street and walked back down to River Avenue, stepping into the cool shadows created by the stadium's right-field wall and the elevated subway tracks. The shops and stores along the avenue, always crowded with fans on a game day, were either empty or closed. There were a few people, probably from the stadium grounds' crew, drinking beer in the

Sportsman Bar, but that was the extent of the action. It was a pretty depressing scene, considering that it was the home address of the famous New York Yankees.

We strolled back to the corner of 157th Street and River Avenue, completing our tour of the block, and I kicked through some garbage in the gutter where Boris had fallen, but I didn't find anything. The scavengers had already picked the place clean, and the blood had probably just washed away.

I put Angus back in the car, then went across the street and wasted some more time talking to a guy from stadium security. He was eager to help because a fan had been injured, but he didn't know much. I was able to confirm that the case had been turned over to detectives from the 33rd Precinct in Manhattan, which saved me a trip to the local station house. But I learned nothing new. On my way out, I ducked into the gift shop and bought Boris a new baseball cap to replace the one he'd left outside in the gutter.

My last stop was the little grocery store where Manny Santos had used the pay phone to call his cousin, Moses. The owner, a tiny man named Ricardo, was very friendly and more than willing to talk. He told me that he'd run outside on the night of the accident because the police sirens were very loud and he was worried about his family. Ricardo had watched the excitement from a distance of about twenty yards. And yes, he remembered the nice white-haired gentleman who'd tried so hard to help Boris. He wanted to know if I was looking for the man so that I could give him a reward. I told Ricardo that we had something very special in mind for the nice white-haired gentleman. I just didn't tell him what it was.

I took the Macombs Dam Bridge back into Manhattan at 155th Street. The Macombs Bridge passes over the site of the Polo Grounds, where the New York Giants used to win pennants. Back in 1923, when Colonel Ruppert built Yankee Stadium for Babe Ruth and the rest of Murderer's Row, he put it right across the Harlem River from the Polo Grounds. Legend has it that

Colonel Ruppert wanted to stand at his office window and look down upon John McGraw, the Giants' manager. Maybe it worked—1923 was the year the Yankees first won it all.

The Giants are long since gone to California, but you can still find old-timers who get misty-eyed when they talk about the team. New York City didn't waste nearly as much sentiment on them. In the early sixties, the city tore down the old ballpark and built an enormous housing project on the site. As you drive across the Macombs Dam Bridge, you're eye level with the ninth or tenth story of the project. The buildings are like many other grim, unimaginative slums, only much taller. If Colonel Ruppert were to look out of his office window today, instead of the Giants, he'd see a couple of filthy brick buildings the size of rocket ships, with laundry hanging out to dry on every balcony. I have a feeling the colonel might just start to miss old John McGraw.

I took a shortcut up Edgecombe Avenue, passed Dykeman House and turned onto 165th Street. Several blocks ahead, I could see the Columbia–Presbyterian Medical Center complex towering over the nearby brownstones and apartment buildings. The 33rd Precinct looked insignificant by comparison. It was a plain-white rectangular building made of prefabricated sections stacked, one on top of the other, like toy blocks. I parked the Nova on the street, but didn't bother locking the car doors. Angus was on duty and it would have taken either a very brave or a very stupid person to chance it. As it turned out, for all the help I got inside, I should have sent Angus in with my questions.

Boris and I have never been on the best of terms with the NYPD or the district attorney's office. Our consulting business exists to help people fix problems the legal system can't or won't resolve. More often than not, that puts us in an adversarial position. But this time should have been different. For once, we weren't meddling in somebody else's business, and that gave me confidence as I stepped through the front door into the precinct.

The desk officer, Sergeant Bandura, was a middle-aged man with heavy bags under his eyes and thinning gray hair. He didn't look happy, but he listened when I introduced myself, which was encouraging. I needed a lot more information than I'd gotten from Manny and Boris, and he was the first step. If possible, I wanted to speak with one of the homicide detectives assigned to the case, and maybe even take a peek at the automobile that had been used to flatten Boris.

I got lucky. Officer Bandura knew all about the car. He'd been on duty the night they towed it into the precinct yard. It was a light-brown Chevy Malibu, about ten years old, which was registered in New York as a livery cab. Unfortunately, the forensic guys had already finished dusting, sampling, and photographing it, and the vehicle had been towed to an impound yard somewhere in Brooklyn. Sergeant Bandura told me it would be hard to forget that car—the trunk had been full of dried blood that had attracted swarms of flies. I tried to press him with a few more questions, but he got nervous and called for reinforcements.

After a long, uncomfortable wait on a wooden bench in the hall, a big, fat, red-haired homicide detective named Bill Sweeney showed up. He was wearing a new, imitation designer suit and a lot of gold jewelry. Sergeant Sweeney was a wise guy, with a smart attitude. To hear him talk, you'd think he was the chief of police.

"Look here, Mr. Donovan . . . it is Donovan, right?" He smiled broadly, trying the honey first. "The guy your buddy, Doctor Koulomzin, and his driver identified, he was a local boy, sold drugs to little kids, liked to think of himself as a big man."

Sweeney kept moving a toothpick back and forth from one side of his mouth to the other. His face was a bright crimson

71

and he smelled of garlic. I tried not to stare, but the toothpick was distracting me.

"What was the driver's name?" I asked politely.

"I dunno, you tell me," he said. "What was it? Santos or somethin'."

"No, no, not Doctor Koulomzin's driver," I said patiently. "I was asking about the driver of the car that ran my partner down. You know, over at Yankee Stadium."

"Oh, right, you mean the local kid. Well, back in Puerto Rico, his momma named him Alberto Rivera, but they called him 'Beetle' out here on the street." Sweeney chuckled. "Boy got squashed just like a bug, too. Lemme tell ya, it wasn't pretty. His neck, back, legs, ankles, they was all busted up like somebody worked him over with a sledge."

"And why do you think that happened?"

"I think the Beetle pissed off somebody that he shouldn't have and that the somebody done us all a favor by killin' the little creep," he said evenly.

Tiny beads of perspiration were starting to form on Sweeney's brow.

"So you think the killing was drug-related?" I asked, resisting the urge to move away.

"Damn straight. What'd you think? You're not gonna tell me he had a grudge against some old college professor. Come on, man, the boy was juiced up. No doubt he dusted your pal, but that was just sport for this guy."

"Is that a fact?" I smiled weakly. "The kid liked to play rough, huh?"

Sweeney nodded and sucked on his toothpick.

"You said Rivera was juiced up. Does that mean the coroner's report showed the presence of drugs in his system?"

Sergeant Sweeney didn't like the question. You could see the change in his mottled red face; a flash of anger. But then the smile returned.

"As a matter of fact, Donovan, the lab reported that the kid was wired up like an I-talian Christmas tree," he said happily.

"I don't suppose you remember what drugs they found in his system?" I asked, taking out my little notebook.

"Huh? You mean like the scientific name?" He screwed his face into a knot.

"Well, yeah, I guess I do," I said. "But if you don't remember, that's okay. Maybe you can recall the type of drugs. I mean, was he high on crack cocaine or heroin or something like that?"

"What's with you, Donovan? You sound like a fuckin' church reporter. I'm giving my valuable time here and you're bustin' my chops. What the fuck difference does it make to you whether the kid was smokin' crack or stickin' Fig Newtons up his ass?"

"Obviously, I'm curious. Alberto Rivera tried to kill my partner, and when he failed, somebody killed him instead. It's reasonable to think there could be a connection. I was only wondering if the drugs in his system were exotic—you know, something he wouldn't normally have been using. That kind of information might provide a lead to the killer."

Sweeney stared at me, his lips twisted into a sneer. Then he began shaking his head slowly.

"Ain't this sweet," he said finally. "Just what I need, a fuckin' amateur detective. Listen up, Sport, the Beetle didn't need a reason to kill your friend. It coulda been just because he felt like it. And believe me when I tell you there were plenty of reasons to snuff the Beetle's candle, too. The guy was garbage. Okay?"

I nodded my head thoughtfully.

"So there wasn't anything unusual about the chemicals in his system?"

Sweeney pulled out a dirty handkerchief and mopped his brow and neck. He took a couple of deep breaths, struggling with his composure.

"The Beetle had some puncture holes in his arm," he said quietly, "but what he put in his veins, I don't know or care about. It wasn't drugs that killed the little dirt bag. Besides, these guys will take anything, he wasn't particular."

The toothpick was flicking back and forth rapidly now, like a nervous twitch. Obviously, he hadn't bothered to check the lab results. Before I could say another word, Sweeney decided to go on the offensive.

"What I wanna know," he said, folding his arms across his chest, "is what you college boys think happened. Somethin' tells me it's gonna be real interesting."

He sat back, waiting.

"Well, Sergeant," I began, "my partner and I think Rivera was hired to deliver a small manilla envelope containing the pictures of three sick people to a crazy white-haired man who plans to execute them. Unfortunately for the Beetle, he screwed up and delivered the package to the wrong seats in the stadium. When the crazy white-haired gentleman, let's call him 'Johnny,' realized the package had been delivered to the wrong party, he forced Rivera to help him get the envelope back. Accordingly, Rivera knocked Doctor Koulomzin down with his car and then white-haired Johnny took over. Posing as a Good Samaritan, Johnny lifted a manilla package out of Doctor Koulomzin's satchel and then tried to slit the good doctor's throat with a razor blade."

I paused for dramatic effect.

"Unfortunately for Johnny, he made two mistakes—he grabbed the wrong package, and he failed to kill my partner. Later, when Johnny learned that he still didn't have the right envelope, my guess is that he got very angry and turned that anger against Rivera, killing him. At this point, we think Johnny's out there somewhere, plotting to get his envelope back."

Sweeney stared at me for a full minute. I expected a reaction, maybe even a few questions, but that didn't happen. He just stared for a while, then blinked a few times, like a man coming out of a daze. All of a sudden, he burst out laughing. He laughed so hard that he started to wheeze and cough. Pretty soon he was holding his stomach and wiping his forehead again. Eventually, he got up and walked away. I sat there on the bench for another ten minutes, but he never came back.

When I finally realized that Sergeant Sweeney wasn't going to return, I ducked out of the police station and drove over to the hospital, which was less than four blocks away. For a couple of dollars, the valet-parking attendant agreed to let me park the Nova out front. He was probably just relieved that he didn't have to get in the car with Angus, but I appreciated the gesture.

I got the canvas bag out of the trunk and walked into the hospital lobby. A few minutes later, I stepped off the elevator onto the ninth floor. As I started down the hall, I passed a nurse I recognized.

"How's the big pain in the neck?" I asked cheerfully.

"How do you think?" she snarled and pretended to shoot herself in the head with an index finger.

I walked down the corridor and pushed the door open just in time to catch Boris as he was lighting one of his black Turkish cigarettes. Before he could react, I snatched it away. He started to whine, but I ignored him. He was sputtering about personal freedom and the Bill of Rights when I pulled the Colt Anaconda out of my pocket.

"You skipped the Second Amendment—the right of the people to keep and bear arms," I said, waving the big gun in front of him. "This little charmer should give you an added sense of security."

He grabbed the weapon from me and inspected it cautiously, as if it might bite. I went into the bathroom and flushed his cigarette, then got myself a drink of water. When I came back out, he was pouting again. I pulled the little straight-backed chair up to the bed. He needed cheering up, so I told him all about Detective Sweeney.

"The man is a troglodyte," he declared when I'd finished the story.

"Okay, if you say so," I nodded. "I'd just like to hear him use the word *spic* in front of Manny. Cop or no cop, it would be the last time he did anything that stupid."

"What made you change your mind about the gun?" Boris asked suddenly.

"Your white-haired friend called the apartment this morning," I said evenly. "We're old friends now. He says I should call him Johnny."

"Is that so?" Boris tried to sit up.

I punched our office number into the telephone on his night-stand, then used our code to retrieve the recording of St. John's call. I watched Boris's face as he listened. He didn't move a muscle. When the recording ended, he handed me the telephone.

"Look, I'm sorry if I doubted you, Boris. But your story sounded so screwy, it was hard to accept."

"That doesn't matter now," he murmured. "I'm more concerned that our man is acting so brazenly. It's as though he has nothing to fear."

Boris picked up the gun and studied the barrel carefully before sliding it under the blanket next to his right hip.

"Should I speak with the police again?" he asked.

I shook my head.

"After the reception I got from Detective Sergeant Sweeney, I'm not so sure."

"This is on my head," he said. "I should have spoken up right away, even if they didn't believe me."

"It's not on your head, Boris. I tried to play the good citizen this afternoon and Sweeney laughed in my face. The cops don't want to hear complicated stories. You got hit by a car. The guy that hit you was a slug and now he's dead. Who cares? It's a tough town, and they've got much bigger problems to worry about."

"Is that so? Well, I hope they've got plenty of room in the

morgue. Because if we don't hurry, friend Johnny is going to start filling it."

That was my cue.

"Listen, Boris, I gotta go. Angus is waiting for me out in the car."

"Ah, and how is my Angus?" he asked, brightening.

"Hungry and lonely," I said. "By the way, I brought everything you asked for, even the candy."

I pulled the dinner cart over to the bed and held up the white confectionary bag. His eyes started to dance.

"Is there anything else I can do before I leave?"

"Would you mind assembling my laptop?"

He was being polite because I still had the chocolates, but it wasn't much of a favor. I unzipped the traveling case, plugged the A/C transformer into a wall outlet, set the little computer down on the dinner tray, and turned it on. There was a low, humming noise and then the screen came to life. I lowered the side rail on the bed and positioned the computer so that he could reach it easily with his good right hand; then I put the phone on the tray table next to the laptop, just in case he wanted to use the modem.

"Hey, I almost forgot something," I said, looking into the bag.

I dug out the Yankees hat. Boris's face lit up and he pulled it on even though the tags were still hanging down. While he adjusted the cap, I put the bloodstained manila envelop containing the original photographs and index cards back on the windowsill, then turned to leave.

"If you need anything else, you can reach me on my cell phone," I told him.

"James." He stopped me just as I reached the door.

"What did I forget?" I asked, coming back.

"Nothing at all," he said quickly. "I just wanted to thank you for being such a good friend. This isn't something I could have managed alone."

"Is that so?" I smiled. "Well, if you really want to thank me, you'll promise not to shoot any of the nurses. Okay? And that includes Nurse Nangle."

He started to say something smart, but I closed the door before he could get it out.

SEVEN

...

When I got outside, Angus was still defending the car like a big rumpled sentry, but he wasn't happy. He needed a fire hydrant the way a sailor needs rum.

We started south along Fort Washington Avenue, turned right onto Broadway, then right again onto West 155th Street, rolled down the hill, turned under the Westside Highway and drove straight into Riverside Park. This was the same park where the cops had found a light-brown Chevy Malibu with Alberto Rivera's body stuffed in the trunk; the Malibu had been parked under a streetlight just inside the front gate.

The afternoon was warm and sunny, which had filled the parking lot and the playground. There were hundreds of people milling about—drinking, eating, listening to music. Little groups of wrinkled old men sat together on the park benches nodding and smoking, while their wives chatted and fussed with the grandchildren. In another section, a crowd of teenaged girls in Catholic school uniforms huddled together and made eyes at a pack of baby-faced boys who were trying to look tough. There were lots of the big Lincoln town cars the livery drivers favor, but in choice spots around the lot, I noticed the shiny little BMWs, with dark, tinted windows, that only the crack dealers could afford. The barbecue fires were smoking, and the smell of rice and beans came floating through my car window, reminding me that I'd forgotten to eat lunch.

I squeezed the Nova into a parking space on the far side of the lot, near a stand of trees. Angus didn't wait for me—he jumped through the open window and ran to the bushes. When he'd finished his business, I clipped the leash to his collar and we walked over to the area where the cops had found the Beetle's car. As we strolled along, I got the distinct impression that my buddy and I stuck out like a couple of unwanted tourists; the looks we got said "Yankee, go home!" It was a problem my new friend Johnny St. John probably had, too. With the big mane of white hair Boris described, it would have been difficult for Johnny to go unnoticed. And in his case, a really low profile would have been pretty important. After all, he was dropping off a dead guy. I made a mental note to put some of Manny's relatives to work canvassing the locals.

While I was thinking about St. John, Angus decided he was hungry and started dragging me over to a guy selling big spicy sausages, hot dogs, and plates of rice and beans. The hot-dog man was friendly enough, but he kept looking over my shoulder, like he was worried that I was scaring his regular customers away. I bought five plain, regular hot dogs for Angus and a fat sausage with mustard and onions for me. I slipped the change and a cold Diet Pepsi into my jacket pocket and carried the rest of it down to the water's edge. We sat on the grass by the river and I divided up the food. Angus made his hot dogs disappear in a few bites, then settled down and glared at the pigeons.

While I ate my sausage, I tried to picture Johnny St. John driving into Riverside Park. Poor Johnny was probably all tuckered out from swinging the sledgehammer he used to break all those bones in Alberto Rivera's body. It had been a long, disappointing day for Satan's helper, so I assumed he was anxious to get back to his lair. Once inside the park, Johnny left the car under a streetlight, which was rather bold, and then probably just walked away from it. The path along the river led right back under the highway, and from there, the subway station was only a few short blocks. In some ways, leaving the car in such a busy location was smart. With so much other activity, it would have been hours, or maybe even days, before anyone paid attention to the vehicle, even longer before they thought to check the trunk.

The afternoon sun was slipping behind the Palisades; it was time for me to get moving. I had given Boris my word that I would continue digging into the information on the index cards stapled to Johnny's photographs. There was the list of Dr. Newmans to run down, and I had a couple of Dr. Liebs to call, too. But I wasn't exactly looking forward to it; getting confidential information out of a doctor's office is nearly impossible, and I didn't even know the patients' names.

We started to make our way back across the parking lot, but I quickly realized that it was easier to go around the big crowd than to try to walk through it, especially with Angus poking his nose where it didn't belong. So we took the jogging path near the water. When I looked at my watch, it was nearly five-thirty.

As we were crossing the entrance road, not far from my car, I saw something swinging from one of the park signs. I probably would have walked right past the thing if the wind hadn't shaken it. When I got up close enough to see what it was, my heart skipped a beat. Someone had wrapped an old navy-blue scarf around the signpost, tying it into a big, floppy bow. The initials BMK were embroidered on it in silver thread—Boris Mikail Koulomzin. It had been a Christmas gift from Madame Karina, the gentle lady who lives in the penthouse above us.

I didn't remember seeing the scarf when I drove into the park, but that didn't mean anything. I walked over to the sign and quickly untied the rag. It was covered with dried, matted blood. I turned and started scanning the parking lot, stopping each time I caught a glimpse of white hair. After about five minutes of fruitless searching, I walked back to the car. I put the scarf in the trunk, where Angus couldn't smell it, then fired up the Nova and slowly backed out of the parking space.

I tried to keep an eye on the rearview mirror in case Johnny

St. John was following me, but it wasn't a very reliable security system. To be on the safe side, I took local streets, ran a few red lights, and backtracked a lot. In fact, I ended up taking a route so complicated, I couldn't have followed me.

My apartment was about fifty blocks south and east of Riverside Park. As I made my way downtown, pulling U turns and backtracking, I passed through neighborhoods that had once been full of Irish and Jewish immigrants. The latest arrivals were predominantly Dominican, but things hadn't changed much. The grocery stores and corner markets looked the same, and there were still plenty of bars. I was driving along reading the tavern names and thinking about my own days behind the stick, over in the Bronx. A lot of the pubs had new signs and names in Spanish, but there were still a few of the old shot-and-beer joints. I passed The Greens Isle and the Bantry Bay before it hit me.

I pulled the car over and reached for my folder with the copies of the photographs Geoff Weir had printed for me. And there it was, staring right back at me in the first picture—three smiling men and behind them, a derby hat etched in the storefront glass. I picked up the cell phone and called information. Before long, I had the names, addresses, and phone numbers for The Brown Derby, The Green Derby, The Queen's Derby, The Old Derby, and My Derby. If you included the names of businesses in Brooklyn, Queens, and the Bronx, the list of places with "Derby" in the name got a lot longer. All the addresses I'd written down were bars or restaurants, and they were all in Manhattan.

Talk about your hard work getting easier. Checking out the pubs was a lot more appealing than calling all those doctors. I filed Johnny St. John in the back of my mind and set a course for The Old Derby, which was on 82nd Street near Broadway. As I walked up to the place, I knew right away that it was a dead end; there wasn't a derby etched in the front window. But when I stuck my head inside the door and noticed sawdust on the floor, I decided to stay for a cold pint of Bass ale. As often happens, one pint led to two pints and then the Yankees' pregame show started, so I stayed for some of that, too. An hour later, I strolled out of The Old Derby with a grin on my face and a couple of big stew bones from the kitchen for Angus.

Next on my list was The Green Derby, which was located off Times Square. I was too cheap to spring for a garage, so I pulled up in front of the bar to see if there was a derby etched in the front window. Unfortunately, the front window was gone and a piece of plywood had been mounted in its place. I made an executive decision and left Angus locked in the car out front while I went inside to ask one of the bartenders if there had been a derby on the missing window. It was a seedy place, jam-packed with the lowlives and drunks who hustled out on the street. They were two-deep at the bar, so it took a while to get the barman's attention. When I did, the answer was negative. Before one of the regulars got thrown through the missing window, the name of the bar and a few shamrocks had been painted on it in green—no derby.

"I think you're lookin' for The Queen's Derby," the bartender said, giving me a strange look. "That's down in the Village, pal. You're a long way from home."

I didn't bother having a drink; the place smelled moldy and the glasses looked dirty. When I got outside, there was a parking ticket fluttering under the windshield wiper—$200 for a ten-minute stop. The cost of a parking garage suddenly looked like a bargain. Grumbling under my breath about malicious civil servants, I unlocked the Nova and pushed Angus out of the driver's seat. I checked the address for The Queen's Derby, then crumpled the parking ticket and shoved it in the glove box before slamming the car in gear and leaving a couple of exclamation points, courtesy of Goodyear tires.

The Queen's Derby Restaurant was squeezed in between an art gallery and a clothing boutique on Christopher Street, in Greenwich Village. Christopher Street is a famous rallying point for New York City's gay community, which explained the look I'd gotten in that dive uptown. I didn't care where the place was as long as it had cold beer. Besides, for a young man with an AIDS-related illness, the West Village probably made good sense.

I drove past the restaurant and there was the elusive derby, etched in glass and looking just like its picture. The chances of finding this place were so remote, I couldn't help feeling a bit smug. When I managed to land a parking space on the street, it seemed like destiny. Before going into the restaurant, I called Boris at the hospital. You could barely hear him over the classical music playing in the background. His voice was stronger and he seemed more positive than at any time since the accident. When I told him about my discovery, he got kind of giddy. In fact, he was talking so loudly, I began to worry that the sugar from all those chocolate-covered nuts was screwing up his blood chemistry.

After all the trouble Boris had been through, it didn't seem right to pop his bubble with a creepy story about his scarf, so I kept that bit of information to myself. After we hung up, I called Manny Santos. I wanted Manny to arrange for a few of his relatives to canvass Riverside Park, just in case someone remembered a white-haired gringo driving a light-brown Chevy Malibu. The conversation with Señor Santos took a while, because I had to start at the beginning and retell the whole story. Boris had skipped the part about Johnny St. John and his razor blade. The news spooked Manny so badly, he started ranting about devils and curses. He finally agreed to send some of his boys over to the park, but they were going to carry rosary beads and little vials of holy water. When he mentioned sacrificing chickens to ward off the evil spirits, I said good-bye. Angus was stretched out comfortably on the back seat, so I shut the car door as quietly as possible and left him to his dreams.

The Queens Derby was set in a handsome old building, with red-brick walls and molded-tin ceilings. The bartop was made from a thick slab of dark mahogany, and there were large, faded antique mirrors in carved frames on the back bar wall. The dining area, which was in a side room to my left, was small but inviting. The tables were set with white-lace covers and little baskets of dried flowers, and each had a small Advent candle that flickered in the dimmed light. Against the far wall there was an old, intricately carved wooden mantel. I noticed that a fire was dancing in its hearth.

The barman finally saw the twenty-dollar bill I was flashing and I ordered an ice-cold bottle of Heineken. When it arrived, I filled a tall, chilled glass and took a long, slow drink. Across the bar, I saw the face of a satisfied man reflected back at me in the mirror. I licked the foam from my upper lip and refilled the glass. A few minutes later, the man next to me got up to leave and I grabbed his stool. When I was comfortably seated, I took a casual look at the regulars who were sitting or standing in different places around the room. It was an average-looking group of people, all the usual sizes, shapes, and colors. At first, I didn't even notice that there weren't any women.

Anyway, I was sitting on the stool, minding my own business, when someone came up behind me and started stroking the back of my head. I don't like people touching me, let alone petting my head. Without thinking, I jumped up and whipped around, knocking the bar stool over with a loud crash. My fists were up, poised for a fight, and all the customers were staring at me in silence. When the room came back into focus, I realized that I'd squared off in front of a tall, skinny kid with stringy blond hair and too much eyeliner.

"You're not planning to hurt me, are you?" he winced, mocking me. Several of the regulars moved to stand behind him, just in case I was.

"What? Ah, no, no. Look, I'm sorry, it's just that you surprised me."

The kid puckered his lips and blew me a kiss. It must have looked pretty funny, because everyone else started to laugh. The blond kid broke into a broad smile, then winked at me over his shoulder as he sauntered down to the other end of the bar. I stood there for about a minute, feeling stupid, then picked up the bar stool and sat back down. This time when I looked in the mirror, I saw a beet-red face and wild eyes. The bartender came over to see if I was all right.

"What's a guy like you doing in a place like this?"

He was smiling, but his eyes were serious.

"I'm trying to find someone," I said quietly.

"Aren't we all?" he asked. "But you'll have to excuse me for saying, I think you're looking in the wrong pub."

"Actually, the only thing I *am* sure about is this bar." I took the photograph out of my folder. "Fact is, I'm trying to find the men in this picture. You'll notice that your front window is prominently featured in the background."

"Is that so, Mister—?" He was asking nicely, but the smile was gone.

"Donovan," I said, handing him a business card. "J. J. Donovan."

"Well, Mr. J. J. Donovan, Consultant, suppose you tell me exactly what you want with those men and then we'll see."

The smile was back in place, but it was only for show.

"I'm afraid I can't do that." "I need your help—there's no question about that—but what I have to say is very personal. I'm not looking for anything and I'm not working for anybody. Believe it or not, I'm trying to do a good thing here. I discovered something one of those men needs to hear and it's important. I'm guessing it's the guy in the middle, because he's obviously the center of attention in the photo, but I'd be happy to talk to any of those guys."

"In that case, you're in luck, Mr. Donovan," the barman said softly, "because that handsome fellow on the left in the photograph is me."

He was pointing at the big guy with the beard. I looked up quickly into his clean-shaven face, then back down at the bearded man in the picture. There was no question about it; I'd found one of the men.

Fifteen minutes later, we were seated across from each other at a table in the empty dining room and one of the waiters was tending the bar.

"Peter Walsh, Proprietor, at your service." The big man extended a hand. "I come from a long line of drinkers and innkeepers. My old father had a gin mill down by the docks in Brooklyn, catered to the sailors. You might say that runs in the family, too."

He laughed so loudly that the little basket of flowers started to shake.

"And now, Mr. Donovan, now that you've found me and we've managed to create a bit of privacy, I think it's time you told me what this is all about."

I took a deep breath.

"Under the circumstances, Peter, I think you'd better call me J. J." I sighed.

It was a long, crazy story to just drop in someone's lap, but it didn't make sense unless I started at the beginning. So I told Peter Walsh all about my aborted vacation and about Boris getting run over, and Johnny St. John trying to slit Boris's throat. From there, I told him about the Beetle getting crushed and about his body getting folded up in the trunk of a Chevy Malibu. It was a good thing I was talking to a man who liked a good story, because someone else, like that fat cop Sweeney, would have thrown me out on my ear. When I was finished, I handed him the photograph of himself and the other two men, then watched as he read the photocopy of the index card I'd found stapled to the back.

"That is one fucking incredible story you just told me, son," he muttered, staring at the copy of the index card. "But I got to admit, this shit is too crazy to make up."

He put the copy back down on the table and stared at me for a minute.

"Look, before I forget, I'm sorry about that business with Riki."

"Who's Riki?"

"Riki's the guy who messed with your hair earlier. He's actually a decent kid. It's just that sometimes people come in here to sightsee, and we don't like it very much. That little show was meant to discourage you."

"Well, it worked," I said, smiling.

Peter Walsh sat looking at me for another minute or so, his right index finger tapping on the photograph. All of a sudden, he stood up.

"Wait right here." He jumped up and stomped out of the room.

Walsh was gone for quite a while, and I probably would have gotten a bit antsy but fresh Heinekens kept arriving. Under the circumstances, it seemed prudent to wait patiently. In the meantime, I tried to figure out what I was going to do. Turned out I didn't really know.

"Okay, J. J. Donovan," Peter boomed, charging back into the dining room. "You checked out."

"How so?"

"I called the Milstein Hospital and asked for that Nurse Nangle you mentioned." He was grinning. "You shoulda heard her lay into me when I said I'd been asked to deliver a pack of cigarettes to old Doctor Boris. Like I said before, you can't make this shit up."

He was laughing hard again, and his face was bright red.

"Does this mean you're going to help me?" I asked, trying not to think about the lecture Boris was getting from Nangle.

Peter Walsh stopped laughing and took a couple of deep breaths.

"You were right," he said finally. "The man you're looking for is the guy in the middle of the photograph. His name is Tim Danner. He's a close friend and he's dying, J. J., just like it says on that fucking index card."

I let that information hang between us for a moment.

"How do I find him?" I asked finally.

"Don't worry about that, pal," Walsh said quickly. "Tim's on his way over right now. We fix all his meals for him, and when he's up to it, he comes in to eat. I called him and told him he needs to speak to you. So he's coming in. The rest is up to you."

He stood up.

"Tim will need some cushions for support," he said, thinking out loud. "I'll move you to that big table by the front window, it'll be more comfortable. You stay right there and I'll bring Tim over when he gets here."

It sounded like a plan. I picked up my beer glass and moved to the other table to wait. From my new seat, I could see my car parked across the street. Angus was awake and sitting behind the steering wheel, as if he was getting ready to take the Nova for a spin. I checked my pocket to make sure I still had the keys, just in case.

EIGHT

. . .

"Mr. Donovan?"

I looked up and Timothy Danner was standing across the table from me, holding the back of the chair. I'll never forget that moment. Every UNICEF poster I'd ever seen flashed through my mind and melded into the face of that one frail young man.

"Yes?" No other words came to me.

"I'm Tim Danner. May I sit down?" he asked politely, "I get very tired these days."

I got up quickly and helped him into the chair. By the time I was seated again, Peter Walsh had come back with a mug of steaming hot tea.

"Green tea for Mr. Danner and another green bottle for Mr. Donovan," he said happily, setting a Heineken down in front of me. "You look good tonight, Tim," he touched Danner gently on the shoulder.

"Thanks, Pete, it's been a pretty good day."

During the next few minutes most of the people I'd seen in the bar came over to wish Tim Danner well and offer words of encouragement.

"I used to work here," Danner said, smiling. "They've been very good to me."

"Yes, I can see that," I murmured.

"And, I hear they had some fun with you, too," he said, still smiling.

I tried to smile back.

"You look a little stunned, Mr. Donovan," he said. "I know it's a shock to see me at first, but don't feel sorry for me. I've made my peace, I'm ready."

Either he was very perceptive or I just looked scared, because it was true—the sight of him frightened me. It was like speaking to a ghost.

"Call me J. J.," I said, rallying, "And, please, don't read too much into my expression, I often looked stunned. It comes from getting knocked in the head a lot."

"Are you a prize fighter?"

"No. I just come from a big Irish family—five older brothers. To survive you had to be smart and quick or thickheaded. I've been relying on thickheaded for quite a few years."

Danner laughed and that made me feel better.

"So, if you're not a prize fighter, what do you do?" he asked.

"Actually, I'm something of a windmill tilter," I said with a smile.

"Is that so?" He stared at me for a moment. "I think we need more of those."

"Take a look across the street," I said, pointing. "Do you see a big black furry creature sitting behind the wheel of an old blue Nova?"

He looked, then nodded.

"That's Angus, my faithful friend and companion. His master and I try to champion righteous causes."

"Am I mistaken, or is that dog getting ready to drive away in your car?" Tim asked with a grin.

"He can't," I said, patting my pocket. "I've got the keys."

A waiter arrived with place settings, cloth napkins, and clean glasses. I started to object, but Tim held up his hand.

"There's no point resisting, they feed me every night. It's either here or at home, but I can assure you that Chef won't take no for an answer. You'll be my guest."

"But you don't know anything about me," I objected.

92

"That doesn't matter to me, J. J. I can't afford to waste time judging people anymore. I just take them as they come and let my intuition be my guide."

He stopped for a moment to catch his breath. Talking was hard work for Tim Danner. He smiled and looked down at the tablecloth.

"Anyway, I'm sure I'd like to have dinner with you," he said, finally looking up. "You have gentle eyes."

The compliment embarrassed me, but I accepted it. Dinner was something Tim Danner needed badly; the poor guy probably weighed less than ninety pounds. The skin on his face was almost transparent and you could see that his teeth were badly discolored and that the gums had receded. Eating, like talking, would be hard work for him.

"It just so happens, I haven't had my dinner yet," I said. "I'd be honored to join you. But there's one condition."

"What would that be?"

"Tonight, the meal is on me."

He blushed again.

"That's all right, J. J. I have money. I'm sick, but I'm not destitute. For that, I thank God and Life Line, Inc."

He made the last part sound like a line from a commercial.

"What's Life Line, Inc.?"

"Ah, well, Life Line is the latest financial innovation for the dying man," he said, smiling. "It's what they call a viatical-settlement company."

I gave him a blank look.

"They bought my life-insurance policy, J. J. 'Cash now, not for the undertaker.' " He was trying to make it sound funny, but I didn't laugh. "They gave me forty cents on the dollar!"

This was too personal, too close to the truth.

"Look, I don't know about any of that stuff. But I insist on buying dinner. Besides, I've already got a tab running for all these Heinekens."

He bowed his head slightly, accepting the offer.

Our dinner was presented on large, warmed plates. There were lots of steaming fresh carrots, little piles of brown rice, and medium-rare, thinly sliced cuts of filet mignon. The waiter brought a basket of fresh-baked rolls, whipped butter, and a large carafe of iced herbal tea. It was a simple feast, designed to promote strength. While Tim picked at his food, forcing down small bites, I tried to set a good example by wiping my plate clean. After dinner, he had a dish of chocolate ice cream, the only food he seemed to enjoy, and I ordered a double espresso.

"That was delicious," I said, leaning back to take the strain off my waistband.

"Yes, the food here is wonderful," Danner smiled.

Without warning, he started coughing, and it was a full minute before the fit passed.

"Are you all right?"

He was breathing with difficulty.

"I'm fine, J. J., but I think the time has come for me to go home and rest. This would be a good time to tell me why you wanted to see me."

"It isn't very good news," I began.

"So, what's new?" He smiled sadly.

Counting Sergeant Sweeney, Manny Santos, and Peter Walsh, it was the fourth time that day that I'd told the story. Tim listened carefully, his eyes focused, taking in all the details. When I mentioned the injuries to Boris, he winced.

"And so," I concluded, handing him all the photographs, "I'm on a mission to find and warn the people in these three pictures. If possible, I'd also like to figure out what you've all got in common."

"You mean other than being sick?" He looked up from the papers. "We're all very sick."

"Right, other than that, or maybe because of that."

We sat in silence for a few minutes while Danner studied the photographs.

"I don't know, J. J. There's nothing familiar about these people," he said finally.

"What about the information on the index cards? Does that make any sense to you?"

I handed him photocopies of the cards that were attached to the original pictures.

"Well, the information about me is *very* accurate," he said sarcastically. "I am suffering from a Microbacterium Avium complex infection, and I was originally diagnosed at NYU."

"What about the name 'Lieb.' Is that familiar?"

"Lord knows, it should be," Tim said emphatically. "She's my doctor."

"That's weird," I said.

"How so?"

"Because I tried to find a Doctor Lieb associated with NYU and got nowhere. I checked the referral service and the AIDS unit. No one knew anything about a Doctor Lieb."

"That's because she's retired, J. J.," Danner explained. "Doctor Lieb is old enough to be my grandmother. Years ago, she was connected to NYU, as a teacher or something, but now she just cares for a few of us who are mostly beyond help. We call her 'Nana.' "

From the earnest expression on Tim's face, I got the message that this Dr. Lieb was something rare and special; a physician, not a technician. There wasn't much else to say about the card. I didn't ask him to explain the nine-to-sixteen months.

"What about the white-haired guy—Johnny St. John. Does that name ring any bells?" I asked, moving away from the cards.

"The Avenging Angel? The only thing familiar about him is his message. There are plenty of angry fanatics in this country. They like to focus on people who are weak or different."

Danner was exhausted, and my news hadn't done much for his spirits. He shook his head, melting into the chair as his strength gave out.

"I'm sorry to bring you more trouble, Tim," I said, "but I want you to know, I'm going to find this guy. I won't let him hurt you."

"You really are a windmill tilter aren't you?" He smiled again, weakly. "You're just one man, J. J. Donovan. You can't save everybody."

I opened my mouth to speak, but he held up his hand.

"Don't bother. I know your heart's in the right place and you'll do what you can. Besides, there's very little Mr. St. John can do to me that hasn't already been done. I just reacted badly because it doesn't seem fair. You know? After all I've been through, to have this fool to worry about."

He shook his head sadly.

"This would make a wonderful tragedy," he whispered. "How ironic, I finally get to play a lead."

"Are you an actor?" I asked, relieved to find a new topic.

"I was an aspiring actor," he said shyly.

"You can tell me about it on the way home."

"On the way home?" He looked surprised.

"Sure. I'll walk you home and you can meet Angus."

I got up before Tim could argue and walked over to the bar to settle up with Mr. Walsh. While I had his attention, I gave Peter my card with the office and cell-phone numbers, in case he needed to reach me.

When I got back to the table, Tim was struggling to get up. I put one hand under his arm and lifted gently. There was nothing to him except ribs and arm bones. The man was lighter than a small child. I fought back my pathetic paranoia about sick people and helped him to the door, trying hard to think about the healthy young man I'd seen in the photograph. When we got to the car, Angus was happy to see us, but he sensed right away that he should be gentle. There was no jumping or exaggerated tail wagging, just lots of wet kisses and some snuggling.

"He's beautiful!" Tim beamed.

That was a first, and Angus shot me a smug look. It was good to watch Tim's strength return as he drank in the big dog's unconditional affection. They played for a little while before I put Angus back in the car. Then Tim and I strolled down Christopher Street toward his apartment building. We walked slowly, and he told me about his life and his struggle to become an actor.

His building wasn't far, but it took us about twenty minutes to walk there, with frequent rest stops. He lived on the third floor of an old brownstone, and I could see the fear in his eyes when he looked up at the stairs. I let him make his own way up the stoop, but once we were in the foyer, I picked him up and carried him the rest of the way. He fussed a little, but not very sincerely. The stairs would have been torture.

After a brief struggle with the keys, he managed to open the front door and we were greeted by a big fat Persian cat named Samantha. She ran to Tim, purring loudly, and started to rub against his legs.

"This is my baby," he said with pride. "We take care of each other."

Cradling Sam in his arms, Tim gave me a tour of his home. It was a small, one-bedroom apartment, with hardwood floors and tall windows facing the street. Everywhere I looked, there were framed photographs of family and friends. I tried not to dwell on his illness, but it was hard to look at pictures of a healthy Tim Danner without thinking about the effects of the disease. Tim went into the kitchen to feed Sam, then he came back and lay down on the couch.

"I can't stay long, Tim," I said when it seemed as if he'd fallen asleep.

Danner opened his eyes and blinked.

"I'm sorry, J. J. I'm just tired."

"I know that, but before I leave, we need to get a few things straight," I said seriously.

I found another business card that wasn't too wrinkled and wrote the cell-phone number and my address on the back.

"I talked to Peter. He knows that somebody might try to harass you and he's going to keep an eye on things for me."

I placed the card on the coffee table between us.

"You can call me any time, and I mean any time. No problem's too small. You got that?"

He looked at me seriously for a moment, then nodded. I went over to the couch and helped him to his feet.

"Good. Now, I want you to lock and bolt the door behind me. I'll check in from time to time, but from now on, you're to show extreme prejudice when deciding who to allow into this apartment. Is that understood?"

"Yes sir, Señor Quixote." He saluted weakly.

As I turned to leave, Samantha came running back into the room. Tim bent down and picked her up. She nuzzled into his neck and the purring started again, only louder. Tim's face melted into a broad smile and he winked at me.

"She's my girl," he said happily.

I don't think I'll ever forget that innocent smile.

NINE

■ ■ ■

I was just maneuvering the Nova's front bumper past the rear end of a brand-new Mercedes Benz when the cell phone began to ring. I flipped it open and was nearly deafened as Boris roared into the receiver.

"James, is that you?!"

"Yes, Boris. And you can stop yelling, the connection is very good."

"There's been some trouble," he hissed, lowering his voice.

My foot slid off the gas pedal and I let the car roll back into the parking space. There was a lot of noise in the background on Boris's end of the line. Several people were speaking at the same time and you could hear loud scraping sounds, as if heavy furniture were being moved. I sat back heavily in my seat.

"Okay, Boris." I clenched my teeth. "Just give it to me straight. Is anyone hurt?"

Another pause.

"Not really."

"Bad answer."

"Well, Nurse Nangle has fainted, but it's nothing, really. She's had a bit of a fright and a little bump on the head. They say she'll probably be fine in a few hours."

"*Probably!* Boris, don't do this to me."

It was too late. Someone cut him off.

"J. J., is that you?"

It was the voice of Dr. Richard Steinman, our neighbor and friend. He was shouting into the telephone.

"Yeah, it's me."

"Well, get your sorry butt up here, pal. Boris has turned this place upside down. There's been gunfire, and some kind of a madman dressed as a nurse has threatened several people with a butcher knife. Do you hear me? This is no joke. I'm talking about pan-di-mon-i-um!"

"Okay, take it easy. I'm coming," I sighed.

Someone else in the room was talking to him.

"Look, Donovan, I gotta go now. Get up here as quick as you can."

Dr. Steinman slammed the phone down.

It took me more than forty-five minutes to get uptown from the Village, but the guard was waiting for me out front. He let me park right next to the front door and even handed me a pass, like I was a big shot. Angus had gone back to sleep, so I didn't bother him. I hurried across the empty lobby to the elevators. On the ride upstairs, I tapped my foot nervously, counting off the floors, wondering just how much trouble we were in. When the doors opened on the ninth floor, I got a hint.

The richly carpeted hallway wasn't quiet or peaceful anymore. Security guards with walkie-talkies were now stationed at the elevators, and nurses were shouting instructions as staff members tried to reassure angry patients and their families. Dr. Steinman was right—it was a messy scene. Some administrator was going to pay dearly for allowing Boris to stay on the same floor with all the VIPs. When word got out about gunplay in the halls, those all-important paying customers were going to flee to other medical centers.

I had hoped to slip past the nurses' station, but Hiram Parker grabbed me before I could take evasive action. He marched me into the staff lounge, where I was confronted by a small band of grim-faced medical professionals. In addition to Parker, who had a vise-grip on my arm, Rich Steinman was glaring at me, and a sourpussed old battle ax in a starched white uniform gave me a look that could have pierced steel. Behind this tribunal stood a sizable cadre of orderlies, practical nurses, and security officers. There were no smiles on any of the faces.

"Good evening," I said, nodding tentatively.

They all began to yap at once. It was pretty intimidating.

"That's enough!" Parker shouted, demanding silence. "Within these last three hours, Mister Donovan, all hell has broken loose in this hospital, and your partner has been at the center of the storm."

"Is that so?" I replied, summoning as much authority as my voice could convey. "Well, I'm going to require a full explanation, Hiram, because frankly, I don't like your tone."

I pointed my thumb at Steinman.

"When I spoke to my buddy, Richard, he mentioned gunshots and something about an intruder armed with a knife. If I'm not mistaken, he said the man was dressed like a male nurse. I didn't think he was talking about Boris."

Hiram Parker stiffened noticeably and inched closer.

"Let's all just try to calm down," Richard suggested, stepping between us. "I'll tell you what we know so far, J. J. An intruder, dressed like a male nurse, got into Boris's room tonight. Apparently, Nurse Nangle walked in on them and that's when things really got out of hand. No one is sure what happened next, except that someone fired shots and Nangle passed out. Boris hasn't been very cooperative, and Miss Nangle has been under sedation ever since the incident."

"You said shots were fired. How do you know they were gunshots? Was anyone hit? Have you found shell casings? Is there evidence of damage from stray bullets? You know, like a bullet hole in a wall or a shattered window."

I kept a perfectly straight face.

"No, there wasn't, isn't, whatever," Rich fumbled uncomfortably. "So far, the only accounts we have are from patients and staff members who heard the noise and smelled the gunpowder."

"What about a gun?"

"We haven't been able to locate a gun either."

"From what you've told me, Richard, it doesn't sound possible for Boris to have been responsible for any of the events you describe. His injuries have him confined to a bed. If you didn't find a gun in his room, and he's incapable of leaving the room to find a hiding place for it, why would you think he's anything but an innocent victim? If there was a gun, your male nurse is the obvious suspect. Though as far as I'm concerned, the noises people heard could have been caused by any number of things."

"Oh yeah, like what?"

"I don't know, noisemakers or firecrackers, something to confuse and scare people while the intruder made his escape?"

Steinman rolled his eyes.

"And what about the butcher knife?" I asked.

"Oh, that was real enough. The prowler threatened several people as he ran down the hall. In fact, he managed to point his ugly knife at Mr. William Coles, a private patient who just happens to be a member of our board of directors."

Rich spoke slowly for emphasis.

"Ouch," I winced. "So what happened? Since we're having this nice little chat, I take it the bad guy got away."

A security guard with gold captain's bars stepped forward.

"The intruder managed to effect an escape by running down several flights of stairs and then crossing into one of the other buildings. To do so, he would have needed a floor plan and one of our coded identification cards."

He stopped and scanned the faces in the room suspiciously.

I almost laughed out loud. Several hundred thousand patients walk the halls of the Columbia–Presbyterian Medical Center each year, and there are thousands of employees and other medical professionals carrying I.D. cards. Access and familiarity wouldn't have been problems. We all just stared at the officer until he melted quietly into the background again.

"Have the police been called?" I asked, breaking the silence. There was some nervous shuffling of feet, but no one stepped forward to answer.

"Hello, I'm asking a question." I snapped my fingers in the air. "Did anyone bother calling the police?"

"No, J. J. We decided not to call the police," Richard Steinman confessed, sounding exasperated. "I thought it would be best to wait until we'd talked to you. This is a hospital, for Christ's sake! The last thing we wanted was a brigade of cops tramping through the halls."

Right on cue, three security guards blundered into the room. The guy with the gold bars told them to scram.

"Is that so? And if your precious Mr. Coles had been attacked, would you have hesitated to call the police for him?"

"Look, Donovan, you and Boris have a reputation. I don't know what you're up to right now and I didn't want to act without speaking to you. Besides, now that I think of it, Mr. Coles *was* attacked, or at least confronted."

"I don't know, Richard," I said slowly. "It sounds to me like you guys dropped the ball. Doctor Koulomzin was also attacked and by someone, maybe even a patient, posing as a member of your staff. Instead of trying to crucify my partner, this hospital should be doing its best to make him more comfortable. At the very least, the police should have been notified. Has it occurred to anyone that Boris may have saved Nurse Nangle's life?"

Steinman was trying very hard to look angry, but the image of Boris as a hero was more than he could take.

"See here, young man, we believe that Doctor Koulomzin discharged a loaded weapon in his hospital room."

It was the Lady Grinch in the starched white uniform.

"As a result, one of my nurses is injured and in shock and the entire floor is in an uproar. You're not going to get away with this, not if I have anything to say about it."

I took a step closer to the old prune. Her name tag read: EVELYN BAKER—SENIOR NURSING SUPERVISOR.

103

"I've had enough!" I announced, turning back to Hiram. "Doctor Parker, Boris Koulomzin is your patient, which means he's your responsibility as long as he remains in this hospital. I suggest you disband this angry mob and get refocused on his care and safety. Either way, this nonsense is over. If we are subjected to further unfounded accusations or harassment from this little kangaroo court, I'll respond by placing calls to my lawyer and the local news media. In fact, I'll make the calls if Nurse Baker so much as opens her mouth again. Is that clear?"

Senior Nursing Supervisor Baker actually tried to speak, but Parker turned on her.

"Button it, Evelyn," he snapped.

I left them to sort it out and headed down the hall to Boris's room.

The door was closed, so I knocked. When Boris didn't answer, I slowly pushed it open. The room was dark except for the glow coming from the screen of his portable computer. As my eyes adjusted to the shadows, I noticed that the books and papers I'd placed on the radiator were now scattered on the floor and that the bed was empty.

"Boris?" I turned the lights on and took several steps into the room.

"James, is that you?" He spoke very softly.

I stopped short and turned to my right. Boris was sitting rigidly, hidden behind the door, his huge frame supported on the little straight-backed chair. His right leg was stretched out in front of him, like a broken spar, and his left arm was supported in his lap. Boris blinked a few times, looking through me; he wasn't wearing his glasses.

"For heaven's sake, Boris," I sighed. "What are you doing out of bed?"

He winced in pain as he tried to stand up. I rushed over to help him and together we managed to reach the bed without doing any damage.

"You realize there's a lynch mob waiting for you out at the nurses' station?" I asked when he was lying down again.

"I've already been introduced," he yawned.

Boris closed his eyes and took several long, deep breaths. In less than a week, his simple sheltered life had been turned inside out. I went into the bathroom to look for the spare set of spectacles he keeps in his shaving kit.

"Okay, Lefty," I said, handing him the glasses. "Where'd ya stash the gat?"

Boris adjusted the wire frames, then stared at me for a minute.

"Are you drunk?" he asked finally.

"Of course not, I'm just trying to lighten the mood a little bit."

"Well, don't," he snorted. "This isn't funny."

"Okay, fine, but I still want to know what you did with my gun. After firing it, I mean."

He gave me a nasty look.

"For your information, this has been one of the worst nights of my life. In case you haven't figured it out, I had another meeting with Mr. St. John this evening."

"So I've gathered. Where's my gun?"

"I'm so happy you're concerned about my welfare, he said sarcastically. "Your precious revolver isn't here."

"What do you mean 'isn't here'? Where is it?"

"I gave it to the nice gentleman with the mop. He promised to keep it for me until things settled down a bit."

Boris had the smug look of a man who's found the perfect solution to a difficult problem.

"You gave my gun to a stranger?" I sputtered.

"Precisely."

"Do you at least know his name?"

"Of course. His name is Howard," he said, losing patience.

"Okay, forget about Howard for a minute. Did you or did you not fire a pistol in this room tonight?"

"Yes, well, as far as that's concerned, it is fortunate for me that Mr. St. John's weapon of choice is a dagger. Had he selected a pistol, I would now be dead."

Boris let that statement resonate for a few seconds.

"The revolver you gave me, cleverly loaded with harmless blanks, neither scared nor deterred him," he complained. "In fact, if anything, it reenforced St. John's delusional belief that a divine source is guiding his hand. Since bullets apparently couldn't harm him, the man left here thinking he's invulnerable. I will admit that the gun made enough noise to disrupt his plans, but under the circumstances, levity seems rather out of place. Wouldn't you agree?"

"Well, I guess so. But since you're alive and I haven't seen the bodies of any innocent bystanders, I'm thinking that maybe the blanks weren't such a bad idea. Why don't you just tell me what happened here tonight?"

He wrinkled his forehead in disgust, then sighed again.

"I was lying here, drifting in and out of sleep, when I heard the creaking of the hinges as the door was slowly opened and then closed. There was no other sound. It couldn't have been Nurse Nangle because she blunders in and out of here like a stray bull. So I opened my eyes and there he was, sitting comfortably in the corner."

Boris pointed vaguely with his good hand.

"The shadows didn't hide him, James. His hair was blue-white like the snow, and he was deeply tanned. For this visit, he had changed his clothes and now wore the white tunic and trousers of a male nurse. If I had to guess, I would say the man is fifty years old, though darkness and the ravages of the sun could have aged him somewhat. St. John appeared to be quite relaxed and sure of himself. He sat there smiling at me, like we were old friends.

"At first, we just stared across the short distance that separated us. But he finally stirred, crossing his legs lazily, like an aristocrat. I took the pistol from beneath the covers and laid it in my lap where he could see it. St. John only chuckled softly, mocking me.

" 'That won't be necessary, Doctor Koulomzin,' " he said calmly. 'I've merely come to claim my property, like a reasonable man.'

"I didn't respond, so he continued.

" 'Now, now, Doctor, fair is fair. Why don't you give me the package and let me be on my way? Your time doesn't have to be now.'

"I picked up the gun, cocked it, and pointed the barrel at the center of his chest. He seemed surprised, though after a moment he began to chuckle again. While he laughed, he slowly unbuttoned his tunic. Grinning like a gargoyle, he reached inside the shirt and pulled out a dagger with a long, thin blade and an ornate golden hilt. He inspected and caressed the knife fondly, then placed it in his lap.

" 'Now, let me see, where could my envelope be?'

"His eyes started wandering about the room. I warned him to stop or I'd fire.

" 'Stop? Why, I haven't even moved, you foolish old man,' he snarled. 'Besides, who are you to command the hand of God?'

"There was no more laughter in his voice, James. The look he sent across the space between us was an angry challenge. I tried to sit up a bit straighter in the bed, but when I moved, he leaped to his feet and darted to the windowsill, where he began to rifle through my papers. Of course he had little trouble finding his precious envelope. Then he turned and began to inch toward my bed; in his left hand, he held the envelope, in his right, the dagger.

" 'We have some unfinished business, you and I,' he rasped, moving forward and raising the knife. When he began to chant scripture, I squeezed the trigger.

"As you probably hoped, the noise was deafening, which

proved unfortunate for Nurse Nangle, who happened to barge into the room just as the shots rang out. She managed one loud scream, then collapsed in a heap on the floor."

I tried to imagine the scene: pistol shots like cannon blasts in that small room, Nangle screaming, and St. John stretching his arms wide to offer a better target.

"I kept waiting for the bullets to materialize," Boris continued. "It made no sense, but I fired again and again. Finally, there was just the clicking sound as the hammer fell against spent cartridges."

He looked at me and I could see the disbelief in his face.

"St. John was grinning like an imbecile. He started to advance again, the blade held out in front, as if it were leading him to me. He was very close, James, seconds from reaching me, when Nurse Nangle started moaning on the floor. St. John stopped to look down, and at that moment, the door crashed open. I'm afraid the door gave Nangle quite an unpleasant thump on the head, because she let out a little cry. Her misfortune was my salvation. Standing in the doorway was a tall, sinewy black man holding a heavy mop in front of him like a lance. He took in the scene quickly, then pressed forward into the room, forcing St. John back against the wall and away from me. There were voices in the hall; the chance to kill me had passed.

"Mr. St. John bowed slightly.

" 'Until we meet again, Doctor.'

"Howard, the fellow with the mop, looked over at me and in that instant, St. John lunged at him with the dagger. Fortunately, the thrust went wide as Howard parried, but the move forced an opening and the fiend was able to dive through the doorway into the hall. You could hear people yelling and shouting as he made his escape. I had barely enough time to give the revolver to Howard. First, the man saved my life, and then he covered for me by disappearing with the weapon as quickly as he had come. Minutes later, the room was full of people."

Boris let out a long, dramatic groan, then lay back heavily

against the pillows. Before he could start to editorialize, I picked up the phone.

"Who are you calling?" he asked peevishly.

I ignored the question. Manny Santos answered on the fourth ring.

"Yo, *como esta?*"

"Manny, it's Donovan. We've had more trouble."

"You at the hospital?" he asked softly.

"Yeah. The creep with the white hair just took another crack at Boris. It's time to get the good doctor out of this place. And I mean tonight."

"You got it, man. What you want me ta do?"

"You're gonna take Boris someplace safe. We can talk about the details when you get here, but I think you'll need at least three men. Okay?"

"No problem."

"Good. You've got one hour."

I hung up the phone and started packing.

TEN

■ ■ ■

Twenty minutes later, Boris was ready to travel; his computer was in its little carrying case and the CDs, reference books, and magazines were stashed in the canvas tote bag I'd brought from home. There weren't any clothes to pack. In fact, there weren't any clothes to wear. Dr. Koulomzin lay on the bed in his hospital gown and stared at the ceiling, looking glum.

"Hey, Boris, I don't suppose you own a nightshirt?" I asked, taking a long shot. "You know, like Scrooge wore."

The big man turned his head slowly.

"In my armoire, bottom drawer," he sighed.

I picked up the telephone again. This time, Santos answered on the second ring.

"Yo?"

"Manny, it's Donovan. How come you aren't in the car?"

"Whoa, man. What's wit you? I'm gettin' my shit togetha, bro."

"Okay, okay, relax. Before you leave, I want you to go up to Boris's apartment and find him some clothes. He can't wear pants because of the cast on his leg, but he says there's a night-shirt in the bottom drawer of his clothes cabinet, the wooden one, with doors."

"Nightshirt?" Manny asked, ignoring my description of the armoire. "What the fuck is that, man?"

"It's something people wore to bed a hundred years ago.

111

Looks like a shirt, but it goes all the way to your ankles."

"Sounds like a dress to me, man."

"Well, it isn't a dress."

Boris turned quickly, his eyes narrowing.

"Tell that old fool to bring me some underwear, my cardigan sweater, several pairs of socks, and my slippers," Boris growled.

"Tell him yourself," I said, holding out the phone. "But make it quick, I want you out of this hospital by midnight."

Boris snatched the receiver and started lecturing Manny about the origin and utility of nightshirts.

I left him barking at Santos and went back down the hall to the nurses' station hoping to find someone willing to discharge the big stiff. Fortunately, Richard Steinman and Hiram Parker were still there, working on damage control. When I told them that their problem patient would be leaving the hospital, they tried to argue, but only halfheartedly; there was relief behind their expressions of concern.

Before we could make our escape, however, a large pile of forms had to be filled out, collated, and signed. Dr. Parker sent one of the nurses to get Boris's chart, then sat down and began writing instructions and prescriptions. I took Rich Steinman by the arm and gently led him down the hall. Boris had apparently finished educating Manny, because the receiver was back in its cradle on the nightstand and he'd resumed his contemplation of the ceiling.

It didn't seem fair to leave Richard holding the bag for all the trouble we'd attracted. So I sat him down in the straight-backed chair and told him what had really happened. Boris listened quietly; his only comment an occasional grunt. It was my umpteenth performance of the day, and the yarn was getting more and more polished each time I told it. When I was done, Dr. Steinman just stared at me for a while, then he turned to look at Boris.

"You know something, J. J.?" he said, finally coming back to me. "I actually believe you. The story is just too far-fetched to make up."

"That's what everybody says." I sighed. "Everyone except the cops."

We had time to kill, so I told Steinman about my visit to the local police precinct. Since Boris hadn't heard about my dinner with Tim Danner, I told them about that, too. Dr. Steinman just shook his head; the AIDS virus was familiar ground for him.

"From what you tell me, it doesn't sound like this young man is doing very well. Why would anyone want to hurt him? Unless he responds to a new therapy soon, the prognosis seems very bleak, probably measured in months. What's the point of killing someone who's already doomed?"

"That *is* the question, isn't it?" Boris mumbled sadly.

Before we could respond, Manny Santos and three of his cousins burst into the room. Santos was pushing a wheelchair.

"Buenos noches!" he shouted, then started barking instructions at his troops.

Without another word, the boys helped Boris sit up, then gently steered him into a large, linen nightshirt and a warm, woolen cardigan. When he was dressed, they lifted him off the bed and deposited him in the wheelchair. The patient was ready, his bags were collected, and the platoon was marching back out the door in less than five minutes.

"Hey, wait a minute," Steinman protested, getting to his feet. "You can't just leave, he's got to be discharged."

"I'll handle all that stuff," I assured him, turning to follow the others.

"But J. J., where are you taking him? How will I get in touch with you?"

Rich was sputtering. I stopped and came back to him.

"That's the one thing I can't tell you, Richard," I said. "In the meantime, keep an eye open for a strange man with a deep tan and a full head of white hair."

It was too late to change anything; Manny and his team had the patient on an elevator headed for the lobby. Reluctantly, Dr. Steinman walked back to the nurses' station with me and I forged

113

Boris's name on all the necessary forms. Hiram Parker was also looking glum, but he gave me a written list of instructions for Boris's care and a little pile of prescriptions. I told Dr. Parker to cheer up, his pal Rich Steinman had a really good story to tell him.

Santos had the Fly Rides leem-o idling at the curb on Fort Washington Avenue, in front of the hospital. We both got in the back with Boris, who had his broken leg stretched out in front of him on a large pile of pillows. My plan was to send them all up to my weekend house on the lake, in Connecticut. It was a temporary solution, but at least we'd have some control over Boris's safety. The big man didn't argue; the second encounter with Johnny St. John had taken most of the fight out of him.

"When you get to Connecticut, put one of the kids on the boat dock and another one at the top of the driveway," I instructed Manny. "Oh yeah, and hide the leem-o in the barn. This thing will stand out like a sore thumb in farm country. If you need to go into town, use the Jeep."

Santos looked hurt, but he nodded his head.

"What about weapons?" Boris asked vaguely.

"You'll find a pair of twelve-gauge shotguns and a twenty-two-caliber bird gun in the cabinet next to the fireplace. And there are plenty of shells in the bottom drawer."

"Live ammunition, how novel."

"There's canned food in the pantry, and the freezer's loaded," I continued, ignoring the attitude. "That should tide you over until I can get up there."

"What? You're not coming with us?" Boris looked panicked.

"Take it easy, will you?" I said calmly. "St. John has his pictures now. Any further business with you can wait. I'm out in front and Johnny's playing catch-up. We want to stay ahead, remember?"

"And just how do you propose to do that?"

"You know, Boris, the medication must be dulling your wits. Timothy Danner answered some important questions tonight and you still don't get it. Remember the names typed on the index cards, the ones in parentheses, after the medical-center names? Well, now we know that those names refer to the doctors treating the people in the photographs. And the medical centers checked, too. Doctor Lieb, formerly at NYU Medical Center, is Tim's doctor! It follows that the lady in the second picture is seeing a Doctor Newman at Yale–New Haven Hospital. And the third guy, the snob in the business suit, he must be seeing a doctor named Conners who works, or worked, at Mount Sinai."

"And I have the list of doctors you printed?" Boris asked, stirring.

"Very good, Einstein," I replied, tapping the side of my head.

A few minutes later, the leem-o turned the corner at 165th Street, headed to Connecticut. Manny's three cousins were squeezed into the front seat, listening to a Ricky Martin tape. Santos was still in the back with Boris, but he didn't look happy. His traveling companion, the man with the long line of black-and-blue stitches, was listening to Anton Arensky's piano trio No. 1 in D Minor on the portable cassette player. Boris's eyes were almost closed, just slits, really; he was hard at work, thinking.

When Angus and I finally strolled into the lobby of my building, we found Richie Suero, Gabriel Caraballo, and little Augusto Matteo at the card table playing dominoes. Manny Santos and his cousins may have been headed to Connecticut, but the game went on as usual. Augusto perked up as soon as he saw me.

"Hey, Mista Donovan, what up?" he asked, popping the tab on a beer can. "Yo, I got somethin' here fa you."

"What's that, Augie?" I asked cautiously; it was too late for games.

"It's some kinda letter or somethin'," he said, holding up a dirty manila envelope.

It was the same envelope Johnny St. John had taken from

Boris's hospital room five hours earlier. I reached out and took it.

"Where did you get this?"

"Some guy come in here about an hour ago an gimme five bucks to deliver it to you. He was a strange cat, Donovan. Man got black eyes."

"Did he have a full head of white hair?"

"You got it, that's the guy."

I stood there looking at the envelope for a minute. Johnny was having fun. He wanted to make sure I knew he'd located my home. It was a good thing Boris was in Connecticut; this little surprise wouldn't have done his nerves any good.

"Yo, Donovan, you okay, man?"

The domino players were all staring at me.

"Did I mess up by takin' that thing?" Augusto asked, looking worried.

"No, it's not that," I said vaguely. "But you guys should know this dude is really bad news. Please, just tell me he didn't get on an elevator or anything?"

"No way, no how."

It was Gab Caraballo.

"We keep an eye on shit happens down here, bro. Nobody comes in or out less they go by us. Chill, Donovan, we'll keep Mista Bad Ass outta here. No problem."

"Sure you will," I mumbled. "Just remember what I said, okay?"

During the long, jerky ride up to the seventeenth floor, I held the envelope in my right hand and tapped it against the palm of my left. It was the same dirty, blood-spattered manila package, only now it was heavier and fatter, and it had been taped shut again. The bulk had me a little concerned. It didn't take very much plastic explosive to make an effective letter bomb. On the other hand, a guy who liked to mete out divine intervention with an ornate dagger probably didn't go in for messy high-tech devices. But that was just a guess.

Once inside my apartment, I put the manila envelope on the kitchen counter and made myself a mug of black tea. I puttered around for a while: opening the mail, checking the message machine, trying to ignore St. John and his head games. I finally ran out of things to do and went back to the kitchen. A smarter man would have taken greater precautions. I got my pocketknife out and slit the envelope open for the second time. Nothing happened—no smoke, no explosions, no toxic gas or chemicals.

I blew air into the envelope, and a boxed CD and a sheet of note paper slid out onto the counter. The cover of the plastic CD case indicated that it contained an opera called *Die Walküre*, by Richard Wagner. My musical taste doesn't run in that direction, but I remembered that Wagner's music was used in the movie *Apocalypse Now.* Very funny. Johnny St. John's idea of easy-listening fare. I pushed the disc to one side and picked up the note. It was written on heavy stock with a fountain pen and the script was very ornate. It was addressed to me:

Dearest James—

Alas, but I missed you again tonight. No matter, we'll get together soon enough. The CD is a gift and a special thank-you because you are making this project so much more rewarding for me.

Hugs and kisses,
Johnny

P.S. Our mutual friend T. D. sends his regrets!

When I got to the postscript, I blinked twice before it clicked. T. D.—Timothy Danner. I dropped the note and grabbed the telephone. The number I dialed was ringing at the other end, but no one answered. I slammed the receiver down, then dumped the contents of my wallet on the counter and spread the little mountain of business and credit cards around until I found the scrap of bar napkin with the phone number I needed. This time, the phone rang twice.

"Queen's Derby, can I help you?"

I asked for Peter Walsh. Another minute or two passed before he came on the line.

"Walsh here," he announced.

"Peter, it's J. J. Donovan," I began.

"Donovan? I didn't expect to hear from you so soon."

"Look, it's about Tim," I said seriously. "He isn't answering the telephone and I'm worried. There was another attack on my partner tonight, this time at the hospital. In the confusion, the white-haired guy, this Johnny St. John, he got all the pictures."

I took a deep breath.

"Peter, when I got back to my apartment, there was a note from St. John waiting for me. It ends with a postscript—'T. D. sends his regrets!' I'm guessing now, but if the creep has connected Tim's name with his picture, then the kid isn't safe."

There was a moment of silence.

"Peter, are you there?" I asked finally.

"What? Yes, of course." Walsh sounded dazed. "Look, I'm on my way."

"And, Peter—" I shouted before he could hang up.

"What's that?" He came back on the line.

"Don't go alone."

There was a pause, and then the line went dead.

ELEVEN

. . .

I raced down the Westside Highway, weaving in and out of traffic. I had promised Tim Danner that no one would hurt him, and I desperately needed to keep that promise. There was a chance that he'd merely slept through the ringing of the telephone. But the knot in my stomach said otherwise; Tim's answering machine should have been on. Angus sensed my mood and moved into the back, where he lay down and kept his head low.

At 58th Street, the highway turned into a two-lane road, with traffic lights every couple of blocks. For one seemingly interminable stretch, I sat idling next to the aircraft carrier *Intrepid* and drummed my fingers on the steering wheel while a couple of drunken hot rods argued over a fender bender. It was more than my nerves could handle. I eased the Nova up onto the curb, navigated around an obstacle course of street signs and debris, then pulled ahead of the accident. After that, I didn't bother stopping for red lights; a police escort would have been helpful. Once I got below the passenger terminal, the highway opened up again and I was able to step on the accelerator.

Tim Danner lived on a side street lined with red-brick townhouses and century-old brownstones. It was a quiet, private lane, with neat rows of elm trees. But when I turned the corner that night, the street was clogged with police cars and there was an ambulance parked up on the sidewalk. I pulled in behind one of the squad cars and stuck my "CLERGY ON CALL" sign on the dashboard.

As I raced up the staircase, I remembered how easily I'd carried Tim up these same stairs earlier in the evening. When I reached the landing on the third floor, I stopped pretending there was hope. The door to Tim's apartment was open and the living room was crowded. Peter Walsh was talking to a couple of uniformed police officers, and there was a detective in a suit taking notes. I nodded to Peter, then began to elbow my way down the hallway. I recognized several customers from The Queen's Derby, and I could hear someone crying. I kept going.

The bedroom was also crowded; more cops, a couple of paramedics repacking their equipment, and an evidence team taking prints. Tim was lying on the bed, his head tilted slightly backward, staring up at the ceiling. His fragile arms were resting at his sides, but the hands and fingers were clenched into tightly knotted balls. He was wearing bright red, short-sleeved pajamas with a paisley pattern. Either they were new or freshly laundered, because the only wrinkles had come from folding. His eyes were open wide, too wide. Even from across the room, I could see that they'd lost the spark I'd noticed at dinner.

On the night table next to Tim's bed, I saw a glass syringe and an alcohol swab with a little dot of blood in the center. There was also an open bottle of Moët champagne, and beside that, a fluted crystal glass that was half full. It was meant to look like a suicide party. But as I continued scanning the room, I saw something that convinced me Timothy Danner hadn't taken his own life. The bathroom door was open and I could see Tim's cat, Samantha, hanging by the neck from the shower rod. The animal's tongue and eyes were bulging from its head. It had been strangled with a length of picture wire, then hung on the rod, like an exhibit in a freak show. Even if Danner had snapped, I didn't believe for a second that he could have injured Samantha.

The dead cat had been put on display to impress me, like tying Boris's scarf to that post in Riverside Park. St. John enjoyed these sadistic games. I was beginning to recognize his signature; like popping the cork on that expensive bottle of champagne to celebrate the ritual killing.

There were other signs that should have raised doubts in an investigator's mind. For example, a person getting ready to self-inflict a lethal injection probably doesn't bother to disinfect his skin first. What difference would an infection make to a dead man? On the other hand, using the alcohol swab was the sort of thing a trained nurse or a doctor might do out of habit. It also seemed odd that the evidence on the nightstand was so neatly arranged. Tim Danner was a very weak, very sick man. It was hard to picture him pumping something deadly into his veins and then stopping to arrange things neatly on the table before lying back to die. In fact, depending on the substance that was injected, there might not have been time. Johnny knew I'd be looking for signs; that was part of his fun.

As I walked across the room, the half-empty champagne bottle caught my eye. A picture of St. John, smiling wickedly and wiping his lips on an expensive handkerchief, flashed into my mind. Unless the coroner found that missing wine in Tim's stomach during the autopsy, someone was going to have to explain where it went. That wasn't evidence, but the doubt it created might be enough to get the cops interested in the bubbly left in the fluted glass. I'm no scientist, but I knew that residual saliva could provide the DNA needed to fingerprint the killer, and that was solid evidence.

I stood gazing down at Timothy Danner's body and prayed he hadn't been made to suffer. The kid didn't look at peace to me; I read anguish in the strained expression on his face. Without thinking, I reached down and shut his eyelids.

"Just what the hell do you think you're doing?" someone yelled from across the room.

Before I could answer, a beefy uniformed cop grabbed me by the arm and started dragging me toward the front hall. Like I said before, I don't like being touched or grabbed, especially when I'm not expecting it. I broke free and pushed the big porker out of my way. He didn't like my pushing any more than I liked his grabbing, and he was just putting his head down to make another charge when Peter Walsh came to my rescue.

"This is Mr. Donovan, Sergeant," he said, stepping between us and holding up one of his powerful hands. "You remember, the man I was telling you about."

An elderly detective with thinning gray hair and a really impressive paunch came out of the kitchen with a mug of steaming black coffee in his hand.

"Donovan? I know that name," he said, moving up closer and peering at me. "Why is that name so familiar to me?"

"I don't know, you tell me," I barked, still annoyed at the other guy for shoving me.

"Now, now, Mr. Donovan, there's no need for hostility. This is a tragic event for all those present. Suicide is always difficult to witness and very hard to accept."

He had a deep voice and he spoke softly, but I wasn't in the mood for a sermon from a cop with a degree in psychology.

"Is that so? Well, this isn't a suicide."

I was tired and aggravated.

"Is that right?"

The veteran cop scratched his chin.

"And you said your name was Donovan? I think I heard that name from an old friend of mine. You don't by any chance know a Lieutenant Negro, Christopher Negro?"

He caught me off guard. Negro and I had worked together when I was helping my young friend Clifford Brice find his mother's killer. It involved a factory out in East New York, Brooklyn. Negro retired not long after that problem got resolved. You could say he went out with a bang. There was no reason to hide the fact, so I admitted that I knew Lieutenant Negro.

"So you know Chris. Well, that's fine, just fine."

The old boy was smiling warmly.

"My name's Gavin, Lieutenant Raymond Gavin," he told me.

"Now, what makes you so sure this wasn't a suicide?"

Lieutenant Gavin motioned to another suit, who flipped open his notebook and stepped closer.

"The name's James Joseph Donovan," I said slowly, so he could get it right, then took a deep breath and folded my arms across my chest defensively. "I have reason to believe that Timothy Danner was killed tonight by a man who calls himself Johnny St. John. Mr. St. John is a middle-aged person with a deep tan and a full head of white hair. He is very smart, very unstable, and extremely dangerous."

The guy with the notebook looked up quickly, but Gavin put a finger to his lips and nodded for me to continue. The lieutenant wasn't in a rush.

"It's a long story," I warned, but Gavin just kept smiling.

"That's fine," he said.

Since he asked for it, I gave him the whole thing, beginning with the attempt on Boris's life on the street corner across from Yankee Stadium. Correcting a mistake Boris made early on, I told him about the envelope and the pictures of the three sick people we'd found inside it.

"My partner, Doctor Koulomzin, believes the photographs and the medical information in the package were being delivered to St. John so that he could seek out and then kill each of the sick people in the pictures," I said seriously.

When Gavin didn't pounce on me, I kept going.

"Earlier today—actually it was yesterday—" I said, looking at my watch, "I received a phone call from this guy, this Johnny St. John. That's how I know his name—he introduced himself. The guy wanted his precious envelope back and he was serious. It's all on tape. Believe me, when he started quoting the Old Testament, it got a little spooky."

I took a deep breath.

"Anyway, after that phone call, it seemed pretty important that we find the people in the pictures and warn them. I made a few phone calls, trying to check the information on the cards, but

123

didn't get anywhere. Then I remembered that there was a hat, a derby, etched in the restaurant window in the first picture. I followed a hunch and got lucky, it led me to The Queen's Derby.

"You probably know the rest of this from talking with Mr. Walsh," I said, glancing at Peter. "Danner and I had dinner together this past evening, at The Queen's Derby. We talked at some length and I told Mr. Danner about St. John. He had never heard of the man and he couldn't think of any reason, other than homophobia, for someone to wish him harm. Tim was weak, Lieutenant, but he hadn't given up on life and he wasn't depressed. The man was a fighter. Before I left him, I made a promise. I said that nothing would happen to him."

I looked around the room, then lowered my gaze to the floor.

"I probably shouldn't have left him all alone," I finally admitted. "But as long as we had the envelope, I didn't think it was possible for St. John to find him. I didn't give Johnny enough credit. While I was dining with Tim Danner, St. John was attacking my partner, again. This time, in his hospital room."

"What hospital is that?" the notebook interrupted.

"The Milstein Hospital, up at Columbia–Presbyterian," I told him. "Doctor Koulomzin is recuperating from multiple injuries sustained in the hit-and-run I mentioned earlier."

I waited for the young detective's pen to catch up with the information I'd supplied. The apartment had gone quiet; all eyes had turned to me.

"It's all right," Gavin said, noticing my discomfort. "Keep going. Tell me about the hospital."

"That's another long story," I warned. "The bottom line is that St. John found his envelope tonight, while I was down here meeting Tim. He has the original photographs and he made the connection to Tim quickly, which means he must have another source of information. When I got home and saw Tim's initials in the note St. John left me, I called Peter."

I stopped again and looked over at Danner's body.

"It's just rotten luck that St. John came here first," I said slowly. "I wasted a whole day making calls and wandering around the Bronx. If I hadn't noticed the derby in the background of that photograph, I might have spent weeks chasing smoke trails. It gives me chills to think St. John could get here that quickly. We're talking an hour or two after he found the pictures. It's spooky."

I took a deep breath.

"Anyway, that's all there is to tell. Take it from me, Tim Danner did not kill himself."

Detective Gavin stared at me for a while. You could hear throats being cleared and feet shuffling nervously, but no one spoke. I was tempted to make a wisecrack, but I'd said enough already. Gavin finally turned to the guy with the notebook.

"Bobby, call Milstein Hospital and see what they have to say about this business. I'm getting a real big headache," he groaned, rubbing his temples.

"Sure thing, Lieutenant." Bobby was eager to please.

The kid asked me to spell Hiram Parker's name, then hurried off to look for a telephone. The rest of us waited in silence as Lieutenant Gavin meandered into the kitchen and refilled his coffee mug from the pot on the counter. He stopped to look out the kitchen window, then scratched the back of his neck thoughtfully.

"Now, Mr. Donovan," Gavin began, strolling back into the room, "you will allow me a little reasoned skepticism. In thirty years, I've met a lot of bad guys, but this would mark my first experience chasing the devil, or even one of his immediate associates."

He smiled knowingly.

" 'Spooky' is not a word that lends itself well to evidence-based criminal investigations," he went on. "However, I register your point. Mr. St. John, by all accounts, is a very disturbed individual who bears careful handling. And I agree, it is unfortunate that the timing didn't work out better for Mr. Danner's sake."

Bobby came back into the room, looking like he'd just won the lottery.

"You won't believe this, Lieutenant," he snickered, "but the story checks with the hospital. Man, did somebody raise hell up there tonight! That Doctor Parker is a very unhappy man. He confirmed that his patient, Doctor Boris Koulomzin, was attacked last night. Shots were fired, and a nut job with a big knife ran through the halls threatening important patients. The guy with the knife had a big head of white hair, just like Donovan said. Anyway, the guy escaped, and now Koulomzin's gone, too. Apparently, some mean-lookin' Spanish dudes came and got him. Man, is this crazy or what?"

Gavin started rubbing his temples again.

"I think we should have a long talk, Mr. Donovan," he said finally. "Why don't we move this down to the station house where you'll be more comfortable?"

He was still smiling, but the warmth was gone.

TWELVE

■ ■ ■

By the time I finished chatting with Lieutenant Gavin, the sun had risen. The old boy sure liked to take his time inspecting the pieces of a puzzle. The only reason I broke free at all was that he knew Angus was waiting outside in the car.

To Gavin's credit, he didn't treat me like a moron or laugh in my face, but he still wasn't happy about the situation. I'd really complicated his life. The apparent suicide of a dying man now involved multiple homicides, across two boroughs and at least three police precincts. And God only knew what other mischief Johnny St. John had caused. Making the job even more difficult, there was very little hard evidence to support the expensive resources the lieutenant was going to need to make a case. My story certainly didn't present him with the kind of solid documentation an officer dreams about. In fact, when Gavin realized that I'd never actually seen the mysterious Johnny St. John, he shook his head and started rubbing his temples again.

Gavin's headache was my good fortune. He was a professional, the kind of cop who can't abide loose ends or unanswered questions. And he wasn't trying to dump the problem onto someone else's desk. My copies of the photographs and index cards and the recording of my telephone conversation with Johnny had gotten his attention. But if there was one thing that really bothered him, the thing that made the back of his neck itch, it was the dead cat dangling from the shower rod.

127

"I've seen a lot of suicides," he said flatly, around five o'clock that morning. "When they decide to take a loved one with them, they usually do it gently. Why didn't Danner just give the kitty a shot? He had the needle sitting right there."

Gavin also agreed that the scene in the bedroom looked contrived, and he wanted to know why there wasn't a suicide note. Tim Danner had been facing an early death for several years. If he'd finally decided that life wasn't worth the fight, he would have left an explanation. Tim wasn't impulsive, and he lived in a community that was all too familiar with death. There were many friends to whom he'd have wanted to say good-bye, friends who wouldn't have judged him harshly for his decision. Johnny had been the one in a hurry.

There was an even better reason for Gavin to believe me, only I didn't know it when I started my diatribe back in Tim's apartment. One of the neighbors, Mrs. Arlene Jacobs, had seen a man leaving Danner's building at about the time of his death. She was an elderly widow who sat up nights and watched the street from the shadows of her darkened bedroom. Mrs. Jacobs had seen a man leave the building at eleven-thirty that evening. She was sure of the time because her favorite radio talk show had just started. She remembered this man in particular—he had an impressive head of snow-white hair. She said it wasn't the sort of thing you'd forget.

All in all, there was enough to keep Ray Gavin busy. A call had also been placed to the commander of the 33rd Precinct requesting that Detective William Sweeney make an appearance. The treatment I'd gotten from Sweeney hadn't played well with Gavin. He was from the old school, and the idea that a man might have died because of a cop's arrogance made him angry. I decided not to linger. It seemed unwise for me to be sitting there when Sergeant Sweeney discovered that I was responsible for his early morning wake-up call.

* * *

Angus was my excuse to leave Gavin, but I really wasn't too worried about him. We had taken a walk before I went into the police station, and I'd left him food and some water. So when I got outside, I was surprised to find that he'd endeared himself to a burly cop sporting a thick, red, handlebar mustache and clutching a large bag of donuts. Angus was sitting on the sidewalk next to the cop, trying to lick powdered sugar off his whiskers.

"Good morning," I said cheerfully.

"This your dog?" the mustache demanded.

"Yes and no," I answered, still friendly.

"What's that supposed to mean? You a wise guy?"

"The dog belongs to my partner, but I'm taking care of him just now," I said.

"You call *this* taking care of him? The poor thing needed water and he hadn't been walked in hours. It was a lucky thing I came along when I did and took him over to the park."

He bent down and scratched Angus's ears sympathetically.

"How would you like it if I locked you up in a little box and didn't let you near a bathroom?" he demanded, straightening back up.

"Now just hold on one minute," I said, stepping into his shadow and poking him in the chest with my index finger. "Does this dog look too thin? Is he dirty? Does he shy away when you try to pet him, like he's been beaten or abused?"

One hundred thirty-five pounds of drooling puppy answered the question for me by bouncing up and down happily and wagging its tail.

"I've had a busy night in there," I said, pointing over my shoulder at the precinct. "I'm working with Lieutenant Ray Gavin on a messy homicide investigation."

The cop's eyebrows and mustache rose slightly when I mentioned Gavin.

"So instead of forcing me to drag your butt inside for an attitude adjustment, why don't you just let me thank you for the

129

donuts and for walking the dog and we'll be on our way."

I started to reach for the door handle, but I was still annoyed.

"Before I leave," I began, turning and pointing at Angus, "you should know that this dog is smart enough to play Othello on Broadway and he'd do so in a minute if he thought it would earn him a few donuts."

Angus grinned and drooled on the pavement.

"Get in the car, you little pirate," I muttered under my breath.

He gave the officer one last hungry glance, then jumped into the car. I got in behind him and we left that big cop standing there holding an empty donut bag.

We cruised uptown on Eleventh Avenue until I located a diner that didn't look too dirty. Inside, I found a comfortable booth and ordered up a big plate of scrambled eggs with bacon, home fries, toast, and a pot of strong coffee. I needed lots of fuel to keep me awake. Angus got nothing; he was full of donuts.

Twenty-five minutes later, I had wiped my plate clean and was back in the Nova, with a hot cup of mud for the road. I tried to punch a drinking hole in the lid and managed to spill most of the coffee into my lap. While I was fumbling around, looking for something to wipe up the mess with, I noticed the present St. John had left for me. It had been sitting on the front seat the whole time I was getting the third degree. Gavin had inspected my copies of the photographs and the index cards with all the medical jargon, and I even let him make a Xerox of Johnny's love note. But we'd both forgotten about the CD.

I took a big sip of coffee, flipped open the cell phone, and dialed my house in Connecticut. The answering machine picked up and I was treated to the sound of Kate's voice as she invited the caller to leave a message.

"Hello, hello, anybody home?" I asked the machine. "I'm looking for a banged-up old Russian grizzly bear."

"What do you mean by *old*?" the grizzly demanded, interrupting the recording.

"Relax, Big Guy, I was just trying to get your attention."

"Is that so? Well, you have my attention. Now, will you please explain why you are waking me at this ungodly hour?"

I'd been hoping to soften the blow with a little conversation first, but there was just no way around such a direct question. Suddenly, a great weight was pressing me into the seat.

"Look, Boris, when I got back to the apartment building last night, there was a package waiting for me in the lobby. It was the envelope St. John took from your hospital room."

He didn't say anything, but I heard his cigarette lighter click.

"When I opened the envelope, I found a handwritten note and a CD inside. The CD is an opera called *Die Walküre*, by Richard Wagner. I figured that was Johnny's idea of a joke. The note was something else, it wasn't funny."

I unfolded the paper and read aloud.

"When I saw those initials—T. D.—I tried calling Tim Danner," I said, remembering again just how helpless I'd felt. "But Danner didn't answer his phone. So I got ahold of Peter Walsh, at The Queen's Derby, and warned him that Tim could be in danger. After that, the only thing I could do was to get downtown as fast as possible."

"And what did you find when you got there?" he growled.

"I found that St. John had gotten there first." I sighed.

After that, there was nothing left to tell him except the details. I was so tired that my voice was starting to sound like it was coming out of a tunnel, far away.

"Gavin wants to talk to you, too," I said, finally coming to the end. "And for what it's worth, I liked him. Get this, the guy knows Chris Negro."

Boris mumbled something about Lieutenant Negro being a poor choice for a character reference, then took Gavin's phone number anyway. His voice was steady, but I knew Danner's murder was weighing on him, too.

"Tell me what's been happening on your end," I asked, hoping for a ray of light.

Dr. Koulomzin didn't have any revelations, but at least his

news wasn't all bad. The trip to Connecticut had been uneventful. They arrived while it was still pitch-dark outside and the Fly Rides leem-o was now safely hidden in the barn. The three cousins, Moses, Hector, and Eduardo, were preparing to sleep, eat, and stand guard over him in shifts. Their fearless leader, Manuel, had gotten up at daybreak and taken the Jeep into town for "provisions," which probably meant rice, beans, and beer.

"What about the leads on the doctors and the medical centers?" I asked without thinking.

"It seemed inappropriate to make inquiries in the middle of the night," Boris said sarcastically.

"Oh, right. Good point," I was looking at the cover of the CD. "So what do you make of this opera Johnny sent me?"

"*Die Walküre,* by Richard Wagner," Boris muttered, and I heard his cigarette lighter click again. "The Valkyrie is the second of four operas collectively know as *The Ring Cycle.* The story is taken from Teutonic mythology and chronicles the fall of the gods, the end of the earth, and—"

"Teutonic mythology . . . as in Thor, God of Thunder, right?"

"Very good. Now, if you will listen, I will explain. In Norse mythology, the gods were not immortal; they had to struggle, much as humans do, against their enemies, as well as their own weaknesses. Odin, the supreme Norse god, broke his word to the giant who rebuilt Valhalla, and it started an era of deception, violence, and warfare that ultimately brought about the destruction of the earth and the gods."

I was starting to nod off, but I was happy I'd been right about Thor.

"James!"

The sudden thunder startled me. Thor banging his hammer.

"What? No, no, I'm listening. Gods in trouble."

Boris groaned, like a teacher with a hopeless student.

"As I was saying," he sighed, "in this twilight period of the Norse gods, the mythological world was torn apart and there was constant warfare. The Valkyries, led by Odin's daughter,

Brynhilde, and her sisters, ranged the world, flying from one battle to the next. It was the Valkyries, or 'choosers of the slain,' who decided which heroes would be killed in battle and then led them off to Valhalla."

"So what's the connection? Does Johnny think he's a Valkyrie?" I asked, finishing the coffee.

"Possibly," Boris murmured, "though that may be too simple. In the past, Mr. St. John's biblical recitations have alluded to ominous events, like the apocalypse. The Valkyrie existed to serve and protect the gods. But in this context, they failed, and as a result, the world and the gods were destroyed. The reference could be St. John's way of taunting you for trying to save those who cannot be saved."

"The guy has such a refined sense of humor."

"Let us not forget that this is a very intelligent man," Boris said. "His mind and his soul are badly corrupted, but we must be wary of his abilities."

I wasn't so impressed with his abilities. A guy who spouted fancy quotes and killed frail, sick people wasn't my idea of a challenging adversary. In fact, I was looking forward to my first meeting with Johnny St. John. In the meantime, I kept my opinion to myself.

"By the way," Boris said, changing subjects, "have you spoken to Kate? I think it would be a good idea to let her know that we've taken up residence in her home."

I hadn't spoken to Kate since we parted at the hospital. I started to miss her right away. Then I remembered the message she'd left about that poem.

"Look, Boris, I need a favor."

"I'm listening," he replied cautiously.

"Kate asked me to read this poem by Longfellow."

"Yes?"

"Well, I was hoping you'd take a look at it for me."

"If Kate asked you to read the poem, then she wants your opinion, not mine."

133

"I am planning to read it," I said. "But it would help if I could discuss it with you first, that's all. I put the book in your bag before I left the hospital yesterday."

"Does the poem have a name?"

"It's called '*Mezzo Cammin*.' "

There was a pause.

"When should we expect you?" he asked finally, without agreeing to read anything.

"I need a shower and a couple hours of sleep," I said, looking at my stubble in the rearview mirror.

"You must be exhausted, James, because you are not making any sense," Boris declared. "You cannot go home, it isn't safe. My God, St. John is probably sitting out front waiting for you. Take a nap in the car if you're tired, but do not go near the apartment building."

"What am I supposed to do with Angus?" I complained.

"What do you mean? Be thankful you have such a charming companion."

Over the past three days, I had napped on a plane, dozed in a chair, and slept in my clothes on a couch. Now I was going to be sleeping in my car. There was a pattern forming. I started the Nova and drove off to look for a secluded parking space.

THIRTEEN

. . .

While I was searching for a place to park for my nap, I decided to listen to *Die Walküre*. After all, Johnny had gone to a lot of trouble on my account. I popped the disc out of the case and stuck it into the CD player. I was prepared to hear a bunch of German women the size of pro-football linemen, with breastplates and those metal hats with horns, singing in German.

There was a moment's scratchy silence and then, instead of a full orchestra, someone started playing a happy little jingle on the piano. Next came the pleasant tenor voice of a trained announcer, who informed me that we were about to enjoy the ninth installment in a series of ten self-help courses. The program was called "Ten Steps to a Secure Financial Future," and Volume Nine covered "The Art of Estate Planning." There was a brief trumpet fanfare, and the announcer introduced Mr. Thomas P. Martin—Investment Counselor to the Rich and Famous.

When Mr. Martin started to speak, I reached for the volume-control knob. The man had a high-pitched voice with a very annoying nasal quality. The lecture was nothing special either, just a lot of canned financial advice. The only person who was going to maximize and retain wealth from this CD was Mr. Thomas P. Martin. I listened for a few more minutes, then took the disc out of the player and checked the label. It confirmed that I was indeed listening to a lecture on estate planning. The author was a guy named Thomas P. Martin. Not Richard Wagner. Turning down a side street, I parked next to a hydrant and reached for the cell phone again. This time, Boris answered instead of the machine.

"Aren't you supposed to be napping?" he asked.

"I'm still looking for a place to park," I announced. "Besides, this is important. I need you to check something out for me on the computer."

"What important event could have occurred within the last ten minutes?" he asked.

"I tried to play Johnny's CD."

"And?"

"And the CD wasn't *Die Walküre*. It's a very forgettable lecture on estate planning, given by a man with an extremely annoying voice."

"Does this gallows humor surprise you?" Boris asked, sounding bemused. "I mean, really, estate planning from a serial killer."

His lack of enthusiasm stopped me for a minute.

"Okay, maybe it's nothing," I admitted. "But since we don't have any other leads, I'd like you to do some background on this course. Even if it's another one of his jokes, St. John had to go to some effort to locate and purchase this CD. Maybe we can find a connection."

"I suppose it's worth a try," Boris yawned.

He wrote down Thomas P. Martin's name and the name of the course, then hung up so he could connect the telephone line to his computer modem.

Although I was tired, the caffeine from all that coffee had finally kicked in, making a nap pretty much impossible. I clipped the leash to Angus's collar and let him drag me around for a while, hoping that would take the edge off. We walked longer and farther than I had planned, and by the time we got back to the car, I was ready to shut my eyes for a while. We were way over by

136

the Westside Highway and the street was deserted. The Nova was parked next to a hydrant, but technically, as long as I was sitting in it, we weren't parked. I stretched my legs out on the front seat and let nature take its course.

After what seemed like just a few minutes, my cell phone started to ring. Reluctantly, I opened my eyes. The sun was so bright, I started groping for my sunglasses. I'd been asleep for nearly two hours. While I was trying to regain my equilibrium, the phone kept ringing.

"J. J. Donovan," I said, feeling incredibly groggy.

"James, good news!" Boris shouted into the receiver.

"What's going on?" I asked through the fog.

"What's going on? Why, we've found him!"

"Found who?" I needed to soak my head in a basin of ice-cold water.

"Thomas P. Martin—Investment Counselor to the Rich and Famous. He's the man in the third picture!"

Boris had started out by searching for the course by name, but that led to a dead end. After a number of frustrating miscues, he finally developed a strategy for the search, which was to approach it through companies that sell and distribute books about finance and business. After that, it had been a matter of time. Once he'd located a company that carried the course, he was able to identify the production outfit, and that led him to the Web site. *Ten Steps to a Secure Financial Future* must have been a big seller, because it was prominently featured. There was a very nice biography of Mr. Thomas P. Martin, the author and moderator of the course. There was also a photograph. It wasn't the same picture we'd found in Johnny's envelope, but there was no mistaking the identity. Martin was our man.

"If that's true," I said, coming to my senses, "then Johnny knows about Martin, too. He's the one feeding us the clues."

"I'm afraid that is correct," Boris said, losing some of his enthusiasm. "Remember, St. John thanked you for making his project more interesting. This is probably his way of spicing up the game. He finds it more exciting to pit his wits against ours."

"So what should we do?" I asked.

"Well, I've had quite a good look at Mr. Martin since I discovered the Web site," Boris said confidently. "I placed a call to his investment firm and spoke to several people there who intimated that Martin has not been to the office for several weeks. I was finally directed to his personal assistant, Gerald; a very officious, obnoxious person. Gerald's calculated reticence and Martin's absence have convinced me that Mr. Martin knows that he is in trouble."

There was a click as Boris lit yet another cigarette.

"Without too much difficulty, I was able to locate home addresses for Mr. Thomas P. Martin in Manhattan and Connecticut."

"What's the New York address?" I asked.

It was in the East Sixties. I knew the neighborhood.

"What do you have in mind?" Boris asked quickly.

"Well, before leaving the city, I thought I might just stop by for a look."

"I do not approve," he said firmly. "St. John could have Martin's house under surveillance just as easily as our apartment building. In fact, he may have already been there."

"Don't worry, I'll be careful," I promised with my usual confidence. "Besides, if Johnny's already been there, it won't make any difference."

"That's not true. He could be waiting there for you."

"I don't think so, Boris. St. John won't do anything to me until all three of the people in the photographs have been found. You said it yourself, he enjoys the sport. Anything premature would ruin his fun."

He tried to dissuade me for a few more minutes, but it was pointless, my mind was made up. I finally had a good lead and I wasn't about to let it get away.

Before I did anything else, though, I decided to call Kate. I still hadn't read the stupid poem, but this thing with St. John was getting crazy and I wanted to speak to her before it got completely out of hand. Besides, the sound of her voice makes me feel good, and I needed to feel better.

"Kate Byrne."

It was her professional voice.

"Hi, honey, it's me," I chimed.

"Jamie, what's going on?" she demanded. "I can't find Boris and I've been leaving messages all over town for you. This morning I talked to Rich Steinman and he hinted something about a problem at the hospital. Are you guys in trouble?"

When I hesitated, she let out a big sigh.

"Oh, J. J. Not again."

"Wait a minute, Kate, this is different."

"I don't have time for a long, convoluted story, Jamie. Please, just give me the bottom line, okay? Should I call Eliot Warner and tell him to get the bail money ready?"

"Look, Kate, I'm sorry you're upset, but someone is trying to hurt Boris. That accident in the Bronx wasn't an accident. And the more I find out about the guy who's responsible the worse it gets. He has already committed two murders and there will be more if we don't stop him. We're dealing with a lunatic, a crazy person who kills sick people. We found him out by chance and now it's too late to walk away. He attacked Boris at the hospital last night, and he's been to my apartment building, so I can't go home either. I just called to tell you that I have Boris stashed in the Brookfield house. It was the only place I could think of that was safe."

There was a long silence.

"Look, I'm sorry things always get so complicated."

"Are you going to be all right?" she asked finally.

"Oh yeah, no problem."

"That's what you said the last time."

"Why don't you call Boris if you're worried? It'll make you both feel better."

"What about you?" she asked softly. "When will I hear from you?"

"I'll call you tonight, I promise. Okay?"

She told me she loved me and hung up the phone. I reached over and scratched Angus behind the ears. Not even a hint about the poem; I'd just gotten a twelve-hour reprieve.

I drove up Central Park West and turned onto the Park Drive at 65th Street. The forsythia bushes at Tavern on the Green were full of little yellow buds, and the sun was shining brightly on another beautiful spring day. It was too bad I couldn't enjoy it. When I got to Fifth Avenue, I turned right, heading south. Thomas Martin's house was on East 63rd Street, between Park and Madison Avenues. A very classy address.

I parked in a garage just off Lexington and we walked over to Mr. Martin's street. It was new turf, so Angus took extra time checking out the sidewalks and buildings. We stopped at the corner of 63rd and Park, and the big puppy sniffed happily while I checked out Martin's townhouse, which was halfway down the block, on the right side of the street. I didn't see anything unusual. There were cars packed tightly into parking spaces on both sides of the street, and what looked like regular people going about their business.

Instead of walking up 63rd Street, I went two blocks over and walked back down to Lexington Avenue. There was a small grocery store on the corner of Lex and 61st, where I bought enough supplies to fill a good-sized cardboard box: canned goods, bread, paper towels, fresh vegetables, and a pound of sliced ham from the deli section. It really didn't matter what I bought, but I was hungry and the honey-baked ham looked too good to pass up. Besides, Angus needed a treat. I had him tied to a parking meter out in front of the store and he was sulking.

The next part of my plan didn't include Angus, which was a problem because you can't park dogs in a garage, not even dogs the size of small ponies. Luckily, I was in the Big Apple, where money talks. For a few bucks, one of the delivery boys from the grocery store agreed to watch him. I left Angus half a pound of the sliced ham and started up the street to Thomas Martin's house. It wasn't much of a disguise. A box of groceries does not a deliveryman make, but it was simple, and sometimes that's all it takes. Besides, I couldn't think of anything else.

The townhouse was a classic red-brick building, with white trim and black shutters. It was four stories tall and worth about a million dollars a floor. There were heavy steel bars on the street-level windows and I noticed a new surveillance camera tastefully mounted above the front door. All the houses on the block were built right next to each other, without side alleys or separate delivery entrances, so there wasn't any way to reach the back. If I wanted to get in, I had to use the front door.

I rang the bell and chewed on a carrot stick while I tried to figure out my next move. Standing there in the street like an idiot wasn't a good idea. I rang the doorbell again, but no one answered. There was an intercom next to the door, so I put my box of goodies down and pretended to speak to someone inside while I tested the front door. The knob didn't turn, but the door gave a little, which meant that the dead bolt wasn't locked. I took out my wallet and slipped a credit card into the space between the door and the frame. I moved the card up and down slowly and leaned against the door, but that didn't work. Finally, I tried jiggling the card and shaking the handle. After about a minute, the door popped open, just like in the movies.

It was too easy. A man who's savvy enough to install video cameras wouldn't leave his front door unbolted, not unless he expected company. I stood on the stoop, which was street level, and waited for about another minute. I expected alarm bells or sirens, but when nothing happened, I grabbed my box of groceries and stepped down into the foyer. I pulled the street door closed behind me, then waited again, listening. Still nothing. Directly in front of me, I saw a second door with a fancy etched-glass panel. I pulled it open and stepped carefully into the house.

It was pretty dark, or else I would have seen the trip wire

stretched across the bottom of the door frame. Lord knows, I should have been expecting something. But it was dark and I was careless. I stumbled on the wire, and the box of groceries went flying as I fell flat on my face.

Before I could get up, someone jammed the cold, hard barrel of a gun into the soft spot just behind my right ear.

"Don't even breathe," he hissed.

FOURTEEN

. . .

There aren't too many arguments as persuasive as a revolver placed at the back of the ear. I stayed on the floor, with my head down and my butt sticking up in the air.

"Now, lay on your stomach and link your hands behind your neck," I was told.

The man spoke slowly and very precisely, but it wasn't Johnny. Not unless St. John had developed a nasal twang overnight. The gunman frisked me with his left hand and quickly found the .32-caliber Beretta clipped inside the waistband of my jeans.

"What have we here?" he squeaked, leaning down and dangling the gun in front of me. His breath smelled of old wine and stale cigarettes. "Gee, and I thought you were just delivering groceries."

He took a step back, then wheeled and kicked me hard in the side.

"What was that?" he asked.

I must have groaned.

"That was a question, Mister!"

He kicked me again in the same spot, which hurt twice as much. This guy wasn't Johnny St. John, the voice wasn't even close, but he was mean. I had to do something fast or my ribs were going to start cracking.

"My name is Donovan, James Donovan," I wheezed. "I have

a license to carry that gun and I am not looking for trouble."

I tried to turn my head, but that just earned me another swift kick.

"Stop kicking me!" I shouted. "Please, take my wallet and look for yourself."

He approached me from the blind side, moving carefully. I winced as the gun was jammed behind my ear again, then cried out in pain as he knelt down, digging his knee into the small of my back. I couldn't see him, but the smell of cigarettes, booze and yesterday's sweat made my eyes water. With his free hand, the little sadist ripped the wallet from my pocket, tearing my pants.

" 'James Joseph Donovan—Consultant,' " he read, finding one of my business cards. "And what sort of expertise do you possess, Mr. Donovan, that entitles you to offer yourself as a gun-toting consultant?"

He stood up, using my back as a springboard, then walked around me slowly.

"I help people solve problems," I said.

"Is that so? Well, I'd say you're the one with the problem, Donovan."

He was enjoying himself.

"Look, before you kick me again or start shooting, at least hear me out," I suggested. "I came here looking for a Mr. Martin, Thomas P. Martin. He's an investment counselor. If you're him, I suggest you listen, because I think you're in serious danger. I came here to warn you."

The man laughed.

"Do you really expect me to believe that nonsense?" he asked.

"No, I don't," I added quickly. "But you can call a cop named Gavin, Lieutenant Raymond Gavin. He's at the Manhattan South Precinct. Ask Gavin, he'll vouch for me."

"Is that so? And why would I want to get involved with the police? I could shoot you now, claim self-defense and be done with the matter. Though, now that I think of it, a shooting would probably involve the police, too."

He sounded amused. The guy had already used me for soccer practice and now he was making jokes about killing me.

"Are you Thomas Martin?" I asked, moving my head to the side and risking a kick.

"What if I am?" He took a few steps back.

"If you're Martin," I said patiently, "then you're a business-man, not a killer. Meaning, you're not going to pull that trigger."

"Is that so? What makes you so sure, Buster?" he stepped up and nudged me with the toe of his shoe.

I'd taken more than enough abuse. Whoever this guy was, I was not going to let him kick me again. Besides, a grown man who calls people "Buster" probably wasn't much of threat.

"I asked you a question," he reminded me, nudging a little harder.

When I didn't respond, he moved in to deliver another kick. Fortunately, he was wearing baggy pajama bottoms and I could hear the fabric rub together as his leg went back. When the leg started forward, I rolled into the little creep, knocking him off balance.

"Oh God, my Imari!" he wailed, desperately scrambling to stay upright.

That didn't mean anything to me, and it didn't help him. He stumbled backward, landing on top of an antique mahogany table directly behind him. It was a nice piece of furniture, but it wasn't very sturdy. The table collapsed under him, scattering the col-orful display of dishes that had been on top. As the plates landed among the groceries I'd dropped earlier, they shattered, making a terrible racket. He let out a loud, pathetic whimper, and then a shot rang out. The gun made a big noise in that little space.

I rolled to my right, into the kitchen, and went into a defensive crouch. In the confusion of falling objects, my Beretta had some-how ended up just across the hall, under the radiator. I could see it, but I couldn't get to it without exposing myself. I looked around the room and noticed that the countertop was cluttered with empty wine bottles. Just what I needed—a mean little guy on a bender, armed and apparently capable of firing. I decided to wait a while before offering myself as a target.

After a minute or two, I peeked into the hallway. My buddy was lying in a heap on top of the broken table, moaning softly. The second gun, the one he'd jammed against my skull, had skidded down the parquet floor. It was less than six inches away, leaning up against the fancy baseboard. It was a custom-made .45 semiautomatic, a showpiece. I grabbed the gun and smelled the barrel, confirming that the pistol had indeed been fired. Then I stood up, using the door frame for support, and limped across the hall to get my own weapon.

"On your feet," I ordered, knocking groceries out of my way as I walked toward him.

When I was close enough to finally take a look at the man who'd been kicking me, I got a big surprise. Thomas P. Martin, if that's who he was, had definitely changed. The prosperity and self-assurance I'd seen in his photograph had given way to something pathetic and grotesque. There was a resemblance, but it wasn't very strong. The man whimpering on the floor was bloated and slovenly. There were ugly stains on his silk pajamas, and his large paisley bathrobe looked as if he'd been sleeping in it.

"Come on, I'm not kidding. Get up," I snapped, poking him in the ribs.

As if on cue, he began to sob.

"What's the matter with you?" I asked.

He was crying really loudly and it bugged me. In fact, everything about the man was annoying—his voice, his manner, his personal hygiene, his habit of kicking people. Instead of answering me, he choked off a few more sobs.

"Are you Thomas Martin?" I asked finally.

He looked up between fits and nodded yes. When he saw the

146

guns I was holding, he began to quiver. The little coward wasn't such a big shot when the tables were turned. I holstered the Beretta and clipped it inside my waistband, then tried to slip the other piece into my back pocket. But, of course, that pocket was ripped. I shoved the .45 into my front pocket and went to look for my wallet. I told myself to be patient. After all, Thomas Martin was a very sick man.

"Okay, okay, stop crying," I said, as nicely as possible. "I told you before, I'm not going to hurt you. So shut off the water-works."

He stopped abruptly and turned on me angrily.

"Is that what you thought, that I was weeping because you struck me?" He looked utterly disgusted. "You ignorant fool, I'm weeping because you have ruined several classic pieces of Japanese porcelain."

He picked up some of the fragments and held them out for me to see, then started crying again.

"Aw, knock it off, you big baby!" I shouted, slapping the broken pottery out of his hand. "You've got some nerve trying to blame this situation on me. Quit blubbering and get on your feet. In about five minutes, the police will be here and they'll want a plausible explanation for this mess. In case you didn't notice, your gun went off when it hit the floor."

He picked himself up and stood looking down at the broken treasures on the floor. He took a handkerchief from his back pocket and wiped his face, then blew his nose dramatically.

"Well?" I asked.

"Well, what?"

"The police. How do you want to handle the police?"

I was worried that Thomas Martin would make trouble for me. After all, I'd entered his place illegally and there are rules about that kind of thing. Fortunately, he was too upset to think clearly.

"Forget the police," he said with a dismissive wave of his hand. "The place is soundproofed."

I relaxed a little.

"The real question is, how to profit from this egregious loss? I believe the insurance policy is in the study."

He turned and started walking away as if I wasn't there, as if he hadn't been kicking me minutes earlier, as if a shot hadn't been fired.

"Whoa, Martin. Stop right where you are!" I yelled. "We've got to talk. The broken dishes can wait."

"You must be joking." He looked amused. "We have just destroyed four perfect Imari plates. Those pieces were made in eighteen eighty-three. They're invaluable."

"They *were* invaluable," I pointed out, "but they're not anymore. So let's stop wasting time."

"Oh, no, no, no, my friend," he stuttered.

"I'm not your friend, Mr. Martin," I said. "Not with these bruised ribs or the sound of that pistol shot still ringing in my ears. I came here to warn you about a man. His name is St. John, Johnny St. John, and I believe he is planning to kill you."

He just stared at me.

"As far as I'm concerned, he can have you," I continued, rubbing my side. "But there are other people to think about, so before St. John comes to collect your worthless hide, I need some information, which means you've got to start talking. Now, tell me, does that name mean anything to you?"

He closed one eye, frowning, then folded his arms across his chest and turned his attention to the ceiling.

"Well?" I urged.

It wasn't that hard a question.

"Well, the name you mentioned doesn't mean a thing to me," he sighed. "On the other hand, I fully expected them to send someone. I mean, sooner or later."

He belched loudly.

"I don't understand. You knew you were in danger?"

"Of course, you dolt. Why else would you find me armed and hiding in the dark? For Christ's sake, I haven't been to my office

148

in nearly three weeks. Didn't you find it strange when you couldn't locate me?"

"You knew I was looking for you?"

"Hello, anybody home?" he asked, speaking into an imaginary telephone. "Someone called my office and asked a lot of nosy questions. Wasn't that you? My secretary, Gerald, knows his job."

He tutted loudly.

"Let's go over this again," I said, trying very hard to control my temper. "If you know that someone's out to hurt you, why haven't you contacted the police or sought protection?"

He strolled past me, into the kitchen, and poured himself a large glass of brandy from a crystal decanter.

"I can't very well go to the police, now can I?" he sighed, holding the brandy snifter up to the light.

"I don't see why not."

"Because, dear boy, I've stolen half a million dollars from the bastards. If I go to the police, I'll have to give it back."

He smiled wickedly, then drained his glass.

FIFTEEN

· · ·

My mouth must have been hanging open, because Martin began to laugh. When I pressed him for details, he got ornery again and refused to say anything more until he'd read his insurance policy, which was upstairs in the study. Money and property, he explained, come before pleasure. There was nothing to do except follow him as he staggered up the staircase.

The study was on the third floor, overlooking the backyard garden. It was a lovely oak-paneled room, with thick upholstered Victorian furniture and stacks of old leather volumes. I sank into a comfortable chair and watched as Mr. Martin sorted through his files. It didn't take him long to discover that the broken Imari plates were insured for much more than he'd paid for them, even after he'd factored in the effects of inflation. Buoyed by the good news, Thomas Martin called his secretary, Gerald, and dictated a phony account of the accident for submission to his insurance company. It was a smooth bit of fraudulent work, especially considering his blood-alcohol level.

"I don't know how I'll ever live without those delicate beauties," he sniffled, trying to hide a smile, "but you know, Donovan, the money will help."

We didn't have time to play games. Johnny St. John had led me to Thomas Martin for a reason, and it wasn't for pleasure. Now that I was sitting in his study, looking at Martin, I started to think that maybe I'd been suckered. The way things stood,

Johnny could have gotten himself a two-for-one deal. It seemed prudent to move the conversation along. I gave Martin a quick summary of the situation, but he didn't seem very interested. The guy had shaken like a leaf when I held a gun on him, but the threat of Johnny St. John didn't bother him one bit. He just sat behind his big desk looking smug.

"What's the matter with you?" I asked finally. "This isn't a joke, a man's been killed. Doesn't that mean anything to you?"

He blinked.

"Look, I'll be really honest with you," I said. "My partner and I don't know where to look for this guy, St. John, and the clock is ticking. Every minute I waste here gives him another chance to harm someone else. Why don't you help me out? After all, your picture was in the envelope, too."

He took a cigarette from a box on the desk and lit it carefully, studying me. I'm no expert, but the guy didn't look sick, not like Tim Danner. He needed a shower, a shave, and lots of black coffee, but he wasn't frail. In fact, the man was so fat his pajama top barely covered his gut. And, for a dying man, he kicked like a mule.

"It's like this, Donovan," he began, leaning back in his big leather desk chair. "My best friend was killed a few months ago. His name was Michael Adams. He was already dying from the AIDS virus, so no one wanted to believe me when I tried to tell them he'd been murdered. The job was very neatly orchestrated to look like an accident. But I know what I know."

His eyes were cold and focused.

"You see, I'm just like them," Martin said tapping cigarette ash onto the rug. "Exploiting opportunities to make money is my one real talent, so I understand the bastards."

He smiled and reached for his brandy snifter.

"Since my friend died—" he began, then stopped. "Actually, Michael Adams was my lover, Mr. Donovan." His words were slurring. "Since Michael's death, I've been wallowing in guilt

152

and self-pity. A Greek tragedy—as usual, resulting from my own hubris."

He sighed dramatically.

"But I'm digressing. I was about to tell you why Michael was murdered. Naturally, it's about money." He reached for his drink. "Michael Adams needed money to pay bills while he awaited his premature death. The medical expenses kept growing and he couldn't work. I tried to help him, but he wouldn't accept my money. Filthy lucre, you know. In the end, the only option was to sell his life-insurance benefits. After all, what good would life insurance be to a dead man?"

Thomas Martin blew an angry blue cloud of smoke at the ceiling and started grinding his teeth.

"Timothy Danner sold his life insurance, too," I said, remembering what he'd said when I offered to buy dinner.

"You're not the brightest lightbulb in town, are you, Donovan?" he quipped. "You don't sell the insurance, you sell the benefits. Tell you what, why don't you just listen?"

I dug my nails into the arm of the chair and tried to smile.

"If Danner was sick, with no hope of survival, then I'm not surprised to hear he sold his benefits," Martin continued. "It has become quite common. Remember, if there's money to be made, there's always a buyer. In fact, the demand for death benefits is so hot right now it's become a niche market. Last year the market grossed nearly three hundred million. And that's just the tip of the iceberg. Blink your eyes and it will top a billion. Imagine the Grim Reaper overseeing a billion-dollar bull market!"

The smirk returned, but Thomas Martin wasn't happy.

"The industry is composed of two- or three-dozen viatical-settlement companies," he continued. "Actually, they're just brokerage firms specializing in death benefits. The word 'viatical' should be familiar to an Irish lad like yourself, Donovan. It comes from *viaticum*, which is the communion given to Catholics during last rites."

I shrugged.

"Skipped your religious education classes, did you?" he snickered. "Well, no matter, it was just a point of interest. Though now that I think of it, you'd be wise to bone up on your Bible before taking on this Johnny St. John. From what you've said, he sounds pretty well schooled in the Good Book. I mean, for a lunatic."

Martin leaned forward and crushed the butt of his cigarette in the ashtray. He immediately lit another.

"Anyway, these viatical-settlement companies are flourishing. You see, the investor's risk is extremely low because most state insurance departments guarantee life-insurance payments, even if the insurance companies themselves go bankrupt. This means the paper investors are buying is pretty much gold. And the rate of return is outstanding, especially when you compare it to things like Treasury bills or money-market funds."

He started rooting around in his desk drawer. After a minute or two, he pulled out a faded newspaper clipping. It was a *New York Times* article, entitled "Now AIDS Patients' Lives Are Drawing Speculators." The article confirmed everything he'd said and more. By selectively choosing people certain to die in a short period of time and then buying their death benefits for a fraction of the face value, the settlement companies offered investors rates of return sometimes in excess of thirty or forty percent. When you compared that payback to five percent or less from T-bills and money-market funds, the investment looked great. At least, it was great if you could get past the fact that you were profiting from terminally sick people.

"There is all kinds of source material," Thomas said, shoving a small mountain of paper across the desk. "I've got advertisements, booklets, applications."

He'd done his homework.

"I hate to say it," I said as I leafed slowly through the papers, "but it seems like a pretty good idea. I mean, if the person who's dying doesn't have a family to provide for, then why not collect

154

some of the benefits while there's still time to put them to good use? Sounds to me like the industry helps sick people who would otherwise have to depend on charity. It gives them a way to die with some dignity."

Thomas Martin rubbed his eyes slowly with both hands, then ran his fingers through his thinning hair.

"Are you some kind of Boy Scout?" he asked finally. "I'm not describing the fucking Salvation Army. It's conceivable that the first company to offer this kind of a deal *may* have had a higher motive, but I doubt it. Wall Street doesn't work that way. The market has grown, and will continue to grow, for one reason and one reason only—there's money to be made on death benefits. The street's not the least bit interested in charity cases.

"Take another look at the business, Donovan. To qualify for a cash settlement, the sick guy, the person with the guaranteed insurance benefits, has to satisfy the viatical company's team of crackerjack physicians that he'll really be dead in less than two years. That requirement is true for every settlement company in the industry. The viatical company then serves as a broker, floating the man's dire medical prognosis to a pool of hungry investors. The broker is supposed to dicker with his investors, skillfully negotiating the best possible offer, but that part's a joke. The brokers are playing both ends. They get paid by the investors, not by the poor dying shmuck with the insurance policy.

"No surprise there, right?" he asked, smiling unhappily. "The offers vary widely, depending on the circumstances. You could hear anything from twenty-five to ninety cents for each dollar of benefits value in the policy. Usually, it's between fifty and sixty cents, though you get much less value if you're in a real hurry. Are you with me?"

I felt the urge to give him another poke, but I nodded instead.

"In Michael Adams's case, they reluctantly gave the poor man seventy-five cents on the dollar, but only because we shopped around and I handled the negotiations. Believe me, seventy-five

155

cents is not the norm. I wanted to buy the damn policy myself and give him one hundred percent of face, but Michael wouldn't listen to reason. The man was as stubborn as an ox."

He stopped, and seemed to drift away. When his gaze came back to me, he gave a start, as if he'd forgotten I was in the room.

"Where was I?" he asked, sitting up a bit straighter and rubbing his eyes again.

"You were saying that Michael Adams got seventy-five cents on the dollar."

"Right. Well, if Michael had lived the full two years, then the buyer would have gotten a very impressive return, more than twelve percent per year for his investment in the goddamn policy. But if the subject dies within a year, the return doubles. If death comes sooner, say it's within six months, the ROI goes even higher. Last year, the average rate of return for *all* of these investments was well above twenty percent. That's not bad when you consider the paltry return from mutual funds. I mean, which investment looks better to you?"

"The sooner the policyholder dies, the better the return on investment," I repeated, thinking out loud.

Then I sat up straighter.

"Are you telling me that Johnny St. John is killing people so he can improve the rate of return for a group of investors?"

"Very good, genius, but you're a little bit off target," he said happily. "Your white-haired friend sounds certifiable; I doubt that he's thinking about rates of return. From what you've said, he's fixated on the Book of Revelations, not on investment strategy. Of course, that makes him perfect for this nasty little scheme. They can wind him up and let him loose on his prey without worrying about the consequences. If St. John gets caught, it won't make any difference. The lawyers will certify him nuts and they'll close the file."

Thomas Martin put his feet down and folded his hands in front of him on the desk.

"St. John is being used, Donovan, only he's too fucked up to understand that. And even if he were capable of making that mental leap, he'd be useless as a witness. Can you imagine the effect one of his biblical tirades would have on a jury? Don't you see, the money men, the guys who conceived of this dirty business, get to reap the profits without getting their hands dirty. It's a pretty slick operation."

"Don't you mean *sick*?" I suggested.

Thomas Martin stared at the floor.

"Of course it's sick, Donovan," he said finally, his voice a whisper. "Even a cynical old pederast like me can see that the business is evil. Do you know how long they gave Michael for his seventy-five cents on the dollar?" Martin didn't wait for an answer. "Three months! They gave the kid three months and then they cashed him in like an old bond. They stole the last few months of his precious life so a forty-four-percent return could drop into some rich creep's retirement fund."

Martin reached for the brandy.

"Yes, even I can see they've got to be stopped," he muttered.

"Is that right?" I leaned across the desk and grabbed his glass. "And just how were you going to make that happen? Was it looking up from the bottom of a quart of booze?"

"Say what you want about me, Donovan," he whined. "God knows, I'm not much of a person. But I loved a man once, and he deserved better. I want to do something about this for Michael's sake."

He was pathetic.

"It may not seem like much," Martin continued, sitting up and raising his voice, "but I did manage to get in the first shot. What did you think I was talking about before? Four hundred and eighty thousand dollars isn't petty cash."

I'd almost forgotten about his daring theft.

"I'm not making this up. I sold those bastards a phony bill of goods. They bought an eight-hundred-thousand-dollar policy from a man who isn't sick."

He slammed his pudgy fist down, then winced in pain.

"Okay, you got their money and their attention," I said evenly. "I'm very impressed. Now, what's the rest of your plan?"

He plopped back down in his chair, looking deflated.

"That's just it," he admitted. "I don't have a plan."

We sat there in silence for quite a while as Thomas Martin considered his predicament.

"I've got it!" he announced, startling me. "I'll hire you and your partner. From what you've told me, the Russian sounds smart enough to figure this out."

"Thanks for the compliment."

"Look, it makes perfect sense. You want to stop St. John and the guys behind him as much as I do, only I seem to have painted myself into a bit of a corner. That's where you folks come in."

"What makes you think we'd do your dirty work?" I asked.

"It's not like that, Donovan. We'd be joining forces, merging strengths. Besides, you're going to continue with or without me. You're not the type to give up."

"If that's true," I asked, "what do you bring to the table?"

"Well, for one thing, I know where to start looking," he said, smiling sweetly. "And if that's not good enough, let's just say I'd also be putting you boys in line to collect a couple hundred thousand dollars."

SIXTEEN

■ ■ ■

Two dollars or two hundred thousand, it was blood money any way you looked at it, and that's not our style. Besides, Martin's plan might have obligated Boris and me to aid and abet him, and we don't commit felonies unless we have a really good reason to.

But Thomas Martin was right about one thing—I wasn't about to give up. And whether he knew it or not, I had no intention of leaving without him. Johnny St. John was lurking somewhere in the world outside and I needed Martin to help me find him. We wrangled for a while, then decided to let Boris set the terms and conditions of our collaboration. That made Thomas happy, because he figured it was a done deal. I just smiled; Thomas Martin had never met Boris.

Deal or no deal, it was time to get moving. I had to retrieve the car, pick up Angus at the grocery store, come back for Mr. Martin, and then drive up to Connecticut. The prospect of riding for several hours in a closed car with a man who hadn't bathed in a week made me queasy, so I told him to shower and change his clothes. Martin acted insulted, but it was a farce. The man was ripe enough to wilt flowers. Before he shuffled off to the powder room, I collected a set of keys to the house and made him promise not to drink any more brandy. I didn't get my hopes up, but a promise was better than nothing. When I heard water running in the shower, I headed for the parking garage, taking care to lock the dead bolt on the front door.

It was a very short drive from the garage to the little grocery where Angus was supposed to be waiting for me. I double-parked out front, but it wasn't the same peaceful scene I'd left earlier. The sidewalk flower stand had been knocked over, and the manager, a very small Korean man, was jabbering at a couple of kids in dirty green aprons as they scrambled to put the displays back together. There was plenty of confusion, but no Angus. I waited for the tiny Korean to take a breath before interrupting.

"Excuse me," I said politely, "but I'm here to pick up my dog."

"Dog? Your dog?" he sputtered, raging. "Very, very bad. Look it mess, very bad. Stupid, stupid, stupid!"

The little man went right on yammering, so I reached into my pocket and came out with the old money clip. The cash had an immediate calming effect on the Korean. At forty dollars, he was still breathing hard, but he'd stopped yelling. When I got to sixty dollars, a sheepish grin began to form. And then, when I peeled off two more twenties and held out one hundred dollars, he broke into a smile so broad I could see all the fillings in his teeth. Unfortunately, Angus picked that moment to come whipping around the corner, dragging the baby-sitter behind him. The storekeeper dropped the wilted fern he was about to offer me, snatched the cash out of my hand, and darted into his store.

Angus must have sensed trouble, because he came over and sat meekly at my heel, while Ronnie Dee, the sitter, listed his grievances. As far as I could tell, the trouble began when an old Park Avenue type and her fancy poodle waddled up to consider the flowers. Apparently, the allure of this rare canine flower proved more than Angus could resist and one thing led to another, explaining the goofy, satisfied expression on the big mongrel's clock. It cost me another forty bucks to bribe Ronnie, who leveraged his position by hinting that the poodle's mommy was looking for revenge. Since I'd paid for it, I grabbed my fern and left before anyone else could touch me for cash.

We drove one block north, then turned left onto 63rd Street and proceeded across Park Avenue. The scene in front of Martin's house hadn't changed in the forty-five minutes I'd been gone, but that didn't mean it was safe. I coaxed the Nova into a tight little space next to a fire hydrant, then took my Beretta out and put it in my jacket pocket. I left Angus behind to negotiate with meter maids and went back inside.

Nothing had changed. The front hall was still a mess of broken dishes and groceries, and the dining room looked like the morning after a party. By the time I got back up to the study, I was in a pretty foul mood. One hundred and forty dollars for dog-sitting, a couple of bruised ribs, and very little sleep can do that to a person. It didn't help to find a freshly showered Thomas Martin posed behind his big desk like a Chief Executive. He glanced up, then pointed to a couple of expensive leather traveling cases, as if I were the bellboy.

"Well, what's been keeping you?" he demanded, jumping up. "Let's get moving!"

He threw some papers into an open briefcase, then pushed past me, down the stairs. Martin was gone before I could say a word, so I picked the bags up and followed him.

The situation didn't improve when we got outside. In fact, Mr. Martin got very nasty when he realized that we'd be riding in the same car with Angus. It seems that the intrepid capitalist was mortally afraid of large dogs, especially big black hairy dogs with menacing white fangs. Martin threw an impressive tantrum on the sidewalk, but it didn't change a thing, so he gave up and got in the car.

Not surprisingly, Angus didn't like Thomas Martin any more than Martin liked him. From his seat in the back, the big pooch rested his chin on Martin's left shoulder and growled softly into the nervous little man's ear whenever he tried to move or speak. If Angus wanted to make amends for the flower-stand incident, he was on the right track. After about six blocks, Martin clammed up and I didn't hear another peep out of him until we got to Connecticut.

Exactly two hours and thirty-five minutes later, we turned onto a private driveway leading down toward the lake and my house. It's a winding dirt road, but the path is usually clear and easy to navigate, even in the snow. This time, we weren't so lucky. About fifty yards down the lane, I had to jam on the brakes because the road was blocked by a fallen tree. When I skidded to a stop, two men in ski masks jumped out of the bushes. They were armed with shotguns.

Angus went berserk. He started barking ferociously and pawing at the windows, which scared Thomas Martin so badly he turned a sickly gray-green color and began to shake again. I killed the engine, then slowly opened my door.

"No *mas*, no *mas*," I implored, stepping out of the car, my hands up in the air.

"Yo, Señor Donovan, *que pasa?*" Moses Santos asked, lowering the shotgun and lifting his mask.

It was probably cruel not to say something when we first pulled up, but I couldn't resist. When Angus heard Moses's voice, he gave a little yelp of joy and scrambled over the front seat. They've been pals since Moses was a small boy. The other kid, a tall, skinny young man with a patchy beard and a wandering eye, was Eduardo, another Santos cousin.

"This is Mr. Martin," I said, pointing.

Martin stumbled out of the Nova and held up one of his hands.

"Where is the bathroom?" he asked weakly.

We all turned and pointed down the lane. The house was just visible through the trees.

"Oh, fuck it," Martin wheezed. He doubled over and vomited onto his shoes.

162

The Santos boys looked surprised, but I waved the sounds of retching away.

"Don't mind him. Señor Martin has had a little too much excitement."

"He is drunk," Eduardo said, taking a closer look.

"That, too," I admitted.

Everyone, except Thomas Martin, had a good laugh. Martin summoned what remained of his dignity and straightened back up.

"Perhaps you could continue your moronic conversation down below, in the house," he snarled.

That just made the boys laugh louder, but they shouldered their weapons and moved the tree, making a path for the car. Martin didn't wait—he was already staggering down the lane, so I tossed Moses the car keys and hurried to catch up with my unhappy guest.

Angus bolted past us down the drive, swerved around the house, then continued on to the boat dock, where he roused some migratory ducks before plunging headlong into the ice-cold water. He paddled ashore, shook himself dry, then looked around, apparently surprised that the rest of us hadn't joined him. When I clapped and whistled, he pretended not to hear.

It didn't matter. The lake is big enough for Angus and the ducks. It stretches south about three miles from where we stood and is a half mile across at the widest point. It's one of the prettiest ponds I know of; crystal-clear and loaded with perch and large-mouth bass. Ski boats aren't allowed on our lake, so the sailboats and fishermen are spared the noise and the chop. In warmer weather, I launch a small skiff and spend hours feeding the fish with an expensive graphite fishing rod and spinning reel.

Our home was built at the turn of the century as a hunting lodge for an old Tammany Hall politician from the Bronx. It sits in the middle of five thickly wooded acres, with a big red barn off to one side of the property and tiers of flower gardens leading down to the water. The old place was designed around a Great Room, with a massive stone fireplace, and a cathedral ceiling framed out with hand-hewn beams. There are big picture windows at the back of the house and French doors leading to a wide porch that offers a spectacular view straight down the lake.

On either side of the living room, there are smaller wings, with comfortable, airy rooms. If you turn to the right as you enter the house, a short hallway leads to the master bedroom, which has a private bath, and two guest rooms that share a second bathroom. If you turn to the left as you enter, you walk straight into a big country kitchen.

The kitchen is one of the nicest rooms anywhere. The ceiling is high and the rough beams are exposed, giving it an Old World feel. Kate has little bundles of herbs hanging to dry, and their smells fill the room. We have a potbelly stove in one corner, near the long kitchen table, and there are tall windows that create a good cross breeze in the summer. Originally, there was a cold-storage room, a pantry, and a wet room, but we gutted them and made a fourth bedroom with another bath.

The house has a simple design, but the old judge made sure it was built well. According to the deed, it stayed in his family until the Second World War ended, after which a series of weekend owners entered the picture. From that point on, the place was used mostly in the summers and it was treated like an oversized cabana. Aside from the occasional coat of paint, it was neglected. Inevitably, decay began to set in and the property and gardens went to seed. When Kate and I discovered it, things had gotten so bad that the barn was on the verge of collapsing.

It was a strange time for us. We had been married, then separated, and finally divorced—from each other—all in the space of ten years. Somehow, we'd gotten back together and needed a refuge; a common ground, separate from our very different worlds. It sounds like the plot for a soap opera, but it's the truth. A local real-estate broker was trying to sell us a sleek, contemporary house nearby, and he made the mistake of giving us a boat tour of the lake. He didn't make the sale he expected, but he made the two of us very happy. If we hadn't been looking in from the water, we'd never have seen the crumbling old lodge.

The real-estate man did his best to convince us that the property was a lost cause, but that just added to its appeal. Compared to the stuff Kate and I had been through together, the challenge of salvaging an old house was nothing. For two years, we spent our weekends rebuilding and repainting the place, then combed antique stores from New York City to Manchester, New Hampshire, looking for furniture. In the end, we had something worth holding on to.

When Thomas Martin and I stepped into the living room, we discovered that my home had been turned into command central for the eccentric Dr. Koulomzin and his merry band of Dominican street guerrillas.

The oak dining table, a grand old Shaker piece, had been shoved up against the wall and converted into an all-purpose desk and workstation for the computer. Its polished surface was covered with dirty cups, dishes, magazines, newspapers, and thick old textbooks. The sofa had also been appropriated by the commandos. Apparently, it was doubling as a bed for some member of the occupation forces, because it was heavily draped in sheets and blankets. The rest of the furniture had been stacked in a far corner, and the carpets had been rolled up.

There was a lively fire crackling in the hearth, and Thomas Martin, looking and acting like the sole survivor of a terrible accident, limped over to warm himself in front of it. I was still checking out the room and trying to find the words to express my outrage, when Manny Santos drifted in from the kitchen, sucking on a long-necked bottle of beer and carrying an enormous sandwich. A slight blond woman hovered in the shadows behind him.

165

"Yo, Donovan, 'bout time, man. What's up?" Manny asked cheerfully.

Before I could respond, the sofa heaved and Boris Koulomzin sat upright, scaring Thomas Martin so badly he threw up again, this time directly into the fireplace.

"My God, man, show some restraint," Boris thundered, fumbling for his glasses. "This isn't a cow pasture."

"Speaking of restraint," I snarled, "who asked you to rearrange my home?"

"Ah, James, you're finally here."

Boris smiled at me.

"Manuel, my chair," he ordered.

"Uh, uh, Doc." Manny shook his head. "You forget the magic word again."

"Oh, all right. *Please!* Please get my chair, you obnoxious little reptile," Boris growled.

"That's betta," Manny agreed, putting down his beer and sandwich.

The object in question was an old-fashioned wheelchair with a caned back and seat. It had adjustable leg rests, each large enough to support a small tree, and there was plenty of room in the seat, which made it ideal for a creature the size of Boris. The wheelchair explained why all the carpets had been rolled and the furniture moved. I helped Manny get the big man into harness; then I dropped into a mission chair by the fire and propped my feet up on the cast-iron grate. Thomas Martin was leaning against the mantel, looking pale.

"This sad-looking fellow," I said wearily, "is Mr. Thomas P. Martin, collector of fine Japanese porcelain, investment counselor, and master criminal. He has a proposition for you, Boris."

I crossed my ankles and looked over at Boris, who raised an eyebrow.

"However, before I go off to bed and leave you to begin *negotiating*, I would like to know how many people are in my house and which rooms they are occupying."

166

"Not a problem." Boris smiled. "In addition to myself, there is Manuel, Eduardo, Hector, and Moses. The charming lady standing by the kitchen door is Mrs. Patricia Gold. Please, Patricia, come in and meet the infamous James J. Donovan."

Mrs. Gold stepped into the light and I got another shock. It was the lady in the picture with the sculpture. She was frail and thin, and looked much older than I had expected. It was obvious immediately that the poor woman was sick. Her color was bad and her skin had the same waxy transparency I'd noticed on Tim Danner. She approached me slowly, and I stood to offer her my chair.

"Mr. Donovan," she said softly, extending both of her hands, "I'm so sorry for this intrusion into your home. I know it must be very disconcerting to have strangers mucking about among your personal belongings. It's obvious that you put a great deal of love into this house."

"I did it with my ex-wife, Kate," I mumbled, suddenly tongue-tied.

"Oh, I'm so sorry," she said quickly.

"No, no, it's not like that," I stammered. "We're together . . . well, not exactly together, because we live apart and we're divorced, but it's still our place."

I had to stop. I was confusing myself.

"The former Mrs. Donovan is a remarkable woman, named Kathleen Byrne," Boris explained. "Kathleen and James rebuilt this home together, several years *after* their divorce became final."

"Well, whatever the arrangement," Patricia Gold said politely, "you and Kathleen have done a marvelous job, and I thank you for offering me such a comfortable, safe haven."

She smiled warmly.

"You are welcome, Mrs. Gold, and I am happier to see you than you could possibly imagine," I said sincerely. "But I must confess that I am surprised to find you here. My partner has really outdone himself this time."

167

"Please, call me Patricia," she grinned. "And you're right about Boris, he's a marvel."

"To finish answering your first question, James," Boris continued, beaming, "Patricia is using the master bedroom. At my request, Manuel and the boys are taking turns sleeping in the guest rooms adjacent to Mrs. Gold. I have confined myself to this room and the porch, leaving the bedroom off the kitchen for you. The bed has been made up with clean sheets."

"What about food?" I asked. "I'm famished."

"You will find a roasted turkey in the refrigerator and a kettledrum of Manuel's rice and beans on the stove. It is not *cordon bleu,* but you won't starve."

"Good. What time is it now?"

"Nearly seven," Boris said, checking the mantel clock.

"Okay, wake me up in about four hours."

I started limping toward the kitchen.

"But, James, we haven't had a chance to speak."

"I'd be wasting your time, Boris," I said, yawning involuntarily. "I've got to get some sleep. Besides, Mr. Martin's quite a talker and he's got plenty to say. Believe me, we'll have a lot to discuss later, when you're through with him."

I kept on going and didn't stop until I reached the refrigerator. When I had a sandwich and a cold beer of my own, I ambled into the bedroom and closed the door. It's a cozy little room, with a full bed and a nice view of the boat dock. I ate my food quickly, sitting on the edge of the bed, then dropped my shoes and lay back against the feather pillows to finish my beer.

I don't remember sleeping or dreaming, but as soon as my head touched the pillows, I was gone. Several hours later, I awoke to the sound of a man's voice reciting verse:

" *'Half my life is gone, and I have let*
The years slip from me and have not fulfilled
The aspiration of my youth, to build
Some tower of song and lofty parapet . . .' "

The room was dark except for a single candle burning yellow on a table in a corner. My first thoughts were of Johnny St. John, but when I opened my eyes, I saw Boris over by the door, sitting in his old wooden wheelchair, reading.

> " 'Not indolence, nor pleasure, nor the fret
> Of restless passions that would not be stilled,
> But sorrow, and a care that almost killed,
> Kept me from what I may accomplish yet; . . .' "

He was reciting slowly, enunciating each of the words carefully. It sounded pretty good, though I got a little distracted watching his glasses slide down the bridge of his nose.

> " 'Though, half-way up the hill, I see the Past
> Lying beneath me with its sounds and sights,—
> A city in the twilight dim and vast,
> With smoking roofs, soft bells, and gleaming lights,—
> And hear above me on the autumnal blast
> The cataract of Death far thundering from the heights.' "

When Boris realized I was watching him, he closed the book and reached for the light-switch, blinding me with the sudden brightness. I sat upright, blinking, and holding my sore ribs.

"Is that the poem?" I asked.

He nodded.

"So, what'd you think?" I sat up and reached for my shoes.

"I think that's a question for you to answer."

Boris reached out and placed the book on the bed.

"When you've had a chance to read the poem to yourself, we'll talk," he promised.

"But I don't know anything about poetry," I complained.

"Please, James, this isn't grade school and I'm not some teacher you're trying to bluff. It is an elegant verse and the meaning couldn't be more obvious. Instead of acting like a child,

169

open your mind to the words. You might just find the experience rewarding."

"Has she called?"

"No, Kathleen has not called, not since yesterday."

Boris sounded worn and tired.

"How are you holding up?" I asked.

"Ah, you finally remembered *my* injuries," he replied. "What gave me away, was it the wheelchair?"

He had a point. I hadn't really paid enough attention to his condition.

"Well, anyway, I am glad to be out of the hospital," he said softly, watching the flickering candle. "And I do feel stronger now than at any time since the accident occurred. There is still a lot of pain and I feel rather helpless, but time will cure those problems. This may sound foolish, James, but I have an intense longing for my own apartment."

I didn't tell him that I'd opened the shades and aired the place out.

"Anyway, with luck, we will all be home soon," he rallied. "The important news is that I finally have a handle on our situation. Your Mr. Martin has been extremely helpful. I take it you know what he's done so far?"

"Well, yes and no. In between the kicking, the wrestling, the gunshots and the vomiting, I only had time for a brief synopsis."

"I thought there was only one shot fired," Boris said, looking concerned.

"Okay—gunshot," I admitted.

"I'm not trying to diminish the offense," he added quickly, "but I need to know whether to believe this man. I'm placing a lot of stock in the information he's providing."

"I wouldn't worry too much about Thomas Martin," I said, rubbing the sleep from my eyes. "The man is crude and selfish, but he's finally committed himself to something other than the pursuit of money and pleasure. It might be the first time in his life."

I thought about it for a moment.

"Check that," I said, remembering the look in his eyes back in the study. "This would be the second time in his life."

"You're referring to Michael Adams?"

"Right."

Boris rubbed his chin thoughtfully.

"Very well, then," he said, coming to life. "I suggest that you take care of this poetic mystery quickly, we have business of our own to conduct. I will wait for you in the living room."

Boris reached back and opened the bedroom door, then tried to maneuver the old-fashioned wheelchair into a turn. It was difficult in that tiny space.

"Boris," I began, grabbing the back of the chair and turning him easily, "what's this poem thing about? Am I in some kind of trouble here?"

He grabbed the door frame with his good hand, stopping the wheelchair abruptly.

"For Christ's sake, man, use your head. The poem's about fulfillment. And it's not about you. It includes you, certainly, but strictly speaking, I'd have to say it's about Kate. Now hurry up and call the poor thing before she starts cutting you out of all the pictures again."

I didn't move.

"Do I need to say it more plainly?" he bellowed. "Hurry up, we've got work to do. Damn it all, James, there's a trap to be set."

SEVENTEEN

. . .

I helped Boris into the living room, where Thomas Martin was dozing by the fire, then returned to the guest room and shut the door. The book of poetry was lying on the bed. After a few minutes of diverting self-examination, I finally picked up the anthology, found *"Mezzo Cammin,"* and read the poem to myself.

I still don't know what the title means, but I forged ahead, reading slowly and carefully. When I was finished, I tried it again, this time reading really fast. That didn't help too much, so I went back to the beginning and read it out loud. That third pass seemed to do the trick. At least I was sure that I'd heard all the words. I went into the kitchen and dialed Kate's number.

The telephone rang five or six times.

"Hello?" She sounded groggy.

"Kate, it's me."

"J. J.?"

"Yeah. Did I wake you?"

I looked at the wall clock; it was eleven-thirty.

"I guess you did," she chuckled.

I felt like a teenager asking a girl for a date.

"Look, Kate, let's not beat around the bush," I said seriously. "Is everything okay? Are we okay?"

"What are you talking about, Jamie?" she yawned.

"You know what I'm talking about," I continued, digging the hole a little deeper. "Are you giving me bad news with this poetry thing?"

"Of course not. What's the matter with you? I ask you to read one poem and you fall apart. God, Donovan, sometimes I don't know why I bother."

The direct approach wasn't working.

"Listen, Kate, I read the poem."

"Did you really read it, Jamie, or did Boris read it for you?"

Uh-oh.

"Yes," I said.

"Yes, what?" she sighed.

"I read it and he read it."

Kate thought about that for a second.

"Well, that's better than nothing," she decided. "So, what did you discover?"

"I discovered that I'm worried. The poem is all about some-body growing old without getting the things they always wanted, right? Well, that just makes me think I'm not giving you what you need."

"Are you really that insecure about us?" she asked.

It was my turn to think for a minute.

"Well, no, probably not," I said. "But I am worried by this poetry thing. We're usually very straightforward with each other. What does Longfellow have to do with us? I'm confused."

"You can say that again. Okay, funny man, I give up. I was trying to make this a special, maybe even a romantic, moment. Anyway, here goes. I asked you to read this particular verse because it addresses the way I feel right now, at this moment in my life. There's something I've always wanted and I've been afraid to face it. I guess I was worried that if I cared too much, this thing I want would never happen. This poem called out to me, reminding me that if I wait any longer, it could be too late. Do you understand?"

I didn't, but it seemed safer to say that I did.

"If you understand, you'll know what I'm trying to say to you with this poem, J. J.," she added quickly. "Think about it, what's been missing in my life? What have I always wanted?"

The only thing that came to mind was hanging on a rack in Saks.

"I didn't know there was anything missing," I finally admitted.

"Okay, forget it, Jamie. Just listen—*I am pregnant!* Is that clear enough? In fact, I'm so pregnant that they tell me I'm going to have twins. Now do I finally have your attention?"

The answer was yes, but I was too stunned to say so.

"Hello, J. J. Are you still with me?"

Kate was giggling.

"Yes."

"And you're all right?"

"Am I all right?" I croaked. "I mean, are you all right? And, my God, the babies, are the babies all right?"

"We're all just great, Daddy," she announced proudly.

"I'm going to be a father," I said softly.

"Don't worry, honey, everything will work out fine. It's still very early, but things look good so far, and the morning sickness has been very mild."

"Morning sickness?" I paused. "What's that like?"

"Never mind. If I tell you the symptoms, you'll start to develop them. Remember what happened when I had the mumps?"

I was beginning to feel a little queasy.

"When did this happen? I mean, we're not talking St. Croix, right?"

"Don't be silly, I'm nearly eight weeks along."

I started counting backward.

"It was after the fund-raiser at Lincoln Center," Kate said confidently.

Apparently it was a good thing I had gotten a nap in during the ballet.

"Since we've established when this happened," I began, "the

next question is: how did it happen? I don't recall making any plans. Did I miss a meeting?"

"No, you didn't miss any meetings," she said softly. "I just decided to give nature a chance and this was the outcome."

Not a very good answer, but I didn't care. My favorite things are dogs, old people and children. Boris has a dog and our favorite neighbors are elderly, so children seemed like the obvious addition to the group.

"Did you know about this while we were on the island?" I asked.

"Yes," she admitted. "And I meant to tell you, only I couldn't find the right moment. Then we got dragged back here and I didn't know what to do."

"Wow, so you were pregnant while we were away."

I was starting to feel guilty about all the wrestling we'd done between the sheets.

"Well, I sure couldn't tell," I added quickly.

"Don't worry, Jamie. I know what you're thinking, and it's all right. In fact, it's still all right."

I decided to change the subject.

"Kate, is this what you always wanted?" I asked her seriously. "Is this the fulfillment you need?"

"Very good, Shakespeare," she quipped. "Tell you what— when the time comes, let me introduce the kids to poetry."

Out of the blue, an idea came to me.

"Kate," I asked, lowering my voice, "do you think we should get remarried?"

"Don't worry about that right now, okay, Jamie?" she chuckled. "Lots of kids have divorced parents."

It's amazing—if I blink, they sail right past me.

"Jamie?"

"Yes, Kate."

"Are you happy?"

"The woman I love is going to bear me not one, but two children, and you're asking if I'm happy?"

176

"Answer the question, Papa," she insisted.

"Kate, this is a little sudden, you know? But I assure you that when it actually sinks in, I will be happy. In fact, I'll be busting buttons all over the room. Just think, I can take the little tots to Yankees' and Knicks' games and the Bronx Zoo and the Natural History Museum, and Boris can teach them music and everything else. This should be a blast. Hey, how old do they have to be before they start to swim?"

"Swimming?"

"Okay, forget about the swimming," I said, plowing right ahead. "There's plenty of other stuff to do. By the way, I just thought of something. What are they? Boys? Girls? Not that it makes a bit of difference, lots of girls enjoy sporting events. Not you, of course, but lots of other girls. On the other hand, now that I think about it, we could have a boy and a girl, which would be a nice balance."

"Hold on there, Daddy. I take it back, you *are* excited." She was laughing again. "I won't know the sex of the babies until I have amniocentesis, which will happen between the fourth and the fifth months. We'll have to wait until then, unless something obvious pops up on one of my sonograms."

If she was carrying a boy, I had no doubt that something would pop up on the sonogram. After all, these kids were Donovans.

"Jamie, if you're this crazy about babies, why didn't you say anything to me?"

"Why didn't you?" I asked, taking a breath.

There was a pause.

"I just didn't know how much it meant until I realized my time could be running out," she admitted.

Apparently we had gypped ourselves for years.

"Jamie?"

"Yes."

"Come and see me," she whispered.

The sound of her voice was so bewitching that I almost

dropped the phone and ran out the back door. Then I remembered Johnny St. John, and my skin went cold. We now had something very special and precious to protect, and it made us both vulnerable.

"Kate, listen to me for a minute," I said evenly, trying not to scare her. "This business with Boris, it involves a madman who's been hurting defenseless people. He is very clever and very dangerous. If I were to come and see you, it's possible I'd be leading him to you. That is not a chance worth taking, especially now."

"I really need you with me, Jamie," she murmured sadly. "It's not fair."

I wished that things could be different, but it never works out that way for us.

"Okay, you might as well get it over with and tell me the whole story," she said. "It's worse for me when I don't know what to expect."

She was right, so I told Kate the whole truth about the accident that nearly killed Boris and brought us racing home from St. Croix. I gave it to her pretty straight, especially the parts about Johnny St. John and my visit with Thomas Martin. I was explaining Mr. Martin's theory about the viatical-settlement companies and the market for death benefits, when I mentioned Michael Adams.

"Michael Adams?" she interrupted. "Jamie, I've heard that name before."

"I don't think so, Kate."

"No, I have," she insisted. "Don't you remember, in St. Croix, the obituaries? There was going to be a memorial service for him."

It came back to me and I shivered.

"How could that be?" I asked. "Michael Adams died almost two months ago. His memorial service wouldn't have been in a newspaper this week."

"Boy, you must have been really hung over," she sighed. "Think again. I found that paper in the closet, it was old."

"I guess you're right," I said, remembering how the news had affected our day. "Well, whenever it happened, it was too soon."

There is only so much bad news a person can bear, especially a woman with raging hormones. Kate burst into tears. I kept my mouth shut; there was really nothing to say.

EIGHTEEN

...

When I strolled back into the living room, it was dark and quiet except for the crackling of the fire. Apparently, Mrs. Gold and Manny Santos had gone to bed, because their chairs and coffee cups were empty. Thomas Martin was still there, but he was stretched out on the couch, sleeping. Boris was slumped in his wheelchair by the hearth, lost in thought. I tiptoed over to the mission chair, sat down, propped my feet up on the grate and closed my eyes.

"James? James, I'm talking to you!"

I blinked and there was Boris, snapping his fingers in my face.

"I'm sorry, what were you saying?" I asked dreamily.

"I was wondering if everything is all right."

He gave me a strange look.

"Right as rain, couldn't be better," I mumbled, turning back to the fire.

"J. J., what is the matter with you?" he demanded.

The news was just too good to withhold.

"I'm going to be a daddy," I announced.

Boris surprised me by clapping his hands.

"I knew it!" he declared. "Ha-ha, I knew it."

He wheeled into the kitchen and came back with a chilled bottle of vodka.

"What's this supposed to prove?" I asked, taking the little glass he offered. "You always have a bottle of vodka in the freezer."

181

"True," he admitted, smiling wickedly, "but this bottle is different."

He held it up for inspection. Not only was the bottle unopened, but the vodka was double-distilled Stolichnya Kristal.

"Okay, I am impressed," I admitted. "Where'd you find a bottle of that stuff?"

"I made some calls and then Manuel drove into Danbury for me. Now, be still and let me make a toast."

Boris opened the bottle and filled our glasses. His face was still swollen and bruised, but he managed a smile so wide it threatened to pop a few of his crusty stitches.

"Vypiem za schyastie i krepkoye zdorovie," he said. It translates to "let's drink to good fortune and strong health."

The vodka went down cold, then turned warm as it melted in my stomach. Boris refilled the glasses and recited something even longer and more serious, also in Russian. When he finished, we knocked back our shots, then broke the glasses in the hearth, like pagans casting a spell.

When the glasses shattered, Thomas Martin jumped nervously, then bolted upright and looked around the room, blinking.

"How are you feeling, Mr. Martin?"I asked politely.

"Not nearly as good as you two are," he snapped. "What the hell are you guys doing, anyway? Is it the Russian New Year?"

"Actually, Thomas, we were celebrating. My ex-wife is pregnant, with twins."

"And you're okay with that?" he asked.

"Certainly. They're mine."

Martin stood up and stretched like a well-fed cat, then shrugged and walked into the kitchen. When he came back, he was carrying three more glasses.

"What the hell," he said, handing them out. "There hasn't been much to celebrate lately."

Boris poured and we raised our drinks.

"You've been given a beautiful gift, Mr. Donovan," Thomas Martin said. "Let's drink to new life and to the hope that it offers us."

We drank to hope, then sat quietly staring into the fire.

"Since we are all present," Boris said, finally breaking the silence, "perhaps we should get back to business."

"First, tell me about Patricia Gold. How did you find her?" I asked.

"Well, actually she found us," he said, smiling. "I scanned Patricia's photograph into the computer and then I attached it to an E-mail describing the sensitive nature of the information we had discovered. The E-mail was sent to all the Yale University oncologists on the list you provided. I made sure to indicate that I was a professor at Columbia and gave them the name of someone in our cancer center who would vouch for me. After that, I asked only that the message be passed along to Mrs. Gold. Three hours later, she called. Moses drove the leem-o to New Haven and picked her up."

"That is impressive work, Maestro," I said sincerely.

There was a bit of blush on his banged-up face. Boris reached for a cigarette.

"Let's move on to our plans," he said quickly.

"I didn't know we had any firm plans."

I looked over at my partner, but he was screened by a cloud of smoke.

"We made some progress while you were sleeping, Donovan," Martin informed me.

He gave Boris a satisfied look.

"Doctor Koulomzin and I work very well together."

"Perhaps I should begin at the beginning," Boris suggested, backing his wheelchair away from the fire. "Mr. Martin's former companion, Michael Adams, sold his death benefits through a viatical-settlement company. Three months later, the unfortunate Mr. Adams was found dead in his apartment. The body was discovered when the day nurse arrived to start the morning shift. The circumstances were somewhat unusual, but the death was still officially listed as from natural causes."

"What kind of unusual circumstances?" I asked.

"The night nurse, Sheila Mooney, wasn't in Michael's apartment when the morning girl arrived," Martin explained. "In fact, she hasn't been seen since the night before his death. The police checked her apartment, but they didn't find her. The television set was on and there was a cold pot of tea on the kitchen table, but no Sheila. If you ask me, the bastards got to Sheila Mooney and then sent someone else, maybe this Johnny St. John, to Michael's apartment."

Thomas Martin got up and started pacing back and forth.

"Of course, the cops don't agree with me," he said. "They think Sheila Mooney was a very bad lady. According to them, she was derelict in the performance of her duties and then skipped town when she realized that her negligence had contributed to Michael's death. That's about as bad as it gets, gentlemen. A widow with no family and a sparkling record of service to the sick and dying turns up missing and the N.Y.P.D. labels her 'negligent.' Pretty amazing, considering that they concocted this character assassination without meeting the woman."

He stopped and turned his back to the fire.

"For my money, Sheila Mooney was a saint. She was the kind of sweet old girl who drinks nothing stronger than tea and goes to church every day. The lady adored Michael Adams like he was her own child and wouldn't have neglected him if her life had depended on it. What's more, if Sheila had been at Michael's place the night he died, she wouldn't have left his side without a fight. I'm talking about a battle; the place would have been a mess.

"This doesn't mean I think Michael was alone the night he died," Thomas added quickly. "I know he wasn't alone, and the day nurse, Nadine Cooke, agrees with me. When she found Michael's body that morning, he was neatly dressed in clean pajamas, not the clothes she'd left him in the day before. Donovan, the poor man was too weak to dress himself. Someone had to have helped him change clothes. He'd also been medicated. Nadine counted the pills and it checked out. The cops won't listen to reason. They keeping pointing to Sheila, claiming she came to work, took care of business, and then, for some mysterious reason, just left him alone.

"Nadine called me first thing that morning, so I got to the apartment before the police ransacked the place. It was a weird scene, but there were no signs of a struggle. Most of the lights in the bedroom had been turned off, and there was a big vase of lilies on the nightstand, like flowers on an altar. The effect was eerie. The bedroom was also freezing cold, because the air conditioner was running. It was forty degrees outside, for Christ's sake, and Michael had pneumonia, but the A/C was blasting away. As if that wasn't bad enough, the poor guy was lying flat on his back. That was probably all it took to kill him. I mean, the odds are pretty good that he just suffocated in his own phlegm. On the other hand, I've never ruled out the possibility that he was given even more direct assistance—there was a pillow lying at the foot of the bed."

Martin took the bottle of vodka from Boris.

"Thomas, please, we talked about this," Boris said politely.

Thomas turned abruptly and threw his glass into the fire.

"We may never know the whole truth about Michael Adams or the unfortunate Mrs. Mooney," Boris said, picking up the thread of the story, "but I am inclined to agree with Mr. Martin. The disappearance of Sheila Mooney and the subsequent death of Michael Adams raise many questions. Unfortunately, the New York City police and the medical examiner's office do not agree with us. The police dismissed Mr. Martin's suspicions, and the coroner ruled that Michael Adams aspirated in his sleep, the final consequence of his Pneumocystis pneumonia."

"That's not the way it happened," Thomas muttered.

"When the police closed their investigation," Boris continued evenly, "Mr. Martin did not. As we have heard, Thomas has his own theory about his friend's demise, which he decided to test. Choosing a rather unorthodox method, he set out to prove his surmise about the settlement company. For this test, Thomas Martin used himself as the bait.

"To establish credibility, he arranged to have HIV-infected laboratory samples substituted for his own specimens during a routine physical examination. He managed this unlawful deceit by purchasing blood and urine samples from a very sick man of the same blood type. As expected, the diagnosis came back positive. Thomas then had the original diagnosis confirmed by a second doctor, substituting specimens in the same manner. When his bogus illness was documented, Mr. Martin approached the same viatical-settlement company Mr. Adams had used and inquired about the possibility of selling his own death benefits."

"It was really simple," Martin bragged. "I spoke to the broker who handled Michael's deal. The guy knew that I was gay and that my lover had died of AIDS, so he didn't waste time or energy looking into my story; the paperwork took less than a week. I expected some trouble from the insurance company, because we were discussing a substantial policy, but it never came. In fact, they did everything they could to expedite the transaction. Remember, if there's enough juice behind the deal, you can get anything done."

"How reassuring," Boris murmured. "In any event, Thomas negotiated a four-hundred-eighty-thousand-dollar purchase price for his life-insurance benefits. The amount was based on a calculation of sixty cents for each dollar of policy value."

"Considering that I was in a big hurry, it was a pretty good sale," Martin boasted. "My lab results showed a low T-cell count, but I also played it well. I acted really pathetic and whined a lot about dying before my time. It was a great performance."

"The fact that you have survived the consequences of this charade," Boris said seriously, "is a matter of luck, nothing else. I suggest you take a moment to reflect on that."

Thomas Martin looked like a kid who'd been scolded.

"When I had dinner with Tim Danner," I said, turning to Boris, "he told me in passing that he'd sold his life benefits. The subject made me really uncomfortable, so I didn't dwell on it. But the name of the company was easy to remember. It was called 'Life Line.' "

"Yes, Life Line, Incorporated," Boris said with satisfaction. "That is the same viatical settlement company used by Michael Adams, and Thomas Martin. It turns out, Patricia Gold is also a client. And Adams, Martin and Gold all dealt with the same broker. I would wager this same man handled Tim Danner's settlement."

"His name is William Francis Kraft the Fourth," Thomas added coldly. "He's a well-polished snake. Right schools, good family connections. I know, because he likes to talk about himself. This guy Kraft thinks his good fortune is a birthright. I'm going to enjoy taking him down."

Martin's swagger was starting to annoy me again.

"The plan we've been discussing is fairly simple—" Boris began.

"Hold on just a second," I interrupted. "Let's go back to the beginning. What arrangement did you and Thomas come to while I was sleeping? He's looking far too smug."

Martin was smiling.

"Thomas is not our client, James. The arrangement with him is more philosophical," Boris assured me. "However, I have told him that we are committed to bringing this evil business to an end, and he has expressed a desire to help. Among other things, Thomas has agreed to donate approximately four hundred and twenty thousand dollars to the project."

"That's all I have left," Martin volunteered. "From the insurance policy, I mean."

"Half a million dollars isn't philosophical, Boris," I said angrily. "Besides, it represents the proceeds for a felony. I don't want anything to do with it."

"I'm surprised at you, James," Boris sniffed. "I mean, really, these funds will be used to help us attain our goal, which is to put Mr. Kraft out of business. My word, you are the last person I would have expected to get on a soapbox over something like this. Believe me, we will put the money to a very good cause."

The telephone rang loudly, startling all of us. I got up and grabbed the receiver.

"J. J., is that you?"

Peter Walsh was shouting over the noise in his bar.

"Yeah, Peter, it's me. How are you?"

"Fine. Look, J. J., is Doctor Koulomzin there? I need to speak to him."

"It's Peter Walsh," I said, covering the mouthpiece. "Did you give him this number?"

"Of course not," Boris grumbled, wheeling himself over to the phone. "Earlier this evening, I arranged to have all the New York calls forwarded."

I felt like I'd been asleep for days.

"Very good, Peter. Thank you," Boris was saying. "Now, you're sure about the numbers? It's important. I see. Good. Fax me the names as soon as you can. This is very helpful."

Boris held up the phone.

"He wants to speak to you again."

Instead of handing me the receiver, he put it down on the table and wheeled over to his computer.

"What's up, Peter?" I asked, making a face at the back of my partner's head.

"I wanted to let you know about the memorial service for Tim," he began.

"Oh right. I was wondering about that," I lied.

"Well, it's next Wednesday," he said. "Just in case you're in the neighborhood."

My stomach turned a loop; churches give me the creeps worse than hospitals do.

"Well?" Boris asked when I hung up.

"There's going to be a memorial service for Tim Danner next week. I told him I'd try to be there."

Boris raised an eyebrow.

"Where were we?" I asked, walking over to my chair. "Oh yeah, you were about to tell me all about this great plan you and Thomas dreamed up. Let me guess—I get to do all the dirty work, right?"

Boris squinted his eyes peevishly, but I wasn't far off the mark. They wanted me to meet with Mr. William Francis Kraft, the viatical-settlement broker, and charm him into making a really stupid mistake. If Kraft didn't embrace me as a kindred spirit, my fallback position was to shift gears and try blackmail. Boris thought I could bully William Kraft by threatening him with exposure. To give this gem of a plan some legal credibility, my good friend Lieutenant Gavin would be invited. But only if he agreed to play by our rules.

"By the way, why was Peter Walsh calling you?" I asked when Boris stopped to light another cigarette.

"Ah, that. Well, Peter has been spreading the word, trying to find other men who have sold their policies through Mr. Kraft or his company. I thought it would be helpful to have as much information as possible about Life Line when you meet with Kraft. Peter has done better than I would have expected. He's sending us a list."

"That's very nice, Boris, but so far, I'm unimpressed. It didn't take too many brain cells to think up this so-called 'plan.' God, why not drop me into a tank full of sharks and see how long I can manage to survive?"

Martin jumped to his feet, but Boris held a hand up, stopping him.

"I realize that it seems a bit crude," he began, "but I promise you, the meeting will be held in a public place, there will be outstanding electronic surveillance, and hopefully, the police will provide backup."

"Assuming Gavin buys any of this," I reminded him.

"I will speak to Lieutenant Gavin myself," Boris promised.

"Oh, big deal. That should make everything fine. Try looking at this from my point of view, Boris. I've got to sell this scheme to Kraft. If it bombs, you two geniuses will be well out of range. I'll be across the table."

Boris didn't say anything.

"You want to know what I think? I think you're both so anxious to do something, anything, that you're rushing me into a very compromising situation. By the way, how does this little scheme of yours enable us to stop Johnny St. John from continuing his extracurricular activities?"

Boris cleared his throat.

"I am expecting Mr. Kraft to lead us to St. John," he said.

"What if he can't?" I demanded. "What if he doesn't play ball?"

"Don't you think you're giving this Johnny character just a little too much credit?" Martin volunteered from the couch. "The man's not supernatural. I'm sure Kraft can give us a line on him."

I turned to Thomas Martin.

"Since when did you become an expert?" I asked. "Last I heard, you were still an investment counselor. Did your junior G-man card arrive while I was napping?"

The phone started ringing.

"Hello," I snapped.

"Well, hello to you, too, my dear!"

I stiffened.

"Johnny?"

"One and the same, darling. And I must tell you, James, it is *so* good to hear your voice. For the longest time, I was getting your infernal answering machine. I refuse to speak to machines."

"Where are you?"

"Oh, come now, let's not waste time with silly questions. We have business to discuss. Is the fat man there? If he is, put him on the phone."

I told Boris what St. John wanted. He nodded and I put the call on speaker.

"Hello, Doctor, can you hear me?"

"I can."

Boris affected a weary attitude.

"Good. And how are you feeling?"

Johnny chuckled.

"Get to the point or I will disconnect this call," Boris ordered.

Johnny stopped laughing.

"I don't think I like the tone of your voice, old man," he said. "I have warned you before."

"If there is nothing further, Mr. St. John, we will say good night."

Boris started wheeling himself toward the phone.

"Wait just one minute, Doctor Koulomzin, I'm not through with you. Your interference is no longer amusing, and it has kept me from completing my work, which is unacceptable."

"Hey, fuck you, you albino bastard!"

Thomas Martin was on his feet, yelling into the speaker.

"Ah, well, Mr. Martin," Johnny said after a pause. "So James found you. It shouldn't have been hard, I practically told him where to look. As a matter of fact, I had planned to join you fellows, but I became unavoidably detained. It *is* Mr. Thomas Martin, is it not?"

"You're goddamn right it's Thomas Martin, you fucking lunatic. I plan to see you frying in hell."

"Tut-tut, such language from an educated man," St. John taunted, "Fear not, Mr. Martin, you and I will meet soon. Of that, you can rest assured."

There was something in Johnny's voice that sent Martin retreating back to the sofa.

"While we're on the subject, fat man," Johnny snarled, goading Boris, "what have you done with Mrs. Gold? I had something very special in mind for her."

"Listen to me, St. John," Boris said calmly. "You are being

used by people who profit from your crimes. Mrs. Gold, Timothy Danner, these are innocent people who deserve your pity and your concern."

Then Boris began to recite.

"Where jealousy and selfish ambition exist, there will be disorder and every vile practice. But wisdom from above is first pure, then peaceable, gentle, open to reason, full of mercy and good fruits, without uncertainty or insincerity. And the harvest of righteousness is sown in peace by those who make peace.' A true disciple of Christ would understand this and refuse to be led astray by false prophets," he said with conviction.

There was an even longer pause, and then it was Johnny's turn. He spoke very slowly and very clearly.

" 'This is the revelation of Jesus Christ, which God gave him to show what might happen soon. God made it known by sending His angel to His servant John who gives witness to the word of GOD and to the testimony of Jesus Christ. Blessed is the one who reads aloud and blessed are those who listen and heed for the appointed time is near!' "

We all stared at the speakerphone, waiting for more. After a minute, a recorded voice broke into the line asking the caller to deposit more change. Thirty seconds later, the connection went dead.

"So, Thomas," I asked, reaching for the vodka, "you still think I'm giving Johnny St. John too much credit?"

NINETEEN

■ ■ ■

It wasn't a great plan, but it was the quickest way for us to make a difference. I was not prepared to sit around waiting for a brainstorm while Johnny St. John sacrificed more innocent people to his corrupted faith.

I stayed in Connecticut for about a week, during which time we each settled into our own routines. Angus spent his days chasing ducks or sleeping; I worried about Kate and the babies; Boris smoked and tried to work on his computer; Thomas Martin studied the *Wall Street Journal* and *Baron's* every day and pestered Boris with questions about probability analyses and economic forecasting; Manny Santos and his cousins pulled guard duty when they weren't eating or drinking; and Mrs. Gold did her best to keep us all on friendly terms; like a very patient baby-sitter.

I hadn't known Patricia for very long, but already she had made a lasting impression on me. She was kind and understanding, almost to a fault. Yet she could stop a nasty argument with a simple look of disappointment. That frail little woman wielded a lot of influence.

I still can't fathom where the lady got her inner strength. Under the same conditions, most people would have folded. Mrs. Gold had been diagnosed with acute myelogenous leukemia. By the time we met, the doctors had run out of ideas for her treatment and they were talking about just making her comfortable.

As a result of the leukemia, she had lost her job as an art teacher, her friends, and finally her family. All of them had edged farther and farther away from her as death had approached.

The Koulomzin/Martin braintrust had decided that I should make contact with William Kraft by applying to his company, Life Line, Incorporated, like any other prospective client. Patricia Gold and Thomas Martin had both gone through the application process, but Thomas gave me a headache, so I turned to Patricia for help. We spent several long days together, making calls and going over the forms. I baked scones, she brewed herbal tea, and we got to know each other a little; a few days was a lot of time for her.

First, we dialed the toll-free number listed in the Life Line, Inc., brochure, which Thomas Martin had provided. An operator answered the telephone and directed our call to a Miss Loretta White, Administrative Manager for New Accounts. It was Miss Loretta's job to ask sensitive questions without making us feel too uncomfortable. She was a soft-spoken, friendly old girl and probably reminded most callers of their grandmother. That reassuring voice on the other end of the telephone was an effective way to establish trust with people who were about to put their lives on the dotted line.

The next day an official application package arrived by Express Mail. The form was straightforward and chillingly frank. Section One asked for my name, address, date of birth, Social Security number, marital status, and place of business. There were also some questions about my legal status. They wanted to be sure I wasn't involved in a lawsuit or bankruptcy action. A legal complication could interfere with the investor's ability to collect my death benefits once I'd earned my angel's wings. Section Two asked for details about my life-insurance policy. It was basic stuff like policy type, policy number, the list of the beneficiaries, but there was also a big, blank space, with room for lots of zeroes, where they requested the dollar amount of my coverage. The third and final section of the application dealt with diagnosis and medical information. It was much longer than the other sections.

I filled out Section One and Two honestly, using my real name and Social Security number, and even wrote down real insurance information where they requested it. But Section Three was a problem. I wasn't sick and I didn't plan on starting a fake paper trail that could follow me for the rest of my days. Instead of making up a lot of lies, we attached a letter saying that I would provide the necessary medical information if and when I decided to sell my benefits.

The only medical question I couldn't ignore was the T-cell count—the benchmark against which the relative health of an AIDS patient is usually judged. According to Boris, counts vary widely, but a normal person would have a T-cell count of approximately one thousand. If that number drops below four hundred, it's real bad, below two hundred and the patient is officially diagnosed with full-blown AIDS. T-cell counts of two hundred also mark the point at which secondary illnesses can be expected. Obviously, a number below one hundred would be dreadful. To whet the appetite of Mr. Kraft and his investor pals, my letter said that I had gotten a T-cell count of one hundred and twenty-five, but that I didn't believe the results were accurate.

If we got lucky, Kraft would conclude that I was in denial. And if we managed to sell him on the illness part, the rest would fall into place. The phony T-cell count was particularly important because that's the number Kraft would use to make an educated guess about my life expectancy. Once he had projected the number of months or years, it was a simple matter to calculate the potential rate of return from my policy. The ROI, of course, became the basis of a sales pitch to the investors.

The application form also requested detailed information about opportunistic infections, like Kaposi's Sarcoma or the microbacterium avium (MAC) infection I'd seen listed on Tim Danner's index-card biography. These other diseases were almost as important to Mr. Kraft as the T-cell count, because they hinted

195

at the extent to which my weakened immunological system had become ineffective. That, in turn, enabled Kraft to fine-tune his estimate of my departure date. In short, the sicker the patient, the more reliable the estimated time of death. I didn't answer any of those medical questions. A man with a T-cell count of one hundred twenty-five was going to sound the bell on their rating scale no matter what; adding pneumonia to my short list of very serious problems seemed unnecessary.

To speed up the review process, the applicant was asked to supply the name of a physician and/or a hospital contact. I filled in Richard Steinman's name and phone number. I had already spoken to Dr. Steinman, who made it perfectly clear that he was more than willing to confirm, to any and all callers, that I have serious problems. That part was easy, he said, because it was true. On the other hand, he wouldn't lie about my physical condition. This led to a discussion about medical ethics, at the end of which Richard reluctantly agreed to confirm that he knew I was applying to sell my death benefits and that he had reason to believe this decision was a reasonable course of action. It was a white lie, and it hardly stacked up against premeditated murder, but we still had to pry it out of him.

The application closed with a series of representations about the accuracy of the information I'd given and a request for my signature. I still had some misgivings about the phony T-cell count. After all, if the plan bombed, there was a possibility I could find myself accused of insurance fraud or worse. But I signed the thing anyway and we sent it back to Miss White the next morning, along with photocopies of my life-insurance policy, driver's license, and Social Security card.

Despite the sympathetic, heartwarming encouragement from Miss White, the back of the form had carried a notice declaring that employees of Life Line, Incorporated were not qualified to give advice on the relative merits of selling death benefits. The disclaimer went on to ask the applicant to acknowledge that he or she understood the seriousness of his or her illness and the consequences of selling the current and future benefits of the insurance policy. I didn't sign that part either. I wanted Kraft to work for his blood money.

Three days later, William Francis Kraft, IV, left a message on the New York answering machine. I gave myself a few minutes to get into character, then called him back. Kraft spoke clearly, though with a rather affected tone, conveying the impression of an urbane, sophisticated gentleman. He introduced himself and his company without rushing into a sales pitch, then politely inquired after my health and general well-being. When he'd spent enough time to imply real concern and interest, he seamlessly moved on to the business of viatical settlements.

Before I knew it, we were talking about deals as if I had already decided to sell my insurance benefits. Once my paperwork was complete, he explained, it would be distributed to a group of ten or twelve private investors. Kraft didn't bother to say where you find people willing to trade in death benefits; they were simply described as reputable private citizens with the necessary resources to make a deal. As my personal representative, William Kraft would take it upon himself to manage the bidding, thereby assuring me of the very best financial terms.

Bill Kraft made a point of telling me that he understood the sensitivity of my situation. He emphasized the need for a close relationship between client and broker. Such a relationship began with trust, he insisted, his voice smooth as silk. To allay any concerns I might have had about his honesty and integrity, he offered to mail me a copy of his New York State license and even provided me with the name and telephone number of the State Director of Licensing Services, in case I wanted to check him out. He also offered to provide personal testimonials and references. William Kraft was charming and accommodating, and he wasn't overly eager.

What impressed me the most was the soft sell. He didn't question my reluctance to list all the sad details of my medical condition. To the contrary, he seemed to understand and share my

197

concern. I was facing an incredibly difficult decision that would have made anyone hesitate, and Bill Kraft understood. The only pressure came subtly, in the context of the conversation. For instance, he carefully explained that it might take as long as six or eight weeks to complete the viatical-settlement process. He was warning me that I shouldn't waste time. It was a simple message—my time was running out—and he managed to return to it frequently.

I tried not to overact or seem too willing. The plan called for fear and indecision, and that's what I delivered. When it was my turn to speak, I made it clear that it would take more than a pleasant chat on the telephone to convince me. Kraft seemed energized by the challenge. We ended that first conversation by agreeing to meet for lunch at a fancy spot in the East Sixties. William Francis Kraft, IV, took the job of representing my affairs personally, and that meant sparing no expense.

I hung the receiver back in the cradle and took a deep breath. I'm usually intrigued, or at least amused, by talented liars, but this time was different. All this talk about death was scaring me. It was like playing with fire. I yanked the top off a cold bottle of Bass ale and headed for my big mission chair in front of the fire.

"How does he get away with it?" I asked, looking around the room. "The guy has a state license—doesn't that mean some-body's keeping an eye on him?"

Boris was sitting over at his computer, but he ignored me. His attention was completely focused on the screen in front of him. When he gets like that, you can almost hear the mental gears grinding. Mrs. Gold didn't answer either; she was dozing in an armchair on the other side of the hearth. Manny Santos and the boys were outside, making Connecticut a safer place for all of us. That left Thomas Martin. He had emptied the contents of his briefcase onto the coffee table and was busy making notes on a legal pad as he sorted through the papers.

"The licensing thing is pretty easy to get around," Martin

volunteered, picking up his coffee cup. "Each year, the state audits the contracts from the previous twelve months, to make sure that consumers weren't handed lousy buyout deals. For example, the regulators would check to make sure that a patient with a dreadful T-cell count got a great offer. The shorter your life expectancy, the more money you should be getting, right? In fact, now that I think about it, this is one of the few instances in life where you get rewarded for doing lousy on a test. Anyway, the data collected during the audits becomes the market standard for payments to people at different stages of their illness."

"But if New York State is conducting audits, why don't they notice that Kraft's people also die quicker?" I asked.

"Use your head, Donovan," he said, tapping his forehead. "The scam works because it exploits weaknesses in the state's system of oversight. New York State wants to ensure some general standards of fair-business practice for these buyouts. They do that by auditing the deals annually, hoping to discourage the viatical equivalent of price-gouging. That's fine as far as it goes, but the kind of foul play we're alleging is way out of their league. The agencies aren't equipped to handle something this big.

"Normally, you'd expect the police departments to assume responsibility for the investigation of suspicious deaths. Only, in this case, the victims are expected to die and usually do so in ways that seem consistent with their illness. What would be the basis for a complaint against Kraft? He's a broker, for Christ's sake, a betting man. Can you imagine a prosecutor trying to argue that William F. Kraft the Fourth was at fault because a dying man had croaked a little bit sooner than Kraft predicted?"

"Actually," Boris said, breaking away from his computer as the printer started up, "the variability between the medical indicators and the eventual outcome is far too inconsistent to logically question the occasional outlying result. Some people with very low T-cell counts have survived far beyond the median, especially with new medical treatments, while others die much sooner. Thomas is right—Kraft would argue that he and his investors are gambling, like any commodities brokers, using a probability analysis as a guide. Being wrong in a guessing game is not a criminal offense."

"So, as long as he's selective and doesn't get too greedy, they'd never catch him?"

"That is probably true," Boris mumbled, sorting his printouts. "Unless, of course, he makes a mistake."

"What gives his scam its sweetness is the fact that the man doesn't need it," Thomas added, smiling. "If you look at the results nationwide, it's pretty obvious that big profits can be had just by investing conservatively. I mean, not all the dealers are killing their customers, right? If you never pay out more than fifty cents on the dollar and you pick your clients wisely, you'll probably double your investment, if not better. We don't know how many people Kraft has passed along to Johnny Saint John, but it's probably a fraction of his total portfolio."

"So what makes a successful guy risk everything?" I asked.

Thomas Martin's smile grew wider.

"His reasons would probably blow your mind, Donovan," he chuckled. "For some people, enough is never enough. I know guys on the street who keep buying bigger houses and fancier cars just so they have an excuse to justify all the money they demand. This one guy I know, he started out buying polo ponies, pretty soon he needed a groom, and then a trainer. Now he's looking into farms and who knows where that will lead? Doesn't matter, it works for him. It helps keep the pressure up. Besides, the asshole pretends he's just a working stiff looking out for the needs of his family. That's the excuse he uses to stick it to anyone who gets in his way.

"Truth is, the justification doesn't even need to be that complicated. It could be a simple matter of ego. I wouldn't be surprised to find out that Kraft just wanted to have the best track record in the business, and a few recreational homicides was a quicker, easier way to get him the trophy than bargaining with his clients. 'William F. Kraft the Fourth—Best Death Benefits Dealer in the U.S.A.!' Makes you wonder what the plaque would look like, doesn't it?"

"It isn't going to be easy to convince Kraft that he's in trouble," I said, leaning back in my chair. "I mean, he seems pretty well insulated. The guy's a respected, properly licensed member of a thriving industry. And I'll bet he's really popular with the investors."

Boris fumbled in the pocket of his bathrobe until he'd located his cigarette tin. When I saw the ugly black Sobraine in his mouth, I snapped my fingers and pointed at Patricia Gold, still sleeping in the club chair. He nodded and put the cigarette away before turning back to me.

"Now, James, let's not take such a dim view of things," he said seriously. "I've been collecting and organizing data that will support any allegations you need to make. At the very least, you will be able to give Mr. Kraft the impression that he has been thoroughly scrutinized. Besides, he may choose to look upon you as the bearer of good tidings. After all, you'll be dangling a substantial purse."

Boris was satisfied, but it was easy for him to sit there, patting his printouts, looking confident. He would be watching the action from the sidelines, like a four-star general. If things didn't work out, he'd turn on the computer and reanalyze the data. It wouldn't be that simple for me.

The next day was a Sunday, but I didn't go to church. Instead I packed the car and left for New York City. Before I said goodbye to the commandos, I dialed Kate's number from the telephone in the kitchen. Her answering machine picked up. I left a short, snappy message, but it didn't hide my disappointment.

Traffic was light and the weather was beautiful, making for an easy ride into town. I got off the Westside Highway at 96th Street and parked my car in the first garage I saw. It wasn't my usual place, but I didn't want to advertise my return to the city. I carried the canvas bag with my clothes and several bags of groceries out to the curb, then hailed a cab for the short ride uptown.

When the driver turned the corner at 101st, I was filled with a sense of relief as I took in the familiar surroundings. The building was right where I'd left it; bruised and battered, but still standing tall. Old Bill Manners was out front enjoying the sunshine. He had all of the dogs with him, which was very unusual. Mr. Manner's rents two small apartments on the fourth floor and shares them with a dozen or more half-breeds. But, it was rare for him to take more than three or four of the puppies out at one time.

"How're you doing, Bill?" I inquired, stepping out of the cab.

"Just fine, Mr. Donovan, just fine. And how is the doctor faring? And his big fella, Angus?"

"Doctor Koulomzin is mending nicely, Bill," I shouted as the pack started barking. "Angus is taking very good care of him. They'll both be home before long."

Old Bill didn't hear the answer. He was arbitrating a dispute between two large mongrels, while also trying to keep all those leashes untangled. I picked up my bag and the groceries and headed for the lobby, happy in the knowledge that some things don't change at all.

"Oh, James, James, you're finally home!" the Polhemus sisters squealed in unison.

They scurried across the lobby, dressed in identical yellow Laura Ashley frocks and headbands. The outfits would have looked cute if the twins had been sixty or seventy years younger. The "girls" are a pair of identical busybodies, seemingly frozen in late adolescence.

"How is he?" Mildred asked, wringing her hands.

"Oh, yes, yes, how is the great man?" Alma chimed.

The sisters revere my partner. His accident and forced absence had been hard on them.

"Don't worry, ladies. I assure you, he'll be back soon."

"Is there some way we could help?" Alma asked confidentially.

"As a matter of fact, there is," I told her. "I want you ladies to keep your eyes open for a man with a full head of white hair."

"Like Mr. Thompson?" Mildred interrupted.

Howard Thompson lived on the eleventh floor. He was ninety-two years old.

"Not exactly," I said. "The man I'm talking about would be about fifty, with a full head of hair."

"Oh," they said in unison.

"If you should see the man I just described, go directly to the telephone and call the police. The man's name is St. John, Mr. Johnny St. John. And you should be extremely careful, because he is a very bad man."

"Oh," they said again, wide-eyed.

I left them in the lobby, staked out behind a large ficus tree. As usual, the elevator whined and complained, but it took me to the seventeenth floor and actually stopped on a level with the hall floor. Before unlocking the apartment, I checked the stairwell and the closet with the garbage chute. The coast seemed clear, so I moved back in to my apartment.

The light was blinking on my answering machine, which meant that Boris had only forwarded our office calls. I pushed the Play button and listened while I unpacked my provisions. There were only three messages that mattered.

Rich Steinman had called to tell me about a conversation he'd had with William Kraft. As expected, Mr. Kraft called to verify my application. Richard used the word "repulsive" to describe Bill Kraft, so I knew we were talking about the same guy. Apparently, Bill had dropped the charm when he spoke to Dr. Steinman; there had been no pretenses about sympathy. Despite his immediate and visceral dislike for the man, Richard had kept up his end of the bargain, saying just enough to encourage and frustrate the inquisitive scavenger.

The second message was from Kate. She had been out for a walk when I'd phoned earlier, and now it wasn't possible to call her back. She was on an airplane heading for Aspen, Colorado, where some sort of magazine crisis had developed around a cover shoot. As far as I could tell, the emergency involved a super model, a photographer, and the model's boyfriend, an actor. Kate didn't sound very happy about the trip. The message said she'd given her housekeeper, Ellen, the week off and didn't expect to be back until Sunday, or maybe Saturday at the earliest. I was going to miss her, but I was also relieved that she'd be out of harm's way for the next few days.

The third call was from my pal, Lieutenant Gavin. He and Boris had spoken at some length while I was still in Connecticut. I heard only one side of their conversation, so I can't quote Gavin, but I know his first reaction wasn't very positive. In the end, however, they hammered out a compromise. The lieutenant agreed to let us go ahead with our little charade, and we agreed that his men would monitor the entire exchange and serve as backup.

Frankly, it was more than I would have expected from the department. But then, Gavin wasn't your average flatfoot. The autopsy and lab reports that came back on Tim Danner proved that there wasn't any champagne in Timmy's stomach. Indeed, the saliva on the glass had come from a person with a different blood type. Those facts, combined with his own suspicions, raised enough questions in Gavin's mind to make him a cautious believer. The message on my answering machine instructed me to be in his office the next morning at seven-thirty sharp.

After the last message played, I made an inspection tour of my apartment, double-checking the door locks and window bolts, then ducked through the connecting passageway and gave the Koulomzin domicile a similar shakedown. I also closed Boris's windows and lowered the shades again. The apartment could have used a few more days of sunlight and fresh air, but I didn't want to completely destroy the ambience.

As I made my tour, it occurred to me that I was completely alone. No Angus bouncing and slobbering on me; no Manny Santos scratching his stomach and burping; no acrid smoke from Turkish cigarettes. I missed my Kate, but peace and quiet was the next best thing. I decided to celebrate my freedom by drowning a few large Spanish olives in a shaker of ice-cold martinis. After that, I sliced up some potatoes for mashing, sauteed an onion and a handful of mushrooms, then seasoned a big, juicy steak and fired up the grill on my terrace.

After dinner, I slipped into clean pajamas and read a book till my eyelids got heavy. The lights were out by nine o'clock and I slept like a baby.

At seven-thirty the next morning, I was drinking coffee in Gavin's office. The room was a little more crowded than it had been the night Danner was killed. In addition to Gavin's side-kick, Bobby, there were four detectives I'd never met—two men and two women—ranging in age from their early thirties to late forties. Turned out, they were going to have lunch with Bill Kraft and me.

The other face in the room was none other than Detective Sergeant Bill Sweeney, formerly of the 33rd Precinct. He was slouched in a corner, his feet propped up on the table in front of him, working a big toothpick in one corner of his mouth. When I said hello to Sweeney, he spit the toothpick at me.

Gavin marched in a little later, looking more serious than I remembered him. He introduced me to his team, then gave us an overview of the case, starting on the night of Tim Danner's death. He had color photographs of the crime scene and described lots of incidental pieces of physical evidence suggesting that the death was not a suicide. And, of course, there was the coroner's report, which proved that Tim hadn't been alone. The only suspect was the strange man with pure-white hair that Mrs.

Jacobs, the neighbor, had seen from her darkened bedroom window.

That was my cue.

I told the assembly about Dr. Koulomzin's accident on River Avenue in the Bronx and introduced them to Johnny St. John, giving a name, or at least an alias, to their white-haired suspect. I told them about the envelope with the pictures and biographies of Tim Danner, Patricia Gold, and Thomas Martin, then produced my photocopies of the originals. While they passed the copies around the room, I described the second attack on Boris up at Milstein Hospital, and told them about my first visit with Thomas Martin. When they had all the background, I outlined our plan to catch William F. Kraft, then asked for questions.

"Yeah, I gotta question," Detective Sweeney said from his corner. "I wanna know what this fuckin' civilian is doin' messin' around in police business? Answer me that, Lieutenant—what the fuck is this guy doin' here?"

He stabbed a chubby finger at me, but the question was for Gavin. The lieutenant walked over to him slowly, like he was tired. When he reached the end of the table, he stood looking down at the big redhead without saying a word. After about a minute, Gavin started to turn away, then reached back and grabbed Sweeney by the cuffs of his trousers and flipped him over backward. There was a loud crash, and even louder cursing as Sweeney scrambled to his feet, puffing for air.

"Now you listen to me," Gavin said, his voice still low, but commanding. "Unless you're deaf, you heard all the words spoken here in the last twenty minutes. What you should have concluded, you dumb bastard, is that this guy Donovan and his partner are the people who made your case. A serial killer was served up to you on a platter, only you were too stupid to figure it out."

Gavin moved in closer.

"I am going to give you a chance to redeem yourself, Billy, because I hate the very idea of a bad cop. But make no mistake about it, son, your ass is mine. If you so much as hiccup, I'm going to make sure that you regret it for the rest of your sorry-ass career. Do we understand each other?"

Sweeney had no place to go, and the other cops were all making faces like he'd stepped in something. After what seemed like a very long time, Bill Sweeney nodded.

The lieutenant looked around the room.

"Any more questions?" he asked.

You could have heard a pin drop.

"Okay, let's get back to work," Gavin said, picking up the seating chart for the restaurant. "We've got a lot to cover between now and your lunch on Wednesday."

TWENTY

■ ■ ■

"Mr. Donovan? I'm Bill Kraft."

He stood up from the table and buttoned his suit jacket, then extended his hand for me to shake. He was smiling, but his eyes weren't friendly. The sight of me had shaken him.

"Glad to finally meet you, Bill," I said, returning his gaze.

"You will have to excuse me for speaking so plainly, Mr. Donovan," he began, sitting again and adjusting the cloth napkin in his lap, "but for a man in your condition, you seem remarkably robust."

I stand six feet two inches tall and weigh just over two hundred pounds, so Kraft's observation didn't indicate a unique sense of perception. We had expected him to be taken off guard when he met me. It wasn't much, but it gave me a slight advantage, and I needed all the help I could get.

"I'm glad you think so, Bill," I said, trying to look flattered. "But appearances can be very deceiving. Why don't we order lunch and get that out of the way? I would like to be able to talk without interruption."

Kraft was a careful man, but I figured once lunch had been ordered, he'd feel obligated to sit through it; he wasn't the sort of man who causes scenes in fancy restaurants. I got the waiter's attention and ordered myself fresh grouper, a mixed salad, and a glass of chilled Sancerre. Kraft didn't bother with the menu; he asked for the chilled cucumber soup, fresh mushroom ravioli, and a dry Gibson. When our drinks were on the table and the waiter had gone, Kraft folded his hands and smiled at me over the centerpiece, like an old friend.

"How can I help you?" he asked.

"Well, you have my application—" I began, but he interrupted.

"That won't be necessary, Mr. Donovan," he said without relaxing his smile, "I think we should just get down to cases. Don't you?"

I was wearing a wire; the flowers were wired, and there were detectives seated at two of the other tables, watching us.

"Fair enough, Bill," I said, looking him straight in the eye. "As you've apparently deduced, the application was merely a device to bring us to the same table."

"You falsified your application?" Kraft put his drink down, looking shocked. "Why on earth would you do something like that?"

That's what I'd asked Boris when he suggested it.

"To make a long story short, Bill," I said evenly, "my partner and I want to make an investment in Life Line, Inc., and this was our way of getting to know you."

Kraft closed his eyes and pinched the bridge of his nose.

"Let's get something straight, Mr. Donovan," he said a moment later. "I am an established viatical broker, not the local bookie. In my business, we deal with lots of private investors, but they approach me in the time-honored fashion, by making an appointment, showing up on time, and stating their business. Most important of all, the people with whom I work are above reproach. Frankly, the very idea that you would stoop to this kind of subterfuge makes it clear that you would not be suitable."

He spoke with a well-bred whisper of outrage. I had a sip of my wine and smiled at him.

"Look, Bill, I'm sorry if this seems unconventional, but we really meant no harm. The thing is, my partner is a stickler for details and he felt that we'd learn something by going through

210

the application process. It was important to our understanding of your business. Not to mention the fact that it gave us a chance to see how you operate on your feet. And I gotta tell you, Bill— you're good."

He actually blushed, which surprised me; Bill Kraft was susceptible to flattery.

"Now, as to our suitability—" I smiled broadly. "We're prepared to show you evidence that should make you anxious to cooperate with us. No kidding. But before we get down to that stuff, I have a few ideas I thought you might be willing to bat around."

Kraft was stirring his Gibson calmly, the onion skewered with a silver toothpick, but his eyes were glued to mine.

"We recently created a specialty fund here in New York City and we're looking for good investment opportunities," I said. "The first deposit was only four hundred thousand, but there could be much more later if we're pleased with the results. Keep that in mind, because what I'm talking about could be an opportunity for you to grow your business, maybe even diversify."

I took a long, slow drink and let that notion sink in. Kraft didn't say anything, but he was nervous; I could feel the tension.

"Look, Bill, you can relax," I said, continuing. "We're not interested in running your shop. You do your job and we'll stay out of your hair. On the other hand, we have resources that you might someday find useful. Let's just say that you would have influential friends with very deep pockets. Okay? The only condition is that you guarantee us a decent return on our money. That's only fair, right?"

Kraft popped the onion into his mouth nonchalantly, but he was interested.

"For the sake of argument, let's pretend I am interested." He was fingering the stem of his glass. "What would you consider a decent return?"

I rubbed my chin and stared over his head for a moment or two.

"How does thirty percent grab you?" I asked.

Kraft was taking another sip of his Gibson, and he actually choked. At first, I thought one of those little cocktail onions had gone down the wrong pipe, but that wasn't the problem. He coughed and hacked, and his face turned bright red as tears streamed down his cheeks. A part of me wouldn't have minded sitting there watching while the guy choked to death, but I needed him to help me find Johnny St. John. Fortunately for Kraft, the waiter arrived while I was thinking about it and he had the presence of mind to pound on the man's back until the choking stopped.

"You'll have to excuse me," Kraft panted, slumping down in his chair. "I was not prepared for your little joke."

He coughed some more, but the fit was over. I waited for him to get control.

"Are you sure you're all right, Bill?" I asked finally.

"No problem, I'm fine." He was damping his forehead with a handkerchief.

"Well, that's good, Bill, because we're really counting on you, Buddy."

I picked up a fork and started attacking my salad. Kraft seemed unsure of his next move, so he latched onto a spoon and began to cautiously sip his cucumber soup.

"About this investment pool," he said finally. "I mean, you *were* kidding about the return, right?"

A forkful of mixed greens stopped in midair and I looked across the table at him.

"I don't kid around about money, Bill," I said. "Why don't you eat your food and we'll get back to this other stuff when lunch is over. Okay? Watch out, here comes my fish."

Kraft had lost control of the conversation. I enjoyed his discomfort and ate happily, bombarding him with small talk. He pushed his ravioli from one side of the plate to the other, without eating much of it. When I was finished, the waiter cleared the dishes and brought us each a coffee.

212

"Wonderful meal, Bill," I said, smiling over the rim of my cup. "This place was a great choice."

He nodded, but it was obvious that he was about to burst.

"Listen, Donovan," he began, speaking so softly I could barely hear him, "I sat through lunch and I kept my peace. Now suppose you tell me what you're really doing here."

"I told you before, Bill, I'm going to put four hundred thousand dollars of my money into a working partnership. All I expect is a decent return on my investment. And just in case you think I'm not looking out for your interests, think again. Bill Kraft gets to keep everything over that thirty-percent figure I mentioned."

He stared at me, bewildered.

"I can't guarantee you a thirty-percent return on your money, Mr. Donovan. My God, what do you think we're doing, killing the clients?" He tried to chuckle.

"Well, no, I don't think you're actually doing the killing yourself, Bill. But, yeah, I think you're killing your clients."

The fake laughter stopped abruptly.

"How dare you?" Kraft sputtered.

"Come off it, Bill. It's your turn to stop playing games. I know all about you. Do the names Michael Adams and Timothy Danner ring any bells?"

He sat up rigidly in the chair, like he'd been stabbed in the back, and his jaw went slack. When he didn't respond, I rattled off about five more names, working my way down the list of the departed Peter Walsh had put together for us. Kraft looked shocked, but he wasn't ready to surrender.

"Since you have the audacity to raise this question," he began, "I will admit that I recognize most of the names you've mentioned. Indeed, they are all former clients and they are all dead. But it is painfully obvious to me that you and your partner, whoever that is, have failed to recognize the most elemental truth about viatical settlements. Let me make things perfectly clear for you—*all* of our clients die prematurely, because they are all very

213

sick. This does not mean that they were murdered."

Kraft was building up steam.

"I find your suggestion insulting and libelous, Mr. Donovan. In fact, before you continue, I think it fair to warn you that I will be consulting counsel about the proper legal response to your nasty insinuations, and in particular, about your falsified application. I am sure that there are laws against this sort of thing."

I had him by the tail and he was starting to squeal.

"Why don't you knock it off?" I said, folding my hands and leaning across the table. "It's a waste of time for you to go on babbling when we both know the truth. Let me try another name on you and see if that doesn't clear the air a little—Johnny St. John. Does that name ring a bell? White-haired gentleman with a deep tan and a penchant for sacrificial murder. I'm told that you know him pretty well."

William Kraft froze in his chair.

"Don't get me wrong," I added quickly. "We don't care who you kill or how you manage it. Really, that part is no big deal. Just don't sit there and lie to me. It doesn't make for a good business relationship. Besides, I've got a lot more to tell you. Remember a guy named Martin, Thomas P. Martin, the invest-ment banker? Well, Mr. Martin is my houseguest and he's doing very nicely, thank you, despite the best efforts of your friend St. John. So why don't we just stop all this crap and get down to business? We're prepared to make you a sizable cash advance as a show of good faith."

I reached inside my suit coat and brought out an envelope stuffed with hundred-dollar bills. I set it down in the center of the table.

"That's fifty thousand dollars, William. Consider it a gift from your new partners."

Kraft took a sip of water, then calmly picked up the money and placed it in his lap. He looked around the room casually, resisting the urge to count the bills. When he was satisfied that the table next to us wasn't eavesdropping, he looked down quickly, just to check. We had him, you could see it in the eyes.

"There's just one other thing," I said as I watched him slip the envelope into a jacket pocket. "I want you to give me St. John."

Kraft stiffened again, but I kept on going.

"As I've already told you, Bill, Thomas Martin is a close, personal friend. He's very sick and I'm concerned that he won't be allowed to end his life quietly. We've tried to discourage your Mr. St. John, but it hasn't worked. Unless you can stop the man, I'll be forced to take appropriate action myself."

"Unfortunately, that's not possible," Kraft said, patting the bulge in his coat.

"This is nonnegotiable, Bill," I fired back, glaring at him.

"First of all, Mr. St. John cannot be taken off a project once it has been assigned to him. Believe me, it would confuse him in ways that might prove very dangerous. Second, you can forget about my giving him to you. My God, have you any concept of the time that goes into finding and then training *talent* suitable for my purposes?" he asked.

Something in my expression must have spooked him, because he suddenly turned and looked around the room, examining the other diners in the restaurant. When he finally turned back to me, he looked scared.

"I'm afraid I don't know what you're talking about, Mr. Donovan," he said, reversing himself deliberately and clearly. "It is obvious to me that you and your partner are of low moral character, intent upon some hideous and illegal game. I plan to make a full report of this conversation to the authorities after consultation with my attorney. Should you contact me again or make any public statements similar to those I've heard today, I will have charges brought against you. I find your actions reprehensible and I will not spend another moment in your presence. Good day, sir."

Kraft pushed his chair away from the table and rose stiffly.

Reaching into his coat pocket, he brought out the envelope and dropped his cash advance on the table.

"You're making a big mistake, Bill," I told him.

"I think not, Donovan," he sneered, then turned and marched out of the restaurant.

The waiter came over to see if everything was all right, but there was nothing he could do. I ordered a brandy and started doodling on the tablecloth with my teaspoon. Before long, Gavin dropped into Kraft's empty chair, opposite me.

"I almost had him," I moaned, as if almost counted for something.

"You let him spit the lure, son," Gavin said, picking up my brandy and knocking it back. "Remember, you've got to hook him before you can reel him in."

TWENTY-ONE

■ ■ ■

"Hey, nice goin', Donovan," Sweeney cracked.

We were inside the surveillance van, parked around the corner from the restaurant. In addition to myself, there were Lieutenant Gavin, the four plainclothes cops who'd been posing as diners, Sweeney, and a technician named Ralph Perillo. It was Ralph's job to monitor the tape decks and the control board inside the truck.

"Very smooth, tough guy. You really worked some magic in there."

Sweeney kept jabbing me with the needle. I had an urge to get up and smack him, but it passed. He was a project I could save for a rainy day.

The portable phone rang.

"It's for you, Lieutenant."

Perillo held out the cellular receiver.

I watched Gavin's scowl turn into a frown.

"How the hell did you manage that, Jack?" he snapped. "The son of a bitch is a preppie, for Christ's sake."

As Gavin listened, the lines deepened in his brow. He'd taken a pretty big risk by letting me participate in an official police operation.

"All right, I got it. Now, get your ass downtown and make it snappy."

He handed the phone back to the technician.

"That was *rookie* Officer Jack Bruce." Gavin sighed, shaking his head. "Kraft slipped the tail. I tell you, man, things are getting worse. We gotta find this guy."

He leaned back in his seat, closed his eyes and began rubbing his temples slowly. The rest of us kept quiet.

"Okay, Ralph, play it again," he said finally.

Perillo pushed some buttons on the console, and my luncheon conversation with William Kraft started playing on tiny speakers built into the walls of the van. When the tape finished playing, Gavin sat up.

"Well, I'd say we've got good news and bad news," he began, rubbing his hands together. "The good news is that Kraft fucked up when he acknowledged a relationship with St. John. The bad news is he knows it. A smart guy like Kraft, he's probably holed up somewhere figuring out his options."

"You'll excuse me for saying so, but I don't think you got anything, Lieutenant," Sweeney interrupted. "So Kraft knows the guy, what difference does that make? It certainly doesn't prove he killed anybody. Besides, it's not like you can produce St. John. I bet the guy don't even exist."

Detective Sweeney was too stupid to leave it alone.

"If I was this dude, Kraft," he continued, "I'd go right on with my business as usual. And I'd do like he said, I'd have my lawyer serve you with papers till you couldn't take a shit without the process server."

He chuckled, but his eyes were mean.

"Is that so, Bill?" Gavin shook his head again, finally giving up on him. "Tell you what, Detective. You head back to the precinct and get started doing the paperwork for this lunch meeting."

Sweeney grumbled under his breath, but he collected his gear and worked his way to the back of the van. He stepped down into the street, then turned and flicked his toothpick at me before slamming the door shut. Lieutenant Gavin sat in his chair looking tired and every bit his age.

218

"You two," he said, pointing at two of the cops who'd been in the restaurant. "I want you downtown. Check out Kraft's apartment building. For all the help he'll be, Officer Bruce will meet you there. Try to be patient with the kid. All right?" They nodded. "And remember, I want to know everything there is to know about this guy Kraft. Talk to the doormen, talk to his neighbors, talk to people in the lobby. And don't worry about causing a scene. It'll be good for his nerves to know we're in the neighborhood. If he shows up, you call me immediately."

Nobody moved.

"That's it, get going." Gavin clapped his hands.

The officers scrambled out of the van.

"Okay, Ralph, start it up," he ordered.

Perillo doubled as the driver.

"You can drop me off at the subway, Ralph," he said. "I'll meet the rest of you people in front of Life Line, Incorporated in two hours. I'm gonna get us a warrant."

He turned to me.

"For the record, Donovan, that rat Bill Sweeney is going to spend the afternoon writing an early retirement appraisal for me. He's a gnat, but he can make trouble. You follow?"

I nodded.

"Now, in a few minutes, I'm gonna pull a State Supreme Court judge out of his courtroom to get my warrant. If things keep going like they been going, I won't have many favors left to cover my ass. Do you understand me?"

I nodded again.

"So, is there anything else I should know, anything you haven't told me?"

I wasn't holding anything back, but I wasn't helping either. I glanced at my wristwatch.

"Look, Ray, I've got nothing to add and I'm probably just in the way here. Besides, I told Peter Walsh that I'd show up for Danner's memorial service. If it's all the same to you, I should get going, too."

Gavin studied my face, but he didn't try to stop me.

"All right, go," he said finally. "But I want you to check in with me later. You got that, Donovan?"

I may have nodded.

Before he switched hats and started driving us to the subway, Ralph Perillo patched a telephone call through to my house in Connecticut. Boris answered on the first ring.

"I'm afraid the news is bad," I said, getting right to the point. "Kraft was playing along just fine, he even pocketed the money. But then, at the very end of lunch, he got nervous and changed his mind. He threw the cash on the table and started ranting about slander and lawsuits. Before I knew what hit me, he'd stomped out of the restaurant. It was close, Boris, I almost had him. The only good news is that he talked about St. John, and Gavin has it on tape."

Boris didn't say anything.

"Are you all right?" I asked.

"I'm afraid I have bad news as well," he said quietly. "Patricia Gold is in the hospital."

"What happened?"

"Nothing happened, J. J.," he barked. "She has leukemia. Her bone marrow has been infiltrated by millions of deadly cells that are resistant to therapy. Apparently, she was recently given some blood and platelets, which fooled us by restoring her energy and making her seem stronger. The poor woman is even sicker than she appeared."

"Where is she now?"

"We've taken her to New Milford Hospital."

"What about Johnny St. John?" I asked, thinking the worst.

"What about him? There's no risk leaving her in a hospital. Johnny will have to hurry if he wants to participate in Mrs. Gold's death. Besides, Moses and Eduardo are standing guard.

Surprisingly, Thomas Martin also went with her. I couldn't dissuade him."

It took a minute to add up the score. Michael Adams was dead. Tim Danner was dead. Patricia Gold was dying. Thomas Martin and William Kraft were our only leads to Johnny. It occurred to me that Johnny St. John could just disappear.

"What do we do now?" I asked.

There was a pause.

"I don't know." Boris sighed.

Gavin and I walked into the subway station together, but we left on different trains. He was in a hurry, I wasn't. Before we parted, he told me not to look so depressed, that things would work out fine. I smiled back at him, but I wasn't too sure they would.

I drifted over to the subway platform and watched some rats scurrying along the tracks. When the downtown local arrived, I squeezed into a seat between a really fat black woman and an old Chinese guy. The car was full, but as usual, no one made eye contact or spoke. Most of the people stared at the advertisements for trade schools, abortion clinics, and bail bondsmen, which were posted on the walls and around the ceilings of the subway car.

After the third stop, a blind man with an empty Dunkin' Donuts coffee cup shuffled in from the car in front of ours. He moved to the center of the train, steadied himself like a sailor on a rolling deck, then launched into a recitation from the Book of Genesis. The old man's hair was an oily black-and-gray tangle, and he was pale as a ghost, hardly a match for Johnny St. John, but he still gave me the creeps. Call me crazy, but when I got off at Houston Street, I waited on the platform until the train pulled out, just in case the blind man tried to follow me.

The Church of the Nativity was in the middle of the block, on First Avenue between Fifth and Sixth Streets, so I headed uptown. It's a rough neighborhood, made tougher for the parish because it has to coexist with the cynical downtown crowd and all the junkies. The pastor, Father Dan Flynn, makes house calls to the sick and the elderly as far west as the Hudson River and north to 23rd Street.

It was still early, so I took a seat in the last pew, near the exit. The church was small and plain, with the usual hard wooden benches and plaster statues, but at least there were fresh-cut flowers on the altar, and the stained-glass windows had been thrown open, letting in sunlight and air. It was a nice surprise; I'd been expecting one of those dark, foreboding places where people speak in whispers.

As I sat in that empty little church, I tried to focus on Kate and the babies, but black-and-white images of Michael Adams, Patricia Gold, and Tim Danner kept blocking out my sun. Death wasn't just a sad inevitable fact of life anymore. Thanks to Johnny St. John and William Kraft, it overshadowed everything I did.

"Hey, man, you okay?"

Peter Walsh was standing next to me in the aisle. I'd been rocking back and forth and tapping my knees, like a speedball junkie. I took a deep breath and tried to shake it off. Peter patted my shoulder kindly.

While I rocked in agitated silence, the tiny church filled, till there was only standing room. In my ignorance, I'd expected an all-male assembly, but there were people of all ages and in all combinations.

As the service proceeded, Tim's friends and relatives got up and shared their memories with us, describing a good man whose life had touched and inspired them. I'd been right about the kid: he was someone special.

Right then and there, I decided there would be no more play-acting or schmoozing with the enemy. The next time I met William F. Kraft, IV, we wouldn't be sharing cocktails, and when we were finished, he definitely wouldn't walk away.

TWENTY-TWO

▪ ▪ ▪

"Thirty-year-old John Jameson's Red Breast. The finest Irish whiskey, unadulterated by ice or water," Peter Walsh informed me, putting a brimming glass down on the bar.

"This makes four, Mr. Walsh," I said, proving I could still count. "It's a good thing I'm not driving."

"And neither am I!" Peter shouted, filling his own glass and raising it. "To Timothy Danner, God bless him!"

Glasses were raised around the room. Peter Walsh drained his, refilled it, then leaned his elbows on the bar.

"So, tell me what the hell happened today," he asked, lowering his voice.

"Lieutenant Gavin says I tried to reel in my fish before he was hooked," I mumbled.

Peter made a face.

"You won't get away with feeling sorry for yourself in here, my friend. Remember, you've already gotten farther than the police would have. Be grateful for small steps—it takes more of them, but you'll get where you're going in the end."

"Is that some kind of homespun wisdom?" I asked.

"Drink more Jameson's, my boy, and it'll start to make sense to you."

I reached for my glass.

"By the way, did I forget to tell you about the babies?" I asked, closing one eye. "My ex-wife, the beautiful Kathleen Byrne, and I are going to have some babies."

"Excuse me?" Peter blinked. "Run that by me again."

"Kate Byrne, my ex-wife, is pregnant with twins. My twins. I'm going to be a father and Boris is going to be an uncle," I slurred happily.

"Well, I'll be damned, Papa. Good for you," Peter roared.

I put a finger to my lips. This was highly confidential news, until we got the results of the amniocentesis. Peter winked and shook my hand on our secret before running off to settle a dispute in the kitchen. The bar and dining room were crowded with people from the memorial service, so he had a lot to manage. I grabbed some pretzels from a basket on the bar and stood up a little straighter, feeling the whiskey in my shaky legs. I was just checking my tie in the mirror behind the bar, when a dull explosion rocked the building.

At first, no one moved, and then all hell broke loose. From where I stood, it looked like a car had blown up. You could see the burning shell just across the street, but the crowd quickly blocked my view as The Queen's Derby emptied out. I stayed where I was and grabbed a bar stool. I didn't need any more trouble. Besides, I was thinking about Gavin. I'd been trying to contact the lieutenant ever since I got to the bar, but he wasn't answering his beeper. Until I heard from him, I planned to stay right where I was.

I was sitting there on my stool, worrying my way through a fog of Irish whiskey, when a middle-aged man with a wild red hairdo came in from the street and perched on the stool next to mine. He was holding his wineglass delicately by the stem, his pinkie extended for effect and balance. I ignored him and looked out the window again, but there wasn't much to see except a lot of smoke and the crowd. Ignoring the hangover police inside my head, I reached back for my glass of Jameson's and choked down a sip. I'd had enough; the whiskey was starting to taste bitter.

"Do you believe this, a car blew up out there," my neighbor said, nudging me with his elbow. "It started a really scary fire."

Outside you could hear sirens and the fire trucks honking.

People were yelling and running up and down the street. I was glad I'd stayed at the bar.

"What can I tell you?" I said, ignoring my inner voice and drinking more whiskey. "Stuff happens all the time in the big city."

We sat in silence and contemplated our drinks.

"I guess you're feeling pretty bad about Timmy?" the red-headed guy asked. "I think I know how you feel. We all loved the kid."

I was going to tell him that if he knew how I felt, he'd know enough to leave me alone, but for some reason, the words wouldn't come out. I tried to lick my lips, but my mouth was suddenly parched. I took another sip of the whiskey, but it didn't help. Something was wrong. I looked at myself again in the bar mirror and my image was quivering. I blinked, but when I re-opened my eyes, my whole body seemed to be glowing. I'd had four drinks, not enough to bring on visions.

I stumbled into the bathroom and knelt down on the floor, grasping the toilet like a college kid at a beer blast. Things didn't get any better. My vision got blurrier and I started to fade in and out, like I was about to lose consciousness. It didn't make sense. If I'd had too much to drink, I would have felt nauseous, but that didn't happen. It was like I'd smoked really potent grass and the THC was messing with my head. I closed my eyes, took deep breaths and tried to remain calm.

Behind me, I heard the bathroom door open and close. After a pause, the door to my stall creaked open. When I turned and looked up, I was kicked in the side of the face. The force of the blow slammed my head into the pipes behind the toilet, opening a cut over my right eye. Before I could recover from the shock, I was dragged from the tiny stall, thrown against the sink and pummeled in the face, chest, and stomach. When the beating stopped, I slumped to the floor and curled up protectively.

"You're not nearly so smug now, are you, darling?"

225

I couldn't see very much. My vision was still blurred, and now there was blood running into my eyes. I wiped my face on my sleeve and blinked until the figure of my attacker started to come into focus. It was the man I'd been speaking to at the bar. I watched as he reached up and pulled off his red wig, exposing a full head of brilliant white hair. Johnny St. John smiled broadly.

"So, Donovan, we finally meet!" he announced happily, then walked over and kicked me hard in the chest.

"That's just for starters," he snarled as I lay gasping for breath. "I warned you and your fat friend not to interfere in my affairs."

I took a deep breath, then threw up on the floor.

"What's the matter, James, the belladonna doesn't agree with you?" he chuckled. "You know what the pharmacists say—'hot as a hare, dry as a bone, red as a beet, blind as a bat, mad as a hatter.' "

St. John laughed out loud and slapped his knee. I stop gagging and propped myself up against the wall. I'd been drugged. At least I could stop worrying about the symptoms.

"Now, let us get down to business, my friend," Johnny began, carefully unsheathing an ornate dagger that had been hidden inside the leg of his trousers. My eyes widened when I saw the blade.

"What's the matter, don't you like my needle?" he asked. "It's bigger than the one I used on young Tim. But then, one must adapt the tool to the need, I always say."

He flicked the blade at me, slicing through my pants and opening a long gash in my thigh. My leg was bleeding freely, and there was a steady trickle leaking down the side of my face, but St. John was just warming up.

"Where are my people?" he demanded. "My patience for this foolishness has ended."

"They're all dead," I lied. "By the way, I met your friend Kraft today, Johnny. He didn't have very nice things to say about you."

226

St. John stepped back, resting the knife casually on his shoulder.

"You don't show me any respect, James. This has been our problem from the beginning. I am a messenger from the Lord God, Himself. And yet, you show me no respect. Your bullets cannot stop me. The police cannot stop me." He spoke confidently. "Let us be honest. I saw you today, you and Kraft and all those ridiculously disguised policemen. Frankly, I should really be angry that you haven't proven to be a more worthy adversary. But then, I am only a servant doing as I am bid."

"Kraft gave you up, Johnny," I wheezed. "They'll be coming to take you back to the funny farm."

"You see what I mean, James?" He lashed out with the dagger again, slicing through my shirt and jacket, leaving an ugly cut in my arm. "No respect at all. You must stop these childish attempts at manipulation. Your lies serve no purpose. I have already tended to Mr. William Kraft. I relieved the poor man of his worldly cares. Unfortunately, I could not spare him the fires of Hell."

Johnny smiled.

"All right now, time to tell me everything," he said, taking a step closer and lowering the blade.

I searched the room, desperately looking for some way to defend myself, but it didn't materialize. As Johnny got closer, I raised my hands and arms above my head, sacrificing them to his blade in order to buy myself more time. I was on the verge of panic: my heart pounding, my breath coming in short gasps. Suddenly, the bathroom door swung open again. It was Riki, the tall, blond kid who'd made fun of me the night I had dinner with Tim Danner.

"Hey, what the fuck! No rough stuff, you two—" Riki began, stepping into the room.

Johnny wheeled and stabbed him in the abdomen before he could finish the sentence. The poor boy clutched St. John around the shoulders and looked down at me, pain and fear replacing his initial shock. I jumped to my feet, the adrenaline pumping through my frame, and grabbed Johnny St. John by his mane of white hair and yanked him backward, off balance. Then I started pounding him with all my strength.

The Right Hand of God was suddenly quite human. I hit him again and again, throwing all my weight into each of the punches. There was a sickening crack as Johnny's nose broke and blood began spurting from his nostrils. Riki had crumpled to the floor, clutching the hilt of the dagger. I gripped Johnny's hair with both hands and slammed his head into the towel dispenser next to the sink. Once, twice, the third time I cracked the mirror.

I had him staggered and bleeding, but I couldn't finish him off. When my grip weakened, St. John squirmed free and ran across the room. He stopped at the door and tried to say something, but I was already screaming at the top of my lungs, the tears and blood streaming down my face.

I blinked and when I looked again, Peter Walsh was standing in the doorway holding a hurly stick like a battle-ax. I tried to take a step toward him, then collapsed as the room went black.

TWENTY-THREE

■ ■ ■

I dreamed in deep, lush colors: dark purples and crimson reds. They were frustrating, violent dreams in which I tried, but never found, a way to make things better. When I awoke, it was morning and there was a crowd hovering around my bed. I felt like Dorothy in *The Wizard of Oz*.

Lieutenant Gavin was standing near the foot of the bed, his hands wrapped in gauze, looking very weary. Peter Walsh was dozing in a chair in the corner. I could see Thomas Martin through the French doors, smoking and pacing up and down on my terrace. Boris had somehow conveyed himself and his oversized wheelchair from Connecticut to my bedroom. He was brooding, his nose stuck in a book. Manny Santos was fidgeting in the background, looking worried. And my loyal friend Angus was sitting next to the bed with his head on my pillow. I could hear his tail wagging.

When I tried to sit up, they all started moving and talking at once. I'd taken a pretty good beating, but I didn't need that much attention. Still, there was no point in arguing. I relaxed and let them fluff my pillows and pour me water. A minute later, Richard Steinman came in from the living room.

"How's the patient feeling?" he asked cheerfully.

I was busy draining a glass of water.

"Atropine," Rich declared. "The bastard gave you atropine. You have, or had, all the symptoms—dilated pupils, thirst, disorientation. When the lab work comes back, we'll know for sure, but I'd be surprised if I'm wrong. Did you taste something bitter in your drink last night?"

I nodded, still gulping down the water.

"And then you became disoriented? Thirsty?"

I nodded again.

"Atropine. Belladonna. It's a classic." Richard seemed pleased. "You had a good long sleep and we did a bit of sewing, but you should be much better by now. Am I right? How are you feeling this morning?"

"Very sore," I said, putting down the empty water glass. "My face feels like one big bruise. Before I start scaring young children, you better let me inspect the damage."

Richard got a hand mirror from my dresser.

"By the way, if you guys are engaged in some kind of weird competition," he joked waving a hand toward Boris, "he is still way ahead on points. You didn't break anything bigger than your nose, and you took many fewer stitches than he did."

I examined my face in the glass. It was red and swollen, but it looked much worse than I felt. There were stitches above my right eye and on the bridge of my nose, but nothing like the huge scar running across Boris's cheek and jaw. The worst injury was to my beloved nose. When I passed out, I broke the fall with my face, squashing my nose. I flexed all the major joints in my body without difficulty, although the sutures on my chest and thigh were painfully obvious.

"Okay, you can all relax now. I'm fine, and I'm getting up," I announced, causing another general panic.

"Perhaps you should try to eat something first, J. J.," Richard suggested. "I find it helps strengthen the legs."

Ignoring good advice, I sat right up and had my feet over the side of the bed before anyone could stop me. But when I tried to stand up, the room began to wobble. I decided that breakfast wasn't such a bad idea after all.

"So, give me the bad news," I said, taking a deep breath. "I can see it in your faces."

No one spoke.

"Okay, let's start with you, Lieutenant. Why are your hands wrapped in bandages?"

Gavin put his hands behind his back, then looked at Boris and Rich Steinman. Richard just shrugged. Apparently, the news wouldn't kill me.

"Come on, Ray, this isn't the time to get cute."

He sighed.

"Well, this Johnny St. John was a busy man yesterday. Before he got to you, he found William Kraft and carved him up like a side of beef."

"Johnny bragged about that, said he'd relieved Kraft of his worldly cares. Only, he wasn't able to spare him from Hell's fires."

"That's real cute," Gavin grimaced. "St. John caught up with Kraft at his office. As far as we can tell, Kraft was shredding files. Anyway, St. John managed to strap Mr. Kraft to a chair with gaffer's tape, then sliced him up pretty bad. Probably used that nasty blade he left in Mr. Berglund."

"Who's Berglund?" I asked.

"Riki Berglund. The kid who walked in on you and St. John."

"Oh, right," I mumbled. "Riki."

"We'll get to that later," Gavin said. "Right now, I'm telling you about your friend William F. Kraft, the Fourth."

Ray Gavin was upset and he didn't know what to do with his bandaged hands. He tried rubbing his chin with one of them, but that was awkward. Finally, he just shoved them in the pockets of his sports jacket.

"Anyway, when this St. John got tired of cutting your man Kraft, he doused the son of a bitch with gasoline and set him on fire. We don't know if Kraft was still alive when the fire started, but he sure wasn't by the time the blaze was out. You see, it took a while to get to the body. St. John had spilled a lot of gas on his way out, burned up a couple of floors of the building."

"And your hands?" I asked.

"Lieutenant Gavin was burned while helping to evacuate the building," Boris said, speaking up for the first time.

I was starting to feel light-headed. I grabbed the pitcher and refilled my glass.

"And, what about Patricia Gold?" I asked between sips.

"Mrs. Gold died yesterday," Thomas Martin said, coming in from the terrace. "It was four o'clock in the afternoon. She was sleeping peacefully at the time."

The walls were starting to close in around me.

"The kid who was with me—Riki. How's he doing?"

Silence.

"Come on, tell me. What happened to the kid?"

"He's dead, too, J. J.," Peter Walsh said finally. "He died on the way to the hospital. I got there too late to help him or to settle up with that white-haired bastard. Can you believe it? I let the man run right past me out the door. We had him and I let him get away."

"Don't go there, Peter," I said softly. "The man is very cunning. You did what you could, and probably saved my life in the process."

The death roll had certainly filled out in the last twenty-four hours. The only names missing from Johnny's list were mine, Thomas Martin's, and Boris's. I had a different list—it had only one name on it.

"Was anyone else hurt?" I asked Gavin. "You said Johnny set the building on fire. And then there was the car bomb outside the restaurant. Was that St. John's work, too?"

"It was a very convenient explosion," Gavin muttered. "It cleared the bar out and that made it easier to get at you. Anyway, to answer your question, there were no deaths at either the building fire or the car bombing, just minor burns and cuts from broken glass."

A dim ray of light had appeared.

"Well, that's good news," I exclaimed, brightening.

My friends looked at me like I was delirious. Fortunately, the clang of the telephone distracted them. It was for the lieutenant.

"Gavin here," he said, gently cradling the receiver with his injured hands. "Uh-huh, right. It was a fancy-looking dagger. Yeah, that's the one. Right, I got that part. You're kidding! No, no, that's great! What's the address?"

He looked up, smiling.

"Somebody get me a piece of paper," he said. "No, I'm still here. This is the best news I've had in weeks."

"Go ahead, Lieutenant," Boris said, producing a pen and pad.

"Okay, I'm ready," Gavin said into the receiver. "The address is One-three-oh State Street, Brooklyn Heights, between Henry Street and Clinton. What's the apartment number? Basement. I've got it and I'm on my way. What? You bet your ass I'm coming out there. This is my baby, Sergeant. I don't want anybody making a move until I get there. Is that clear?"

He hung up and turned to us.

"We got a break, people. They lifted prints from St. John's dagger and made a match. Johnny St. John is a registered nurse named James Phalon. He lives in Brooklyn Heights. That's all I know right now, but they're putting a complete bio together."

I threw the covers off again and made another attempt to get out of bed. This time, the room didn't rock or sway, but it didn't matter. Gavin wouldn't let me go with him.

"Get your ass back in that bed," he ordered. "You're done, kid. This is police work and we're good at it."

He picked up the phone and called his driver. The car was waiting out front, so he started running.

"Don't worry," he yelled back over his shoulder. "I'll let you know what happens."

*   *   *

After all the excitement, it was kind of anticlimactic to be left behind while Gavin put Johnny out of business. Don't get me wrong, it was good news. I had just assumed that I'd be there at the finish.

"So what are we supposed to do now?" I sighed.

"Why don't you try to relax and get your strength back?" Rich Steinman advised. "I have patients to see up at the hospital, so I'm leaving. Put some food in your stomach, sleep as much as possible, and drink plenty of fluids."

"Oh yes, Doctor," I said with exaggerated humility. "I'm planning to eat enormous Spanish olives and hydrate myself liberally with brimming, ice-cold vodka martini's."

"No you're not," he snapped. "I'm not kidding J. J., I'll be checking in."

Boris sighed impatiently.

"Thank you for everything, Richard. Manuel and I will see that he behaves himself."

"Well, good luck."

Dr. Steinman picked up his medical bag and left us to fend for ourselves.

I didn't much like the idea of Boris and Santos as my sitters, but it wasn't worth an argument. I grabbed the hand mirror and took another look at my broken nose. While I was busy inspecting my swollen profile, you could hear pots and pans banging in the kitchen and a woman's soprano voice issuing rapid-fire instructions in Spanish. Manny and his wife, Gina, had arrived with my food. Thomas Martin and Peter Walsh went to help her, leaving Boris and me alone for the first time since I'd left Brookfield. We looked like a couple of broken old warriors.

"So, how are you really feeling?" he asked.

"Sore. Uncomfortable. Weak. Excited that they've found Johnny. I was starting to worry that he'd simply vanish into thin air. How're you doing?"

By way of an answer, Boris stood up and reached for a pair of crutches leaning against the wall. His movements were awkward and he dwarfed the slim aluminum braces, but it was progress. I also noticed that the stitches were gone from his face, leaving a long, pink, healthy-looking scar. The old Boris was beginning to emerge.

"Hey, that's great, man," I said as he moved around the room. "What about the casts? When do you get to shed the plaster?"

"In a week or so," he said proudly. "I must say it feels good to be home again. Oh, and thank God for take-out food. If I had to eat any more of Manny's rice and beans, I think I'd wither away."

Boris didn't look like he was in any danger of starving to death, but he did seem more preoccupied than usual. He hobbled back to his wheelchair and sat down heavily. As we talked, it became obvious how deeply the loss of Patricia Gold weighed on him. When Gavin had called to tell him about the attack in the bathroom, Patricia was already dead, so Boris and Thomas had decided to come out of hiding. The Santos boys had closed up the Connecticut house and they'd all come back to New York City.

We sat in silence for a few minutes.

"What's wrong, Boris?" I asked. "Do you think we screwed this thing up?"

He took a long time before answering.

"No, James," he said at last, "I don't think we did badly, all things considered. This affair was thrust upon us by chance, or fate. We barely had time to react, let alone plan an intelligent response. Events have unfolded much too quickly for us to assume the blame. It's just that I'm left feeling so very mortal."

"Hey, join the human race, pal."

"Right," he smiled. "Well, let's hope this business really is over."

"What makes you say that?" I was surprised.

"You don't expect them to find St. John so easily, do you?" Boris asked.

"The man took a good beating last night," I boasted. "He's

235

got to go somewhere to lick his wounds, and Brooklyn's as good a place as any. Even if he's not at home, they've got enough now to track him down."

Boris looked up quickly, then shook his head, erasing the thought.

"What?" I asked.

"It was nothing," Boris replied. "It's just that I forgot to tell you that Kate called."

I brightened instantly.

"When?"

"Last night."

"And? How's she doing, how's Colorado?"

"Well, that's just it." Boris hesitated. "She's back already. It seems she took care of business in record time and caught an early flight. She's at home, on the East Side. I didn't tell her about your injuries. It seemed unwise to upset her. I mean, with the pregnancy and all."

He was nervous.

"You were right, of course," I said, but my nerve endings were dancing, too. I picked up the telephone and dialed Kate's apartment. The call was answered on the third ring.

"Hello? Jamie, is that you?"

It was Kate's voice.

"Hi, honey. How was your trip?" I shouted, relieved to hear her voice. "Are you feeling all right?"

Before she could answer, a second voice came on the line.

"Don't worry, honey, she's just fine. And Jamie, I want you to know, she's keeping me really amused."

It was Johnny St. John.

TWENTY-FOUR

■ ■ ■

"Listen to me, you bastard," Johnny hissed. "With a flick of my wrist, your woman and the children she carries will cease to exist. So I warn you, be very careful."

I sat on the edge of the bed, afraid to breathe.

"I heard you talking to that homo bartender last night. It was pathetic. You were so drunk you were slurring your words."

Johnny was panting.

"And don't misinterpret the events of last evening, Donovan. You cannot hurt me. The Lord was merely teaching me a lesson by empowering you. Conceit and overconfidence are dangerous vices. Thankfully, I have seen the error of those ways."

My heart was pounding so hard I was afraid he'd hear it.

"And now, to business," Johnny said, the tension in his voice easing. "I want you to pretend this call is from your pregnant girlfriend and that you're having a pleasant little chat. There's no reason for us to involve your visitors at this point. Do you understand me?"

"Yes," I murmured, wondering how he knew I wasn't alone.

"Put some imagination into your answers," he snapped.

"Oh, come on, Kate, you know me," I ad-libbed.

"That's much better," Johnny said happily. "In a few minutes, I will expect you and that fat partner of yours to drive over here to Sutton Place. I believe you know the address?"

"I can't wait to see you," I said truthfully.

"Good boy, you're performing very well." Johnny sounded calmer. "And James, make sure to bring Mr. Martin with you, too. I just happened to see him prancing about on your terrace earlier today. Imagine my surprise—Thomas Martin isn't dead after all."

A shiver coursed its way up my spine. He'd been watching the building. Johnny started to chuckle again, then stopped abruptly.

"Be forewarned, little man," he snarled, "that if you speak to the police or alert anyone else, I will kill your little sweetie. Is that clear?"

"Yes."

I allowed myself a deep breath as Johnny began to recite: " 'Each of them was given a white robe, and they were told to be patient a little while longer until the number was filled of their fellow servants and brothers who were going to be killed as they had been.' "

The words came out with difficulty, his voice cracking. Johnny St. John was losing his tenuous grip, decompensating a bit more with each radical mood swing.

"Okay, great, how are you feeling, Kate? Is everything all right at work?" I asked, hoping to bring him back to reality.

There was a long, uncomfortable silence.

"You mean is your little whore safe?" Johnny whispered, finally. "She's just fine for the moment, Donovan. Now, do as I say and get over here. You have one hour. If you're late, she dies. If you, Martin, and the Russian are not alone, she dies. If you follow instructions and arrive on time, the good news is that she may live."

There was another torturous interval with only the sound of his uneven breathing. Then Johnny began to giggle.

"Unfortunately, the three of you will not be so lucky," he said at last. "That's the price, my dear—you and your friends for the lady and her babies."

I held my breath, afraid to speak.

"Now, say good-bye, and come face your destiny."

Boris was holding his head with both hands, staring at me. He could read the news in my expression. I opened my mouth to speak, but words refused to come. I was terrified. There wasn't time for planning or discussion, we had to act immediately. I yelled down the hall to Manny Santos, Peter Walsh, and Thomas Martin, then started getting dressed.

"Yo man, wha's up?" Manny asked, bounding into the room.

"I need the leem-o," I said, wincing as I pulled on my trousers.

"Can't do, babe. Dr. Steinman said you gotta rest. So, no car for you."

Manny was in a good mood again.

"Listen up, Santos, this isn't a joke!" I yelled. "He's got Kate!"

Manny gave me a blank look.

"The white-haired guy, St. John, he's got Kate!" I shouted again. "So you get that car now. Please, Manny. There's no time to lose."

He turned to Boris, who nodded; then he ran for the front door.

"You're not serious?" Thomas Martin asked, going pale.

"Oh yes I am."

I pulled the drawer of my nightstand open and took out my Beretta.

"Dead serious."

Forty-four minutes later, the leem-o screeched to a stop in the cul-de-sac next to Kate's building, on 55th Street between Sutton Place and the river terrace. We'd taken the big car because Boris couldn't ride in my Nova, not with his leg in a cast. I killed the engine and ran for the lobby, leaving Thomas Martin to help Boris out of the car. The gilded entrance foyer was deserted; no doorman, no porter, no one coming or going.

There wasn't time for an elevator. I darted up the stairs, leaping two at a time. When I reached Kate's floor, I stopped and caught my breath; no point racing into a death trap. The hallway was empty. At the far end, the door to Kate's apartment was ajar. I walked slowly down the corridor, my footsteps hushed against the carpet, then stopped again at the entrance.

Using my left hand, I pushed the front door open slowly and peeked inside. Kate's handsome marble foyer was awash in blood. There was a big, oblong, sticky puddle in the middle of the floor, and there were dark spatterings on the baseboards and walls. The artist had left his signature, emphatically stamping his handprint on the mirror hanging on the opposite wall.

At the far end of the foyer, on the floor below the archway leading into the living room, I could just see the soles of a man's black oxfords. The man was still wearing them. He wasn't moving.

Behind me, the elevator bell rang as Boris and Thomas Martin arrived. I turned and watched Boris struggle with his crutches. His face was so pale it seemed almost translucent, making the long pink scar on his cheek and jaw line glow. I took a deep breath and crossed the threshold into the living room.

Nothing happened. I walked over to check on the shoes. Their occupant was one of the doormen, a nice enough guy, named Bobby Biolsi. Too nice a man for this kind of death. Bob's throat had been slit from ear to ear, cutting right through the spinal cord. It was a vicious, bloody wound. His head was barely attached to his shoulders. Johnny had obviously honed his technique since his botched attempt on Boris. I reached my hand back and checked to make sure the Beretta was still clipped to my belt.

There was nothing to do for Bob Biolsi, so I moved on, drawn to the bedroom by a hint of light under the door. Behind me, I heard Thomas Martin gasp when he discovered the unhappy remains, but I ignored him. I was focused on the bedroom. Reaching the door, I knocked softly.

"You may enter," Johnny called out from somewhere deep inside the room.

I grasped the knob, turned it quickly and threw the door wide open. It was an eerie scene. The blinds had been drawn and the lights were off. The bedroom was dimly lit by several small votive candles, whose flickering wicks cast dancing shadows on the walls. As my eyes slowly adjusted to the light, I searched the room for Kate. I found Johnny first.

I've thought about that moment a hundred times. Why didn't I just pull out my gun and shoot him? God knows, it wasn't because I'm gun shy. The answer is simple. I hesitated because I knew that Johnny expected me to do something rash. It was really hard, but I forced myself to wait.

St. John was seated in a large, upholstered wingback chair next to the bed. The self-appointed Angel of Death was casually dressed in black jeans and a red turtleneck sweater. His legs were crossed and he was leaning back, smirking at me, only he didn't look so good. One of his front teeth was chipped, his nose was badly swollen, and there were dark ugly bruises on his face and chin.

Kate was lying on the bed. She was wearing black stretch pants and an oversized white T-shirt. Johnny had tied her ankles and wrists to the corners of the antique four-poster. There was duct tape across her mouth, but she was struggling to speak and frantically rolling her eyes, pleading with me to get away. I started toward the bed.

"Don't move!" Johnny shouted.

He produced a large carving knife, and leaning forward, held it against Kate's stomach.

"One more step and I will terminate your future," he snarled.

Kate stopped struggling and lay quietly, staring up at the ceiling. She was breathing heavily and her shirt was wet with perspiration. I turned back to Johnny St. John, with hatred in my eyes.

"For God's sake, Donovan, spare us the melodrama," he muttered.

"You can put that weapon aside now, Mr. Phalon. We have all arrived, as you wished."

At the sound of his real name, Johnny flinched. Boris stood filling the doorway, supported on his aluminum crutches. Thomas Martin was behind him, peeking over his shoulder.

"Ah, finally the good doctor and, with him, my wayward lamb, Mr. Thomas Martin. Welcome, gentlemen." Johnny smiled.

"We have come as directed," Boris said slowly, his lips barely moving. "Now, release the woman."

"I'm sorry to say it isn't that easy, Doctor. First, some preliminaries. Donovan, you will oblige me by securing your fat partner and his pudgy gay friend in those chairs."

Johnny pointed to a couple of dining-room chairs near the bedroom door. There was a roll of silver duct tape on the seat of each chair. No one moved.

"Why all the killing, Mr. Phalon?" Boris asked.

"Phalon? Who is this Mr. Phalon?" Johnny blinked, then looked from side to side.

"Very well." Boris sighed. "I direct the question to Mr. St. John." There was a pause, as Johnny sat up straighter in his chair.

"It is the Lord's will, Doctor," he finally whispered.

"Then I take it your god is somewhat flawed," Boris replied. "I am surprised to learn that, Mr. Phalon. Very surprised."

"The name is St. John, fat man," he snapped. "And, no, my god is not flawed. Quite the opposite—my god is infinite and perfect."

"So, then, I repeat the question—why all the killings? These people you've been sacrificing are already dead with disease. A perfect god wouldn't need to strike twice."

"It is His will."

"Do you mean it is God's will to see people suffer?"

"Yes. It gives Him pleasure."

"Ah, then your god is flawed," Boris repeated. "A Perfect Being could not find pleasure in the pain and suffering of lesser creatures. I am sure you see the point."

If Johnny saw the point, he didn't say so. Instead, he stared at Boris and slowly licked his lips.

"You will sit in the chairs as I've asked," he said softly, lifting Kate's T-shirt and setting the blade against her bare abdomen.

"Fine. As you wish," Boris conceded, moving awkwardly into the room.

When he and Thomas Martin were both seated, I took duct tape and strapped them tightly to their chairs. It was a sickening feeling. I was immobilizing the only people who could have helped.

"Stand back, get away from there," Johnny ordered when I finished the taping. "I have something very special in mind for you, Donovan."

Johnny stood up and started giggling. The big carving knife was gripped tightly in his right hand. In his left, he held a pair of handcuffs that he dangled between his thumb and index finger.

"You will kindly remove your shirt," he snickered, unable to suppress his excitement.

I stripped out of my shirt and threw it on the bed. Kate was moving again, her chest rising and falling as tears began to well up in her eyes. Johnny was far too busy with me to notice. He'd even lowered the blade as he focused on the ritual he was staging for me.

"Oh, very nice," he said, admiring the stitches in my arm. He threw the handcuffs at me. "On your knees, Donovan, hands cuffed behind the back."

Kneeling, I clipped one of the handcuffs to my right wrist, then put both hands behind my back. The second cuff made a distinctive clicking sound as it locked shut. Johnny stepped away from the bed and started toward me, his knife gleaming in the reflected candlelight.

"This is going to be a distinct pleasure," he began. "I want these other people to see just how painful and final the judgment of God can be."

He raised the knife and came at me quickly, covering the distance between us much faster than I'd expected. I rolled to my left and came up in a crouch, both hands in front, firmly holding my Beretta. Johnny stopped short, obviously surprised that my hands were free.

"Move a muscle and I'll put a bullet between your eyes," I shouted, the locked handcuffs dangling from my right wrist.

Johnny ignored me. He feigned a move toward Kate, then jumped in the opposite direction. I fired, missing badly. Kate started struggling wildly against her restraints, distracting me long enough for St. John to shove the big wingback chair at me. I fired a second time, grazing his shoulder, but it didn't faze him. Johnny was diving at me, the knife held out in front of him. I fired again and tried to roll out of the way, but it was too late. The knife caught me in the gut, on the right side, just above my belt.

The blade went in hard, the pain searing into me like a hot poker. I grabbed Johnny's wrist and held it while we struggled for my gun. The blade was moving, grinding away at my insides while we fought. The pain was unbearable. Johnny must have sensed my weakness because he let go of my gun hand and tried to punch me in the face. I absorbed a hard blow to the forehead, and somehow managed to get off another shot. This time, I fired point-blank, putting a crease down the side of his head. The force of the bullet knocked Johnny back off his feet, leaving a bright-red part in his white hair.

Without thinking, I reached down and pulled the long, skinny knife out of my side, nearly fainting in the process. It was a fateful choice; I should have plugged St. John. Before I could react, he was up and running out the door. As he came past me, he planted a foot in my chest, knocking me flat. The Beretta flew across the room and I lay stunned for a moment, coughing and sucking for air. Refusing to give in to the pain, I managed to roll onto my stomach and crawl over to Boris.

Finding Johnny's knife, I sawed through the duct tape strapping him to the chair. When Boris was free, I stumbled across the room and retrieved my gun. Boris cut Thomas Martin loose, and they went to help Kate. I took several deep breaths, clearing my head, then hobbled over to the bed. I picked up my shirt and tied it around my waist, stemming the flow of blood from the wound in my side.

Kate was staring up at me, her cheeks wet and spotted from crying, her eyes wide with fear and full of questions. I reached down and pulled the tape off her mouth, but she didn't speak. Her lower lip began to quiver, and the tears came again. I leaned over and kissed her full on the mouth, then gathered her in my arms.

When she stopped shaking, I looked deep into her eyes promising things I couldn't guarantee. Then I stood up and headed for the door.

TWENTY-FIVE

■ ■ ■

I reached the street just in time to see Johnny St. John steal a big, expensive off-road safari vehicle. He was more than half a block away, at the corner of 56th Street and Sutton Place, but his head of blue white hair stood out like a beacon.

The driver was out of the car, lying in the street, curled into a protective ball, and Johnny was savagely kicking him. The poor man had probably been sitting at the red light, minding his own business, when St. John bushwhacked him. The man couldn't know how lucky he was that Johnny didn't have his knife.

I yelled, and St. John paused long enough to look back. When he saw my face, he beamed like a kid who doesn't want the game to end. Laughing hysterically, he kicked the hapless driver one more time, then jumped into the vehicle. I ran to the corner and got into the leem-o, keeping Johnny in sight. I was just pulling away from the curb, thinking I'd never be able to make up a three-block lead, when I saw Johnny run the red light at 57th Street and drive straight into the side of an old Checker taxicab.

Bad for Johnny, good for me. I gave the leem-o some gas, closing the distance between us. Up ahead, St. John threw his stolen tank into reverse, disentangling it from the cab. He backed up about twenty feet, shifted gears and gunned the engine, ramming the old Checker again. The second blow destroyed the cab, undoubtedly crushing any passengers. It infuriated me. I held the gas pedal on the floor and braced myself, the nose of the leem-o aiming directly for Johnny. I caught up to him just as he was backing up for another assault on the crippled taxi.

Braking enough to keep control, I put my head down and drove into the back of Johnny's stolen vehicle. I caught the rear panel and bumper, spinning it around one hundred and eighty degrees, away from the cab. The leem-o absorbed the blow, then skidded sideways into a lamppost. Both cars stalled, and we sat facing each other through our windshields as we pumped gas pedals and worked the keys in our ignitions.

All around us, cars were honking, and I could hear the wail of a siren. Johnny's car started first and he flipped his middle finger at me, before peeling out in a cloud of pebbles and broken glass. The leem-o finally started, but it took me some time to navigate around the twisted shell of the taxi. When I got clear of the wreckage, I pointed the big car up 57th Street and floored it again. This time, the leem-o choked and hesitated instead of picking up speed.

A block and a half ahead, Johnny made a right turn onto the Queensborough Bridge entrance ramp. It was a bad choice. The bridge is always congested, especially in the early evening. But St. John wasn't thinking about traffic. He raced up the ramp and plowed into the back of a big silver Mercedes Benz. The Mercedes was stuck behind a long line of cars inching its way across the bridge, and the force of the collision started a chain reaction. The Benz hit the car in front and that car hit the next one, and so on. Moments later, I came chugging up behind Johnny's car, the leem-o smoking like a steam locomotive, and blocked his escape.

A crowd was forming as owners and passengers from the damaged cars tried to figure out what had happened. Johnny stepped down from his vehicle and confronted them with a snarl. He was bruised and battered, with blood running down the side of his face from the bullet wound to his scalp. The group fell back in silence, clearly afraid. Without saying a word, Johnny pushed past them and took off on foot across the bridge, headed for Queens.

In the past twenty-four hours, I had been drugged, slashed, beaten, and then stabbed. A footrace was the last thing I needed. Struggling to get out of the leem-o, I braced my right arm tightly against my side, and started to jog after him. I wasn't sure of exactly where he'd gone, but I knew he was in front of me.

When I passed the first tower, the road surface moved under a heavy mesh covering. I kept on jogging till my gut started to burn, then I slowed to a walk. Traffic was bumper-to-bumper in both directions on the bridge, but no one paid much attention to me. A crazed, shirtless man with a stomach wound, staggering onto the bridge at rush hour, was no big deal. No questions asked. No help offered. Welcome to New York.

The sweat was running off me and I was breathing hard, wondering how I get myself into these situations, when a hefty chunk of metal whizzed past my head, destroying the windshield in the car next to me. I ducked behind a girder and searched for Johnny in the cobweb of wires and steel overhead. When a second bolt flashed past me, I spotted him crouching up in the superstructure of the bridge. Drawing my Beretta, I aimed and pulled off two quick shots.

The bullets went a bit wide of the mark, but they came close enough to startle him, upsetting the bucket of rivets he'd been using for ammunition. As the heavy steel bolts rained down on the cars below, breaking windows and denting finishes, Johnny began to climb. I put my gun back in its holster and took a deep breath.

My three basic phobias are hospitals, churches, and heights; meaning I'd been served a psychic hat trick in the last week. It wasn't really that hard a climb; there were plenty of hand- and footholds, but the wind was blowing at about thirty miles an hour and the tower I was about to climb was two hundred feet above the East River. An impressive fall, even by circus standards. I took another deep breath and started climbing.

Johnny wasn't doing so well either. Every once in a while, he would stop and look down at me, sizing up my progress. He had been knocked around pretty well the night before, and now I'd dinged him with at least two bullets. He was moving slowly, and more than once, I saw him lose his grip. Up ahead of him, at a point where the central truss was bolted to the tower, I noticed some sort of platform. Johnny was headed right for it. I was less than fifty feet below him, but he would have the advantage if he got settled on that platform and was able to defend himself against me from above.

When he turned his back to continue climbing, I moved sideways, out of his line of sight. That put me on the outside of the superstructure, directly over the murky river flowing far below us. Because of the angle of the superstructure as it approached the center span of the tower, I was now in for a much harder climb. On the other side of the bridge, the Roosevelt Island tramway car went sailing past; the passengers were glued to the windows watching us. Apparently, New York City was finally taking notice.

If you're afraid of heights, they say you should never look down. I took a good look, and I can tell you they're right, it makes things worse. I could see boats moving on the river, and lots of tiny, flashing lights as police cars and emergency-services vehicles slowly made their way through the traffic. I didn't have any way to know it, but Lieutenant Gavin had commandeered one of these emergency medical trucks and it was carrying Boris and Thomas Martin to the bridge, so they could all watch me do a belly flop from the high dive.

When the shaking in my limbs subsided, I worked up the courage to start climbing again. I tried to dry my sweaty palms, but that was just a waste of time. Fortunately, I now had the advantage because Johnny couldn't see me. And with the wind howling, he couldn't hear me either.

"Come on, Donovan, come and get me!" he shouted.

It took about ten minutes and most of the strength I had left, but I made it to the top of the span. Grabbing hold of the high-tension wires, I pulled myself up on the cap surrounding the top of the tower. Johnny was less than fifteen feet below me on the work platform jutting out over the water. He was very agitated, leaning over the side looking for me. It never occurred to him that I had simply climbed past him.

I took out my Beretta and checked the clip. There were two bullets left; not exactly an arsenal. Fortunately I had painted a little white-out on the sites, making it easier to aim in the semi-darkness. A police officer, looking down at the suspect from above, would have had to consider the appropriate use of force and Johnny's civil rights. I didn't have any rules to follow. Besides, we'd already tried having a meaningful dialogue.

So I shot him.

The bullet struck Johnny in the right hip, knocking him flat. I was aiming for the knee, but the wind was a factor and my hands were shaking from the climb. To be honest, as long as it dropped him, I didn't really care where it hit him. Using one of the steel cables, I slid down to the platform.

Johnny moved to one side and raised himself to a sitting position. He was bleeding pretty good, probably from the exit wound in his butt. I kept my gun pointed at his chest.

"I suppose you think this is some sort of victory," he said.

"All I know is that you're done with killing innocent people."

I was breathing hard and had to keep blinking my eyes to stay focused.

"You can't be serious, Donovan. It's not over. You cannot stop the Hand of the Lord."

A searchlight suddenly flashed on, lighting up the sky and startling both of us. Below the platform, policemen in dark jumpsuits were rapidly climbing up toward the tower.

"You're a sick man, Mr. Phalon," I said. "If I didn't think that was true, I'd give you a little shove and see how well you can fly."

251

"My name is Johnny Saint John!" he screamed, struggling to rise. "You would do well to keep that in mind, you odious creature."

When Johnny stood, I stood, my gun still trained directly at his chest. He slowly raised his hands above his head and began to invoke the twisted revelations of the "god" who spoke to him. He lifted his voice over the sound of the wind, and bore into me with those black eyes.

"The beast was caught and with it the false prophet who had performed in its sight the signs by which he led astray those who had accepted the mark of the beast and those who had worshipped its image. The two were thrown alive into the fiery pool burning with sulfur."

Johnny St. John finished speaking, but continued to stare at me across the short distance that separated us. Below we could now hear the voices of the SWAT team officers as they drew closer to us. I blinked, fighting exhaustion and the pain in my side. In that millisecond of time, he lunged for me, grabbing the handcuffs locked on my right wrist, then rolled backward off the platform. He was a big man, and his weight almost carried me over with him. Luckily, I was able to hook one of my legs around a heavy cable, and hung on for dear life. My head and arms were over the platform, stretched painfully by the dead weight as Johnny dangled in midair. I dropped my Beretta and grasped St. John's wrist with my left hand.

Time seemed to move slowly in the surreal glow of the spotlights now trained on our high-wire act. A helicopter swooped in low over our heads, and ropes spilled out, uncoiling onto the platform. Dark shapes emerged from the cabin as policemen began sliding down toward our tiny perch.

"Donovan?"

It was Johnny.

"Hold on!" I shouted.

"Donovan, I'm talking to you!"

I looked away from the helicopter and the rescue team and down at Johnny St. John, the muscles of my arms stinging, the pain in my side growing unbearable. He stared up at me and smiled.

"Fuck you, Donovan," he shouted above the wind and the sound of the helicopter. "I'll see you in Hell."

Then he let go of the handcuffs and started wriggling, trying to break my hold.

"Hey, Johnny, wait a minute!" I yelled, hoping to buy some time. "I need to ask you something."

He stopped fighting and looked back up at me.

"Before you leave, I need to know what happened to Sheila Mooney."

He didn't say anything.

"You remember Sheila, Johnny," I shouted. "She was the little old lady nurse who looked after Michael Adams."

I was grabbed from behind by several strong men who held tight and began to secure me into some sort of harness. There was silence from Johnny.

"Well, I'm waiting!"

James Phalon, otherwise known as Johnny St. John, looked around slowly, taking in the breathtaking lights of New York City sparkling in the night all around us. Then he raised his face till our eyes met again. I turned cold, remembering the fear in Boris's voice as he described those shadowy black eyes. Instead of answering my question, Johnny smiled. It was a wicked little grin. Then he licked his lips.

I probably just lost my grip.

One moment I had him, the next he was falling backward into the night, looking up at me until the darkness swallowed him and I saw the water splash.

EPILOGUE

▪ ▪ ▪

I'd be lying if I told you I climbed down from that bridge by myself. They had to strap me in a stretcher-sized basket and fly me off in the helicopter. I spent the next four days in the hospital.

Ironically, I ended up on that fancy ninth floor of Milstein Hospital, just like Boris did. Unfortunately, Nurse Nangle had taken a leave of absence, so she wasn't there to tend to my wounds. Instead, I was assigned to a big, gruff ex-marine who was nice enough, but definitely not an angel of mercy. For some reason, they also posted a security guard outside my door.

The local media had a field day with the story. It was in all the newspapers, and there was even some amateur videotape of me desperately trying to hold on to Johnny. I let Ray Gavin handle all the interviews. The last thing I wanted was publicity. Besides, it put Ray in line for a promotion, and he used his enhanced clout to see that my pal Bill Sweeney got a nifty new job collecting tolls on the Triborough Bridge.

Thomas Martin got a break. With William Kraft dead and all the company files destroyed in the fire Johnny set, he was able to keep the money he swindled out of Life Line, Inc. However, under intense pressure from Lieutenant Gavin, Boris and myself, he decided to make substantial donations to a short list of charities we presented. The recipients included a foster home for kids in Catskill, New York, Hiram Parker's orthopedic rehabilitation center and the AIDS Clinical Trials Unit at Columbia-Presbyterian Medical Center.

Kate and the babies came through the ordeal better than ex-pected. Gavin had her rushed to the New York-Presbyterian Hospital Cornell Campus, at 68th Street and York, where she was given a thorough checkup and a bed for the night. In the morning, her housekeeper, Ellen, collected her and they checked into a suite at the Waldorf.

Under the circumstances, Kate didn't want to go back to her apartment. The condo on Sutton Place went on the market three days later and sold in less than a week. It's amazing what a murder can do for market value. Kate realized a tidy profit on the transaction and plunked the whole chunk down on an old house near the Hudson River in Westchester. She has to commute farther to work, but the kids will have safer streets and a great yard.

It is a very large domicile, and the ex-Mrs. Donovan claims there's room for me. In fact, there's even a barn on the property with an apartment upstairs, should Boris and Angus deign to grace the estate with a visit.

We'll see. The negotiations have only just begun.

They didn't find Johnny St. John right away, which got Manny Santos all jittery. He claimed that the body sank because Johnny was possessed. Instead of talking sense to him, Boris stirred things up by citing centuries of folklore in support of the theory.

I didn't get into it with them. James Phalon was a sick, evil man, but there was no point in giving him more credit than he was due. Besides, he bruised up pretty good for a member of the spirit world.

Nonetheless, until the body was found, I wasn't allowed any peace. Phalon had no family, and I'd gotten the best look at him. I was getting calls from the coroner's office every time they pulled a "floater" out of the East River, and they were fishing them out right and left.

Finally, after about four weeks and as many visits to the morgue, I got a call that sounded like it could be the real thing. They'd landed a white, middle-aged male with a bullet hole in his left hip. I was asked to come back one more time, to see if I could identify the remains.

The taxi took me to the corner of First Avenue and 20th Street—Bellevue Hospital. When I told the cabdriver my destination, he raised his eyebrows and took another look at me in the rearview mirror.

The cabbie's reaction didn't surprise me. If you were to stop the average New Yorker on the street and ask where they take dead bodies, the answer would be automatic: Bellevue. There are county morgues and psychiatric centers in each of the five boroughs, but the place most people think of when the subject turns to the dead or the crazy is Bellevue Hospital.

In a given year, nearly seventy thousand people die in New York City. Most of those people, approximately 64,800, die from natural causes, like old age or cancer or heart disease. The ones who don't die from natural causes fall into three categories: seven hundred are probably suicides; about two thousand die in accidents; and the rest are homicides.

I paid the cabdriver and walked into the lobby of the medical examiner's office. There was a Latin inscription on the wall and I asked the guard if he knew what it said. It must be a common question, because he delivered the translation without looking up at the text.

" 'Let conversation cease. Laughter, take flight. This place is where death delights to aid the living,' " he recited, smiling.

Appropriately, I was coming to visit someone who found death positively delightful.

I signed in and one of the staff pathologists took me down to the morgue. It was a busy, crowded place, with gray-concrete walls and lots of mess. We walked in single file, threading our way past doctors, technicians, family members, police officers, and lots of stretchers. As we skirted the ambulance bay, I noticed uniformed workers unloading more inventory. It's one business where there's never a shortage.

When we got to the cold-storage room, I signed some forms and the technician took us into the morgue. He rolled the subject out for viewing, but the body was wrapped in an opaque plastic shroud and I couldn't see anything through it. I stepped to the side and waited while they fiddled with the packaging. It was cold and the place smelled weird. I remember wishing they would hurry up.

A few minutes later, they motioned me over to the table. The body I looked at had been in the water for nearly a month and it was extremely bloated. In fact, it was so swollen and distorted that I couldn't immediately locate the bullet wound in the hip. The flesh was a mottled collage of pinks, purples, and reds set against a waxy gray field. It was the body of a man. His thick white hair was a rotting, tangled mess. I leaned over to look into the eyes, but the sockets were empty. The pathologist thought they'd probably been eaten by some animal in the river. It must have been a really hungry creature.

I didn't need a lot of evidence. The repulsive cadaver was a good likeness of Johnny St. John. Still, I checked to make sure that the front tooth was chipped and that there were flesh wounds to the scalp and shoulder. It was him, all right.

I stepped back, thinking about the damage this man had done, about the loss of life and the suffering he'd inflicted. How do you forgive someone whose madness is the very definition of evil? I decided to leave that question to the moral philosophers up at Fordham University.

Outside, the sun was shining and the air was brisk and clear. I took a deep breath, hailed a cab, and went over to the Waldorf to visit Kate. It seemed like a good day to listen to the babies' hearts beating.

ACKNOWLEDGMENTS
■ ■ ■

Most of the time invested in the writing of a book is time spent alone, the keyboard often clicking eerily in the middle of the night. But I would be remiss should I fail to mention the names of people whose assistance was essential to the completion of this novel.

There was a lady named Susan at NYU Medical Center who humored me while I tested J. J. Donovan's methods of searching for doctors. Dr. R. B. MacArthur, Director of the Columbia-Presbyterian Research Pharmacy, helped me to concoct a *Mickey Finn* for J. J., and his colleague, Dr. Sasha Beselman, provided a simple Russian toast. My friend, Dr. Jay Dobkin, a Director of the AIDS Clinical Trials Unit at Columbia-Presbyterian Medical Center, helped me to understand the gravity and magnitude of this terrible epidemic. Another friend, Dr. Dan Petrylak, a medical oncologist at Columbia-Presbyterian's Cancer Center, explained the treatment and progression of myelogenous leukemia. And my brother-in-law, Dr. Chris Meriam, of Barre, Vermont, illustrated the delicate carpentry an orthopedic surgeon practices on broken wrists, ribs, and femurs.

I should also thank the police officers at the 33rd Precinct in Washington Heights for not physically removing me when I showed up to snoop around their station house.

For Biblical translations, I turned to *The New American Bible*, a text produced in 1970 under a decree of the Second Vatican

Council (*Dei Verbum*), which ordered that "up-to-date and appropriate translations be made in the various languages, by preference from the original texts of the sacred books." This translation was meant to bring the Bible to the widest possible audience and that is my intention as well.

Last, I need to acknowledge my wife, Lynn. She is my editor, sounding board, critic, and number-one supporter. It was her belief in my work that first led me to write a novel. She listens, she encourages, and she loves me.